Praise for *Good Money*

'Gritty and terrifically engaging, this hardboiled story with its matching prose had me hooked from the first page. Leading lady Stella Hardy is a charming mix of chaotic and cool. She had me grinning like an accomplice as I read. The authentic characters and dry humour lift *Good Money* to that most satisfying place—unique, intriguing, quality crime. Green is an assured and bold new author doing already what great crime novelists do—delivering a bloody good story.'

—HONEY BROWN, award-winning author of
After the Darkness and *Through the Cracks*

'Stella Hardy is certainly a witty and engaging heroine, although as a Saints supporter clearly doomed. A satisfying romp through corporate and political corruption, love, drugs, sex and the Western suburbs.'

—ANNIE HAUXWELL, author of
the Catherine Berlin thriller series

GOOD MONEY

J.M. Green studied professional writing at RMIT. *Good Money*, her first novel, was shortlisted for the 2014 Victorian Premier's Literary Award for an unpublished manuscript. She lives in Melbourne's western suburbs.

GOOD MONEY

J.M. GREEN

SCRIBE

Melbourne • London

Scribe Publications
18–20 Edward St, Brunswick, Victoria 3056, Australia
2 John St, Clerkenwell, London, WC1N 2ES, United Kingdom

First published by Scribe in 2015

Typeset in Sabon 10.7/16pt by the publishers
Printed and bound in Australia by Griffin Press

 The paper this book is printed on is certified against the Forest
Stewardship Council® Standards. Griffin Press holds FSC chain
of custody certification SGS-COC-005088. FSC promotes
environmentally responsible, socially beneficialand economically
viable management of the world's forests.

National Library of Australia
Cataloguing-in-Publication data

Green, J.M., author.

Good Money / J.M. Green.

9781925106923 (paperback)
9781925307177 (e-book)

1. Detective and mystery stories, Australian. 2. Kidnapping–Victoria–
Melbourne–Fiction. 3. Melbourne (Vic.)–Fiction.

A823.4

scribepublications.com.au
scribepublications.co.uk

For Clinton and Morrigan

1

MY BEDROOM. Population: one. I was horizontal under the covers, imitating sleep, when my mobile buzzed. I felt my way around the dark room to my coat hanging on the doorknob, and reached in the pocket. 3.56am. Good news then.

My finger swiped the screen. 'Yes?'

'This is Constable Ross, Flemington Police. Am I speaking with Stella Hardy?'

Raewyn Ross was a serious, square-bottomed recruit with whom, for my sins, I had occasional dealings. I was tempted to tell her she was mistaken, that there was no such person. Instead, I allowed my feet to slide across the carpet until my arse came to rest on a pile of clothes. 'Yes.'

'Sorry to call so late. I'm with a Mrs Chol, from the flats here. She's asked me to call you. It's her eldest boy, Adut.'

'Is he okay?'

'Ah. Not as such, I'm afraid. Actually, that person is deceased.'

She spoke in the monotone favoured by some members of the force. I suspected they had their personalities drained during basic training.

Social workers, on the other hand, were another genus entirely. *Bleedingus heartius.* I did a professional development course once, and the trainer was one of those personality-test fanatics. He said social workers were all the same, always figuring in the same quadrant — an excess of empathy, surplus imagination. But that was years ago. I was in my forties now, and running low on both.

I called a cab and then foraged the flat for my least-dirty jeans and a jumper. I brushed my hair — tufts of dark frizzle, uncut since Jacob (this was not because of some oath; rather, for the melancholy, grooming was a chore, and chores were the first to go). My energy went into breathing, going to work, watching TV, then repeating ... and had for over a year.

1

The taxi showed and I ran down to the street. It was a filthy night: the wind was whipping the trees about, and rain was hammering the footpath. The taxi dropped me outside the Flemington Housing Commission complex on Racecourse Road. Mrs Chol's flat was near the top of one of its towers. I dashed into the pong of the graffiti-stained foyer. In the lift, I wondered who else I might see in Mrs Chol's place — cops from the African Liaison Unit perhaps, maybe a grief counsellor. A woman I didn't know opened the door with a hushed '*Ahlan wasahlan*'. I looked past her. Other than fellow residents of the flats, all of them women, there was only Ross. '*Ahlan biiki*,' I answered, and the woman who held the door nodded, and gestured for me to come through.

Compared to my modest quarters, the commission flats were spacious. Mrs Chol's flat had a large sitting room that opened to the kitchen, with the bathroom and three bedrooms down a dark hallway. It had an easy, comfortable feel; but every time I visited, it was the view that impressed me. It took in most of the south-west corner of the city, round-the-clock glittering.

Constable Ross was sitting forward on the bones of her arse on the best seat in the room, looking acutely ill at ease. More neighbours arrived, bringing food. Two women speaking Amharic were working in the kitchen next to a woman in a sari, who was making tea. Mrs Chol was nowhere to be seen, but then she came into the room, aided by two women, and dropped onto an armchair. I knelt on the floor beside her. Her swollen eyes looked at me without recognition, until her arm came around my shoulder and she bent her face to mine.

'I'm here,' I whispered.

'Thank you for coming.' A terrible duel for control was going on. Her hands shook but her expression was opaque and her back was erect, the chin raised in defiance.

Sitting on the sofa were the three little Chol girls. One held a small plastic doll and was singing softly. I realised with a shock it was a modified version of Lorde's 'Royals'. I sat next to her. 'Our brother died,' she told me calmly.

Lost for words, I touched the doll's blonde hair. 'She's nice. What's her name?' But the girl kept singing and didn't answer.

'Our uncles will be here tomorrow,' said the oldest girl, who was about nine and had her most serious-looking expression on. She had her arm around the youngest, who was five.

Mabor stood by himself, leaning against the wall. He was nothing like Adut. Rather, he was straight-laced and academically gifted — he worked hard at school, kept to himself, and studied on weekends. I had seen him at the Union Road library more than once. He told me it was better than his school library because it was quiet and he always got a computer. Tonight, however, he was kitted out like some hooligan, like his brother, in a Nike hoodie and with his jeans slung low on his hips. There was a dark stain above one knee. He glanced in my direction, our eyes met, and he looked away.

I approached Ross, who had a plate of cake balanced on her lap, and she gave me a grateful look. 'Hardy.' She nodded at me. 'Bad night.' And she bit off a chunk of cake.

'Soaking rain, the good sort. Keeps the farmers happy.' A private joke with myself, since farmers were never actually happy.

Ross concurred with frenzied nodding. It was a pity she was so credulous; her humour deficit didn't do her any favours with her colleagues at the station.

'Any details?' I asked.

Ross fished out her notebook, still chewing, taking her time to swallow. 'Just before midnight, a person employed as a kitchen hand from the Knock Knock bar and restaurant in Kensington was taking the bins out to the alleyway at the rear of the property when he saw a youth of African appearance staggering towards him. The victim was clutching his chest, then collapsed.' She looked up at me. 'Blood pissing out everywhere, he reckons. Pretty brutal attack.' She went

3

back to her notes. 'That person then called the ambulance, but the teenager was pronounced on the way to hospital.'

'That's it?'

'Looking for security-camera footage in the area.' Ross put the notebook away.

'No witnesses?'

'Not yet, early days.' She yawned and eyed the kitchen. 'Aren't they at war or something?'

'If you mean the Ethiopian women, I guess they left all that behind. Mrs Chol is a nice neighbour who needs their support.' I looked at Ross, at her dull, uncomprehending eyes. 'Because it's tragic — the kid was only sixteen.'

'Lifestyle choice, criminal gangs.' Ross shrugged. 'Think I'm still needed here?'

'No, you go.' She was depressing me with her tough-cop act. 'Talk to you tomorrow.'

She handed me her empty plate and slipped out the front door. I took the plate to the kitchen thinking that, of all the kids to end up murdered, Adut Chol was not the type. He didn't have that self-destruct gene you sometimes see in the risk-takers, the death-wish types. You do all you can for them, but a short life or a long stretch was on the cards. And he wasn't one of those passive kids who breathed bad luck in from the family gas chamber, soaked in it, always seeming to attract catastrophe. He wasn't even a proper delinquent. He could be sweet, he loved his sisters, and he helped his mother. Then, again, it was true that most of his friends were street thugs — an inept crew that started the day with a morning bong or snort, and spent the rest of it half-pissed, looking for low-grade trouble. Because he was smart, I had thought it was a phase. I thought Adut Chol's *gangsta* shtick was bullshit.

Mrs Chol was staring at the floor, distress and pain now setting in. That sight would not be easily erased from my memory. I was thinking of leaving, when she fell off the chair to her knees and, with a sudden fury, started hitting herself, slapping her face, and rocking and sobbing. I got down next to her and held onto her hands. Other women came to comfort her. In the commotion, she howled and we held her down, all of us.

The eldest daughter came and took her mother's hand, pulling her. Together, we helped her to her feet. The neighbour who'd let me in, a calm woman with grey hair in a neat bun, put her arm around Mrs Chol's shoulders. 'Rest, now,' she said, in a soothing voice. 'Time for rest.' She took one hand and I held the other, and Mrs Chol allowed herself to be taken to her bedroom. At the doorway, she called for her daughters. They ran to her and climbed on the bed. The neighbour pulled the bedspread over them all and shut the door.

I went to the window near Mabor and pulled the curtain back a little. The city lights dazzled, and the neon spokes of the mutant Ferris wheel strobed wildly. It seemed excessive, like a Dickensian urchin, unfortunate and trying too hard to be liked. Behind me, a woman's voice was singing a terrible lament. It took me a moment to recognise it was Rihanna. It stopped when Mabor put his mobile to his ear. He walked away, whispering, and disappeared into the hallway.

The women were leaving. The last two were in the kitchen finishing the dishes, and they refused my offer to help. I went down the hall to the bedroom that Mabor shared with Adut. The door was ajar, and I pushed it open. Two single beds were separated by a table piled with textbooks. All the drawers of a dresser were open and empty. On one of the beds were little towers of clothes. On the other was a sports bag, unzipped. Mabor stood beside the open wardrobe, a small stack of books in his arms. I knocked on the doorframe.

'Get out,' he said, and dumped the books in the bag.

'It's a terrible thing, to lose a brother,' I said.

He looked at the ceiling and breathed through his mouth. 'You reckon?'

I came in and moved a pile of clothes to sit on a corner of the bed. He watched me warily. 'You know who Adut was seeing tonight?'

'Don't know, miss.' He leaned his head against the wardrobe.

5

'Okay. But if you know something that might help the police —'

'No.'

'Sorry?'

'You expect me to tell other people his business?'

'To help find his killer.'

'Adut was right about you. He reckoned you were a fake, you were up to something. He told Mum not to trust you.'

I blinked. 'Mabor, I don't want anyone to get into trouble.'

'Just fuck off and leave us alone.' He turned his back on me.

I stood up, and some clothes toppled onto the floor. I bent to pick them up. Under a T-shirt was a tattered exercise book. My fingers caught hold of the back cover — and, as I raised it, I glimpsed the last page. Only two lines were on it, written in juvenile print and circled over and over. A wave of shock went through me. I read it twice before I was sure. It was my address — my flat, in my building in Roxburgh Street, Ascot Vale. I risked a glance at Mabor. He had his head down now, zipping up the sports bag. I turned over the book to study the cover. *Adut Chol, Year Ten, English*. A couple of years old — he must have been using it as a notebook. I let the book slip to the floor, and with my foot I shoved it under the bed, just as Mabor's gaze returned to me. 'You going or what?'

'Take care of your mum,' I said, and left.

The rain had stopped when I walked from the building, but water continued to drip from lemon-scented eucalypts in the car park. I stood beside the white trunk of a venerable giant, keeping an eye on the entrance. A wind gust shook the wet leaves and drenched me; I cursed and turned up my collar. Then the foyer light went on, and Mabor stepped out. He shifted the sports bag to his shoulder and lit a cigarette, his fourteen-year-old face wretched and grave.

I moved further into the shadows. On a similar late-night call, in the same building, six years before, I'd made the biggest mistake of my life — a single lapse in judgement that saw me descending in the lift, wads of cash in my bag and my adrenalin through the roof. Time passed, as did the sleepless nights and the regrets and remorse, and I had started to relax, to believe I was out of danger.

A four-wheel drive pulled up on Racecourse Road. Mabor yanked up his hood and ran out to it. If he got in, I would go back to the flat to get the book.

He passed the sports bag through the open, passenger-side window. A fat envelope was passed out to him. Raised voices drifted towards me, but they were indistinct. Then the window rolled smoothly up and the car drove away. Mabor stuffed the envelope into his back pocket, piffed his smoke, and headed back inside.

I took a tissue from my bag and dabbed the drips of water on my face. Fatigue weighed on me and with it a bleary-eyed sadness. No one could leave their past behind. Sooner or later the truth always came out, just as Adut had discovered the truth about me. This was the only possible explanation for why he had written my address in his exercise book. How he had found out, I didn't know; at the time, he was only ten years old. Odds-on, someone had seen me and told him. Six years was a long time for whoever saw me to keep a secret — the weight of it perhaps became a burden. So Adut wrote down my address and intended to exploit that information somehow, like blackmail or extortion, or God only knew what. For me, the consequences would have been ruinous — if someone hadn't murdered him.

2

I STOOD by the curb and waited for a passing taxi. It was not yet daylight, but the traffic was approaching gridlock, drivers already feeling the tension. I decided to walk home through the slumbering backstreets. I took my time, dawdling and thinking about how the good citizens in their beds were not troubled by thoughts of death. A picture of my dad came from nowhere. He had one knee on the ground, and though his hat was pulled down so I couldn't see his eyes, I knew the impatient glare was on me. 'Get on with it.' The knife — a small bread knife — was in my bag with my homework and my uneaten apple. No time to go all the way back to the farm for the shotgun. The ewe was lying on the wet grass, head down. The lamb was dead, in raw, bleeding pieces. The ewe saw us and struggled, eyes wild. Good on you, I thought. Trying, wanting to live. He could have taken the knife from me — a quick flex of muscle and it would be over — but he said it was better if he held her. She kicked, but he clamped her down with his body weight. Blood gushed from her neck.

'Your dog,' I said. 'You do it.'

He tipped his hat back. 'Come on. Get it done, then we can get back for a feed.'

I was hesitant, cowardly. It didn't go well. Instead of committing, I made half-arsed tearing and sawing movements, wanting it to be over. It seemed to go on forever. Afterwards, he wiped the blade on the disgusting hanky he always seemed to have, and slapped me on the shoulder. 'Let's go. I'm so starving I could eat two helpings of Delia's bloody casserole.' Men could do that — trade blows, then five minutes later shake hands, kiss, and make up. Meanwhile, I burned inside for years.

I reached Roxburgh Street as dawn broke. My street mainly

comprised respectable brick Edwardian houses with well-tended gardens. I walked up the gentle incline towards my building, an incongruous 1960s box. Say what you will about austerity architecture, compared to the brutalist concrete mausoleums popping up in the area, my place was good, honest ugliness. At some point, the brickwork had been painted white and a Norfolk Island Pine planted in the front lawn. Now gigantic, the tree dominated the street. Mounted above the portico in metallic letters was the name *PineView*.

I climbed the stairs. As I reached the top landing, she teetered towards me on her noodle legs, feet shod with wooden stilts, blonde hair in a twist.

'Off to work, Tania?'

'Yes.' She clattered down a few more steps, but then stopped. 'Tonight still on?'

'Sure,' I said, and went inside and fell face-first on my bed.

At about eleven, I woke, showered, dressed, and headed to Buffy's on Union Road.

'Bit late today, Stella.' Lucas started making my takeaway flat white as I entered his café. He was good that way.

'Worked late last night. Got a *White Pages*?'

He tipped his head in the direction of a sideboard; above it, a couple of phonebooks stood upright on a shelf. I flipped through the A-to-K, while he scalded the milk, until I found my listing: *Hardy, Stella J.*, followed by my full address and land line.

I'd been tired last night, and my judgement was impaired. Surely I was mistaken about Adut and his silly schoolbook. I had worked with some very disturbed people in the course of my professional life, and had never concealed my home address. There'd been no threats, no abuse, no unwanted attempts to contact me. No problem ever. The whole address thing was an innocent coincidence — another explanation must have existed that I had not yet thought of. After all, Adut wasn't a psychopath. He was a smart kid. Not Mabor smart, not academic. But street smart. He'd signed up for all kinds of programs for disadvantaged kids, and left as soon as he got the free backpack or the myki with twelve-months' free public transport. That was not merely smart, it was cunning.

God help me. He knew. He knew.

How could he know? It was impossible. I took a deep breath. I needed to have another look at that book. But I had to be patient.

I boarded a city-bound tram and scored a seat to myself. I drank the coffee and stared out at the cold congested streets as the tram conveyed me to my place of work. At a stop along Racecourse Road, I stepped off and walked to the offices of the Western Outer-Region Migrant Support — or WORMS. The organisation rented a shopfront on Wellington Street next to the Flemington Police Station. The place was deserted. We'd lost half our staff in two years. Those lucky few who had hung onto their jobs, it seemed, were currently either at meetings or seeing clients.

I went to brief Boss about Mrs Chol. His name was Brendan Ogg-Simmons, so we called him Boss. Also, he was my boss. He was short and balding, with an accountant wife and two young children. Despite this, he was usually cheerful.

'Before you say anything, Hardy, you need to put a visit from Pukus in your diary. Next Monday.'

'*Next* as in next week?'

'No. That's *this* Monday — I mean the one after.'

'That Monday's a holiday, Boss.' Public holidays were highlighted in my calendar. 'The Queen, birthday girl.'

'Tuesday then.'

State politics was a bore, but I knew who Pukus was. I'd even met him. He was Marcus Pugh, formerly the Human Services minister, until a recent cabinet reshuffle had put him in charge of the Victorian police force. He used to swan into our program launches, take the credit, drink a cup of tea, pose for a photo with some unsuspecting woman in a headscarf, and then swan out. *Pukus*, we called him — *Mucous Pukus*.

I made a note on my phone, and added a sad-face emoticon next to it. 'Isn't he Police Minister now?'

Boss sighed. 'Yes. Just when we thought we'd seen the back of him, this time he's here announcing the new partnership between Justice and Community Services.'

'Speaking of justice ... Mrs Chol, she's going to need ongoing support. If they arrest someone, she'll need guidance just to get through the hearings, the trial — handle the media.'

Often in these situations, Boss would start saying that he couldn't spare me, how the cuts stymied every program the agency ran, how we all had to do more with less. But this time, he surprised me. 'Justice has announced some funding. New money. Migrants affected by crime. Put together a submission and I'll sign it today.'

I went to my desk and found a yellow envelope with my name on it sitting on the keyboard: the usual guff about the next round of redundancies being unavoidable — the agency was looking for volunteers to take a package. A part of me wanted to go, right then and there, to clear my few possessions and drop my pass card on Boss's desk. Instead, I wrote the damn submission.

At lunchtime, I dropped into the police station next door to see Raewyn Ross.

Some new guy, a baby-face with the measurements of a knitting needle, scoffed at my enquiry. 'The Khaleesi? Not here. Probably taken a sickie.'

'Khaleesi, as in —'

'*Game of Thrones*.' The needle smirked.

He was in the place five minutes and had already joined in disrespecting Ross. I let it slide. 'Homicide been to visit Mrs Chol yet? Collected Adut's stuff?'

He looked at me like I was speaking Lithuanian. 'Couldn't tell you.' I waited with raised eyebrows. He sighed. 'Want me to ask?'

'Not to worry.' I made it to the door before I turned around. '"The Khaleesi". Is that —?'

'Yep. Irony.'

A door opened behind him and a disembodied voice said, 'Mrs Chol is at the coroner's. Plain clothes told me, said he was taking her.'

It was wishful thinking, but maybe, just maybe, the plain clothes detective was so busy helping Mrs Chol through the process, that he hadn't ordered Adut's room to be cleared yet. In any case, with Mrs Chol not at home, there was no way to get into her flat. I said my thanks and walked back to work. Tomorrow it would have to be.

The rest of the day, I rang clients and answered emails. At five o'clock, one of our regulars came into our waiting room and fell asleep. Boss and I tried to rouse him, but he wouldn't budge. This vexed me as I had plans to get home, drink half a cask of wine, and watch *The Walking Dead*. Boss called the Salvation Army while I tried to get some sense out of our guest. We tried to get him walking, and had an arm each when he decided to vomit down the front of his shirt. My gag reflex wanted to join in. Then he shat himself. I unrolled a kilometre of paper towel.

It was past seven when I finally walked into the foyer of my building. Letters jutted from my letterbox. I juggled my bag and sorted through them: bill, bill, catalogue, postcard. Postcard? I checked the address: wrong flat. I read the message — *We're having the best time! Just love Fiji!!! Joyce and Frank* — and dropped it in the correct slot, feeling put out. *Fix your sloppy handwriting, Joyce. Can't tell your 5s from your 9s.*

I flicked the lights, cranked up the heater, and put two slices of bread in the toaster. I had only just opened the fridge door when I heard the modest tap that Tania used for a knock on the door. I let her in, and she brought her fresh-faced, sweet-smelling *joie de vivre* with her. She had ten centimetres on me in flats — and she wasn't wearing flats — so I had to tilt my head back to see her white teeth smiling down at me. She handed me a bottle. 'How was your day?'

'Acceptable. You?'

'Awesome.'

'Come off it.'

'Not gonna lie. I like my job.'

'The paring of human skin? Inhaling carcinogenic chemicals?' I opened a cupboard, took down two glasses, and started twisting the bottle cap. The cap was stubborn; I couldn't gain any purchase on it. Since last night, everything sucked — I couldn't even think straight, let alone open a bottle. All I could think, over and over, was how could Adut have found out? There must have been a witness. Someone living in the flats. Everything was coming apart — except the damn bottle cap. I wrenched it, and drew red welts across my palm to no avail.

Tania bit her lip. 'It's a cork,' she said tentatively.

'Really?' I looked at the label: *Beaujolais Village*. No local gut-rot for Tania. She favoured French wine, and it was always excellent. 'Oh, right.'

'Do you know when they're going to fix the security door on this building?'

I found a corkscrew and started screwing. '*When?* You mean *if*. It's been like that since I moved here.'

This news displeased her considerably. 'Well, I wouldn't have signed the lease if I thought the security was compromised.'

'*Compromised?* Ha! This isn't the Pentagon.'

'But don't the other tenants care?'

I thought about them — the ones I knew well. 'Nope.' Not even the owner-occupiers like me and Brown.

'Aren't you afraid?'

'Afraid?'

'I mean, concerned.'

I poured her a glass of wine, trying not to laugh. 'Not really.' I tried to reassure her. 'You're safe with me around. I killed a sheep with a knife once.'

'Stella!'

'I'm not proud of it.'

'Oh my God, I can't believe I didn't notice before.'

'Wait, what?'

'Your feet. I bet we're the same size.'

I studied her face: she seemed genuine. 'So?'

'I've got these shoes. I was going to chuck them out, but —'

This time I laughed, full and free. It had been a while, and it came out as a squawk.

'They're too tight across the toes, but I bet they'd fit you.' She beamed at me.

There was much wrong with this state of affairs. Her excessive generosity, for one thing. The fact that my toes were hidden inside a pair of Blundstone boots, for another.

'They're in my flat,' she was saying. 'I'll go and get them.'

'No rush,' I said. She didn't hide her disappointment. So I added, 'But I was just thinking how fabulous your taste in shoes is.'

'Oh my God! I know!' She looked at them admiringly for a moment. Then she addressed me. 'Stella, I have loads of clothes you could borrow, and nice shoes. And, well, don't take this the wrong way, but I was going to suggest a makeover.'

'But you look fine.'

'Not me ...'

My mobile trilled. *Saved*, I thought, *by the default ringtone*. I swiped the screen. It was Mrs Chol: 'Stella, the police are here.'

I held my breath. They were probably conducting a thorough search. 'Do you want me to come over?'

'No. It is all right. My brothers are here with me now. Stella, listen, I need to tell you something.'

All I could think was that Mrs Chol was about to reveal the existence of the book, with the cops standing in her lounge room listening to every word. 'No!' I shrieked.

'Pardon?'

'I mean, I'm doing something. Can I call you back?' I put down

14

the phone, and found Tania staring at me.

'You've gone grey.'

'Hmm?'

'In the face.' She gestured at my head. 'You're all sweaty. Are you okay?'

I had trouble focusing. 'Sorry, Tania. I think I need to have an early night.'

'Yes, I think you do.' She stood by my door then turned back to me, an anxious expression blighting her perfect facial structure.

'Would you like me to walk you home?' I said, half joking. Three steps, and we were there.

'Yes, please. That would be brilliant.'

I chocked open my door and we went out. The stairwell was in darkness. The third-floor collective was quiet. Brown Cardigan in 9 had the TV on low volume; and Amber and Jack, the joined-at-the-hip hipsters from number 11, were in Hobart at some music festival. I waited while Tania turned her key in the door to flat number 12. Once inside, she wished me well and shut the door. I heard a bolt slide, a second lock snap shut, and the chain slide into place.

I smiled a little at her nervousness. Melbourne wasn't dangerous; it wasn't up there with New Delhi or Caracas. But as I walked back to my flat, I realised that, despite her skittishness, I liked having Tania around. Flat 12 had been empty for ages, and it gave the third floor a cold, creepy vibe. Then, a couple of months ago, Brown reported seeing a young woman carrying boxes inside, and concluded brilliantly that the flat had been leased. At first I was wary of this apparent interloper and interrogated Brown for information, but all he had managed to learn was that she was from Western Australia. But then I bumped into her in the foyer one evening, and she tottered towards me on spiky heels, offering her hand. 'It's Tania, by the way. Bradshaw.'

I gave her cold mitt a hearty shake. 'Stella Hardy.'

'I know, the old guy told me.'

'What? The gossipy old bastard. Better watch what you tell him.'

'Totally!'

Brown had said she was pretty — a colossal understatement. If I'd had to guess, I'd have said TV journalist, or fashion ambassador to a large department store. Turned out she was a beauty therapist. She seemed tolerable, but was kind of ingratiating. Or I was a soft touch. In any case, she inveigled an invite, and we drank a bottle of wine at my place one Thursday. Somehow it became a regular Thursday thing. It was my favourite day of the week to get a skinful. No one cared if you came to work with a hangover on a Friday. Who did work on a Friday?

Once inside, I called Mrs Chol.

'What have the police found?' I asked, trying to sound nonchalant.

'They have found the man,' she said. 'The alleged man.'

The news was good, excellent, and so fast. Yet I felt panicked. 'Who?'

'The police received a call to go to a house in Deer Park.'

'An anonymous tip-off?'

'Yes. The man lives there with his mother. They did a search and found Adut's phone. Wait a minute.' I waited. She came back. 'The police lady wants to talk to you.'

'Hardy?'

'Ross? I thought you called in sick?'

'No. Who told you that?'

'No one. Wires crossed. What do you have?'

'Blood-stained clothes and the likely murder weapon. They've got him in the cells.'

'Who is it?'

'Darren "Clacker" Pickering. They're charging him with murder.'

3

MY WATCH and handbag were conveyed in a plastic tray through an X-ray machine the size of a truck. As my belongings emerged, a guard opened my bag, and took out a teaspoon I kept for emergency yoghurt-snacking and put it behind the counter. I rushed under the metal-detecting arch to confront him.

'Oh, good on you! Can't be too careful with *spoons*. Lethal. I could use it to tap His Honour on the noggin like a boiled egg.'

The guard folded his arms and smiled with the smug righteousness of those with limited power. I waved my newly received Department of Justice ID at him, but he was unmoved. I glared at him, snatched my bag, and headed to court, struggling with my watchstrap. By the time I entered the courtroom it was nearly full. I saw Mrs Chol in the public gallery and eased past her supporters, neighbours, and relatives, to sit beside her. She gave me a grateful look and a quick squeeze of my hand. I had to look away; since the night of Adut's murder last week, my obsession with his exercise book took the place of proper professional regard for my client — it made me feel like a traitor. If I had managed to get hold of the damn thing, maybe I could concentrate on other things, but every time I went to her place to try and get my hands on it something or someone hindered me. Like Bruce Copeland, the homicide detective who was in charge of the case.

He sat two rows from us playing a game on his phone. With his tortoise-shell spectacles and good manners, he was more librarian than hardened cop. I liked him because he had been in constant contact with Mrs Chol since Clacker was arrested and she had found him reassuring. But I was also annoyed with him because whenever I went to retrieve the exercise book, bloody Copeland was there and I had to leave empty-handed.

I glanced around the court. Staff of both legal teams were having last-minute whispered conferences. Clacker stood in the dock. He had a carrot-top with russet freckles and buckteeth. He wore a suit that only made him seem dodgy. The clothes, plus his slouch and botched tattoos were a biography of his childhood poverty, limited education, and time served. His tendency to use an unblinking angelic look, one I'd seen delinquents use many times, was a tell-tale sign that he was lying and gave the impression that Clacker was still a child. He was twenty-nine.

Verity Spinks, the prosecutor, stood and I leaned forward. There was CCTV footage, she said, that showed Clacker in the area of the Knock Knock restaurant at the time the kitchen hand saw Adut staggering down the alley having suffered fatal knife wounds. Items found in Clacker's house included Adut's phone, a knife matching the murder weapon, a large amount of cash, a small quantity of marijuana, and twenty grams of the drug commonly referred to as 'ice'. It was, she concluded, a straight-forward case of aggravated robbery, resulting in the tragic death of a promising young teenager.

The grave personage of Finchley Price, dark-haired with a touch of grey at the temples, was barrister for the defence. He denied the significance of all of the prosecutor's evidence. He sighed, shook his head, used the word *circumstantial*, and said he was bewildered as to why we were here wasting His Honour's time.

At one point, I drifted off and started planning my evening — a two-step programme: go home, hit the cardboard. The disturbing thought arose that perhaps the wine cask in the fridge was empty, in which case, new plan: hit the bottle shop.

Eventually His Honour signalled he was ready to make his pronouncement. It appeared he did not like to see time wasted either. 'I find sufficient evidence for the defendant Darren Clyde Pickering to stand trial for the murder of Adut Chol.'

Darren's mother pointed at him. 'You lyin' fuckin cunt.'

At that moment the gallery erupted. Clacker's supporters were yelling abuse at the magistrate, the press, everyone. Security guards and several cops stormed in and started removing people. His Honour called for calm, pounding the desk like a carpenter on crack.

Mrs Chol accepted words of comfort from her supporters, and when the courtroom was cleared we went out together. Near the main entrance, Copeland was waiting for us. He clasped her hands in both of his. 'Do you understand the verdict?'

'Yes, Bruce,' said Mrs Chol.

'There'll be a trial. It's a way to go yet, but we'll get there.'

'Thank you, Bruce,' she said.

Copeland gave a sad little smile and pushed his glasses back. He shot me a parting look — for what, I didn't know — and went out, where the waiting media mobbed him.

We waited inside until the photographers and journalists who were surrounding Copeland had gone further along the street. The day was becoming gloomy, and low clouds gathered over the city. Heavy drops of rain splattered around us as we went down the steps of the old court building.

'How's Mabor?'

She frowned. 'Quiet.'

'Back at school?'

'Yes. He walks his sisters to the primary school then he goes on by himself to high school.'

'Maybe I should come over and see how he's going? Like tonight? How's tonight?'

'No, Stella, thank you. Lately, Mabor likes to keep to himself. After school he goes to his room, does his homework. He comes out only to eat. But if you want to come and visit with me, have some coffee, it would be all right. Maybe tomorrow?'

I swallowed, one more day. 'Great. Tomorrow then.'

She hailed a taxi and I watched it meld into the sour Melbourne traffic. Taxis were expensive. If she took one to court and back every

19

day of the trial she'd be broke in a week. I'd offered to arrange a lift for her but she was determined to travel alone by cab. To her, the cost seemed irrelevant, which puzzled me.

I turned to leave and caught sight of Finchley Price pacing down William Street. He was bleating into a mobile. His arrogant demeanour had been replaced by a hunched, anxious whispering as he made for his chambers. He looked stately though, with the black silk gown billowing behind him. The man rocked a wig and robe, I'd give him that. For my part, I fought the evening commuters for a seat on the next tram heading to West Maribyrnong. I sat down and looked out the window, but all I could see was myself sitting in the dock, humiliated and condemned, while Verity Spinks waved around Exhibit A: a battered exercise book.

Between the tram stop and my home, I detoured via the local fish and chip shop. While waiting for my order, I let my gaze linger on a wall-mounted television, a fast moving series of images: rain, floods, water washing away once firm ground. Then some perky newsreader came on, skimpy camisole, big hair, and inappropriate smile. News, entertainment — who could tell, these days?

> And in finance news, mining company CC Prospecting has urged the government to maintain foreign ownership rules and disallow the entrance of non-Australian companies in the bidding war for control of the Shine Point refinery. CC Prospecting is in a bidding war with Chinese and other foreign companies for the project.

I cared not. The rain had eased to a drizzle. Passing headlights shone on the wet Union Road tram tracks. A stocky man stood across the street from my building, apparently waiting for someone. Fool, I thought, wearing shorts and thongs in this weather. He made me cold just looking at him. At least he had had the good sense to pull his hoodie up over his head, against the rain.

20

Entering my apartment, I dropped the parcel of minimum chips and grilled flake on the coffee table. I was in my bedroom changing out of my work outfit and into tracksuit pants when I heard the clack of heels on the landing. I opened the door to Tania, hair in an up-do and dressed in skinny jeans.

'Hey,' I said. 'What's up?'

She seemed confused for a moment. 'Oh. Are you busy?' She had her handbag over her shoulder and a David Jones shopping bag in her hand. In the other hand, down by her side, I could see a bottle of wine.

'I'm not exactly *busy*, as such.' Was it Thursday again already? Yes — a week had passed since I first sighted the book. Dear God, I still didn't have it.

'I have the shoes.' She handed me the David Jones bag.

'Wow. Great. I'll try them on later.' I went to close the door.

'Wait.' She fished in her handbag. 'I got you some DVDs. I know you like movies. I thought you might like to add them to your collection.'

They were pirated — the kind found in markets all over Asia. I sorted through them: *The Breakfast Club, The Blue Lagoon, Ferris Bueller's Day Off.*

'These aren't really my thing,' I said. I'd seen them all except *The Blue Lagoon.* I had to draw the line somewhere. The others were average, and granted that Ferris Bueller knew how to have a good time, I didn't want them clogging up my DVD library, sitting next to quality like *Alien* or *A Muppet Christmas Carol.*

'Stella, please take them. As a favour to me.'

'What do you mean "a favour"?'

'Could you look after them for me?'

Look after them? She made it sound like she had just handed me a puppy, or a pot plant. But I was nothing if not a good neighbour. 'If you like.'

'You never know, you might want to binge on teenage movies.' She laughed and continued to stand there smiling at me.

I glanced at the bottle, one of her fancy French labels. 'Like chips?'

'Love chips.' She came inside and closed the door. 'I'll put these away for you.' She went to my wall of indifferently assembled Swedish bookcases and found a spot for her DVDs on the top shelf, paying no heed to my filing system. I made a mental note to refile them later. She lingered by the shelves scrutinising the titles.

I got out some plates and glasses and cut my fish in half. I put a portion on her plate with a handful of chips. There was a bottle of tomato sauce in the back of the fridge. I put everything on a tray and carried it to the coffee table.

'Want to watch one?' I asked.

'This.' Tania handed me the *Hornblower* series. Really, she could not have impressed me more if she'd gone for *The Lord of the Rings*. Bonus points for *The Two Towers*. I slotted the disc, and she sat on my sofa and kicked off her shoes.

'Colour's gone,' she said.

It was a relic, my television, and everything on the screen was a shade of purple, but I couldn't be bothered fixing it. 'I'm used to it.'

And so, while we watched Horatio sail his frigate into a nest of Dons, we dined on fillet of shark and salted *pommes frites*, paired with smooth Bordeaux. For her part, she stuffed the chips in her mouth by the handful like a hungry adolescent boy, while I drank most of the wine. To my relief, she was not one to talk while I was trying to watch TV, but every so often she checked her phone.

'Expecting a call?'

'Not really,' Tania said. 'I meant to ask — how did the hearing go?' She blinked her black lashes at me.

'It's going to trial,' I said and skulled my wine. My thoughts lingered on Finchley Price. He was in his element striding around the court but I couldn't imagine him having the same air of supremacy in, say, the TAB or the greyhound racetrack. 'Heard of Finchley Price?' I asked.

'No, what's that?'

'That,' I said, 'is a barrister. Nice looking.'

'Ew! Are you insane? Barristers are ugly. They're all creepy hunchbacks with pasty faces and feathery hair.'

'Hunchbacks?'

'Totally gross.'

'Calm down, I get it. I didn't know you were so familiar with the legal fraternity.'

'I used to do the mail for Faurtinaux Bath.'

I hadn't figured Tania as the itinerant-worker type, with actual life experience. 'When was this?'

'Straight after school. Gap year. My friend Jimmy and I got the job together. We called them "Fart and go Barf".'

I didn't know what to say that. I looked at her for a moment, while she stared at the screen. I was onto my fourth glass of red and feeling carefree. 'Tania, can I ask you something?'

'Hmm?'

'Have you ever done anything you were ashamed of?'

'Oh God! All the time! I sent this tweet once. I was drunk and —'

'No, I mean like *wrong*.'

'You mean like killing a sheep?'

'What? No!' I clearly couldn't confide in this ninny.

She made her hurt face, which I ignored. After a moment she said. 'How's your client holding up?'

'The unfathomable Mrs Chol? Who can say?' I rubbed a chip in tomato sauce. 'She seems pretty tough.'

Tania nodded eagerly. 'She sounds amazing. Raising five kids on her own. Well, four now.' She cringed. 'But you know, starting a new life in a foreign country. Incredible.'

'Yeah.' I shrugged. *Whatever.* I sipped my wine, wanting Tania to stop yapping so I could concentrate on the fetching lieutenant dangling from a rope over a shark-infested sea. On cue, Tania took her handbag and went to the bathroom. I hit *pause*, and dropped

23

the empty bottle in the recycle bin and dumped the plates in the sink. I tried to push the chip paper into the bin but it was stuffed to capacity. I took off the lid and leant on the rubbish with my knee until it surrendered.

The difference in years was an issue. I preferred the company of women my own age.

My former best friend, Phuong, and I had known each other since our university days. Sure, we were temperamentally different. She was reserved and cautious and thought men were an optional extra, and I was brash and loud and needed men — a boyfriend, to be exact — like an addict, like a punter at the track, desperate for a sure thing in the last race to recoup her losses. On the plus side, we shared similar values, a love of horror movies, and had the verbal shorthand of an old married couple. As friends, we had the kind of bond that tolerated normal human misconduct in the other. We validated. We supported. We enabled. It was what we did. That was before Phuong found Buddha and became a sanctimonious bore.

Tania reappeared with freshly applied makeup and we watched the rest of *Hornblower*. When it was over, I stood, rather unsteadily, to walk Tania to her door. She unlocked her door and flicked on the light.

'All clear,' she said, a little bashfully.

I turned to leave and she grabbed my arm. 'I've just had the most awesome idea.'

I looked at the indentations her nails were making in my forearm. 'That's nice.'

'A gold triple! We go to the salon early, before it opens.'

'Gold triple?'

'It's three kinds of treatment, all of them fantastic for your skin.'

'My skin?'

'Yes, if we go before it opens, I can do it for free.'

'When?'

'Tomorrow. Be here early, before seven.'

24

Seven? 'Look Tania, I'm not sure —'

'No, you have to! Promise you'll do it. Promise.'

'Um. I promise.'

'Afterwards we can go shopping for a new outfit, the beginning of the new you.'

'Great,' I said. 'See you tomorrow.' And I got the hell out of there before any other promises were made.

4

AT THE prearranged time, way too early for my liking, I crossed the landing to number 12. I'd spent a sleepless night filled with thoughts of the mythical gold triple — and how the scouring of my defective dermis symbolised the emergence of a wonderful new me. Crazy shit like that. I'd kept my end of this mad bargain by setting my alarm an hour earlier than usual and dragging my tired bones out of bed. I found a pair of jeans on the floor, and turned my black jumper right-way out; then I put on my black boots, my coat, and my scarf. I looked a fright but I didn't care. Today, it was Tania's job to fix that.

I beat a musical *rat-a-tat* on Tania's doorframe. After a little while, I put my ear to the door. I could hear no morning sounds, no showering, no FM radio. I knocked again, long and hard, on the middle of the door. The rest of the building was getting into gear: doors slamming, shoes clomping in the stairwell. Disgusted, I gave her door one last thump and then rang her mobile. It rang out and went to voicemail. I recorded thus: 'Tania, I'm outside, open your fucking door.'

I went downstairs. Her Mini Cooper was in her allocated parking space.

I walked down to the road and looked in both directions. Roxburgh Street was in full morning-transit mode. Single-occupant cars, chauffeured school kids, mothers in dressing-gowns doing drop-offs: the usual free-for-all of noxious congestion to which we'd all become accustomed. I stood in a stream of pedestrians, young men — facial hair, suits, messenger bags — and young women — skirts, scarves, handbags over forearms — striding to the railway station, and I looked towards Union Road. Had she gone for takeaway coffee at Buffy's? I checked my phone: 7.15am. She'd told *me* to be on time, the nerve of her. I cursed her and her whole non-committal generation, a bunch of irresolute shape-shifters.

I headed to Buffy's.

'Has my neighbour been in this morning? Pretty blonde girl, mid-twenties.'

Lucas put my coffee next to my newspaper, on the counter, and accepted my coins. 'No. But tell her I would like her to.'

The world outside tried to sweep me up in its pointless activity. But I stood there, newspaper under my arm, a determined lost soul. I thought I was a pretty good judge of character. I could not quite believe I had misread Tania, she was no mystery, with her heart four centimetres beyond her sleeve, her face an open pamphlet, her simple needs, her inability to practise the dark art of ... well, any of them. We were a kind of *before and after*, she and I. Except I was what happens when ... *Ah bugger it*, I thought, *might as well just go to work.*

I boarded a tram and glanced at the front page of *The Age*: CC PROSPECTING FILED ACCOUNTS LATE. The Australian Tax Office intended to bring charges against a Western Australian mining company for a massive unpaid tax bill on the $2 billion profit. The company was contesting, with legal representation by — what do you know — Faurtinaux Bath. Below that, in the bottom corner, an ad for an adult beanbag, only $600 — the definitive omen of civilisation's collapse; next stop, post-apocalyptic dystopia.

Tucked away on page four: MY CLIENT IS INNOCENT: PRICE. Nice photo of Finchley. I thought about cutting it out. What was I, twelve? I checked the Melbourne forecast, the Queen's birthday long weekend was going to be pretty standard: cold, overcast, windy, showers. I held my takeaway cup in my bare hands and sighed.

In the Flemington shopping precinct, I stepped off the tram and walked along Wellington Street to the WORMS premises. I sat at my desk and stared in the manner of an over-tired infant. I rubbed my eyes and groaned. The long day stretched out before me.

I switched on my phone and hit *redial*, Tania's phone rang out. I declined to leave a message. By now, I was worried. I had dismissed her security concerns as the anxieties of a small-town girl in a big city. But what if she was being pursued by a dangerous ex? It was possible that, while she'd never mentioned a boyfriend to me, one may exist. My office walls were covered in posters decrying violence against women. How had I missed the signs? I needed to check with the people in her life who knew her better than me. Her salon seemed a fairly obvious place to start. I found the number for Superlative Skin Sensations, located at the nearby shopping centre known as *Knifepoint* by locals, and rang them on the work phone.

'Superlative Skin Sensations, this is Kiara,' said the girl who answered.

'I had arranged for a treatment this morning and —'

'With who were you booked in with?'

The Catholic within cried out at so many grammatical errors, but I remained stoically mute. I'd gotten into trouble in the past for correcting people's grammar. 'Tania. I'm her neighbour,' I added. 'I was booked in for a triple golden.'

'Gold triple,' the girl said coolly. 'I can't see any booking. Are you sure?'

Now I remembered Tania had said it was off the books. 'I might have the day wrong. Is she there?'

'She hasn't come in today. I have to call all her clients.' The whiff of martyrdom in this remark put my dander up. Higher. I wondered how Tania stood the place.

'Where is Tania?' I heard a female voice in the background ask.

'It's not like her to not show up.' I heard another girl say.

'I'll try her mobile again,' said the receptionist, who then hung up on me.

I sat at my desk staring at the screen. On a whim I looked up on an online trader and ordered the box-set of *Breaking Bad*. Then I went back to rubbing my eyes and groaning. I was doing this when something soft rested on my shoulder. I looked, but a swollen belly obscured my view.

'You okay?' It was Shaninder, a colleague with expert knowledge of domestic violence statistics, the locations of all the women's refuges, and the best Indian restaurants in the western suburbs.

'Self-harm.'

'I see.' She laughed. 'Was it fun?'

I thought of Tania, her crazy generosity, the lovely French wine, Horatio Hornblower. 'It was a variety of fun.'

'Good girl,' she said.

I nodded to her bump. 'How's it going?'

'All very good. She gets the hiccups.'

'Really? Didn't know they did that.'

She patted her belly and turned to go.

'Hey Shaninder, I have a friend who might be in a DV situation.'

'She still living with him?'

'No, but I'm concerned. She's not answering her phone.'

'Flat battery?' She smiled benignly.

'But she's not at home and not at work. Could you check the refuges?'

'This conversation, we are not having.' She gave me a look that said I should know better, and left me to go back to rubbing my face.

The hangover was working its way through my eyeballs. I needed to take something. I walked down to Racecourse Road and into a nearby café. Taking a seat in a booth, I ordered tea. The place had mirrors along both walls and from a certain angle an endless-image thing happened — like a cheap special effect on *Dr Who* — making it almost impossible to avoid my reflection. The horror I experienced each time I saw myself was worsening incrementally. I rummaged in my bag for a packet of painkillers and swallowed two capsules. The tea, when it arrived, had soap bubbles on the top. I jiggled the teabag, took a cautious sip, and started to relax.

Why was I anxious for the safety of a woman that, in all honesty,

I barely knew? A fear, based on a suspicion, due to a feeling, with no proof — that was what I had. What I needed was advice — low key, discreet counsel on the best course of action. I had contacts. I knew people who helped people. There were the good people of the free legal services. I also knew lots of union people, advocates and advisers and mediators and counsellors. There was my mother. Scratch that. There were priests and nuns and bishops. Rabbis and imams. There was my local member of parliament. There was Phuong.

And there was Mabor.

Right there. Mabor Chol, Adut's younger brother, sitting in a booth across the aisle. Opposite him, sipping a cappuccino, was a man in a purple velvet dinner jacket, open-necked shirt, and aviator sunglasses. Normally, this would be amusing — deserving a chuckle, at least — but at that moment in time, my brain was incapable of humour.

I slumped down to avoid him seeing me. In a semi-crouch, with my face down, and still holding my tea, I squeezed out of the booth and headed to the back of the restaurant. Then I doubled back and slid into the booth behind Mabor. If I glanced in the mirror on the opposite wall, I could see Mabor mangling the straw in his milkshake.

Bits of their conversation drifted back to me.

Mabor, fidgeting: 'He has to fucking suffer. Like me and Mum and the girls. Like we all are suffering.'

His companion looked pious, like a priest hearing confession. 'Nobody wants it more than me, believe me.'

'You could have done it, man. Before he went inside.'

'It's better this way. I told you that. I keep telling you. These things are easier done inside.'

'You said you'd protect him.'

The man reached across and smacked Mabor's face. 'Watch your tone.' He sat back.

Mabor didn't move, or flinch or touch his face, but instead gazed coolly at the man.

'How could I protect him?' said the man. 'He doesn't do as he's told.'

'What are you talking about? He worked hard, man, worked the whole area.'

'You heard.' The man dressed like a gangster sat back and pulled at his cuffs, calming himself. 'I had a little job for him and he refused.'

Mabor thumped the table in front of him. 'Bullshit.'

The man sniffed. 'Lots of snow coming down,' he said. 'On the hills. Heh heh.' He leaned back in the booth, arms akimbo. 'You should take advantage. Know how to snowboard?'

Mabor stood and gathered several plastic shopping bags. 'Do it. Soon. Okay?'

'Don't get ahead of yourself. I can't work miracles.' The man sniggered, like he could work one if he wanted to. 'In this business, you need to be patient. I've lost people over the years. Money too. Cops rip you off. Lost a shitload in a deal that went bad. What you have to learn to do is wait, bide your time then ... *wham*!' He slapped a hand into his fist. 'Take revenge.'

Mabor was shaking, legs, shoulders, nerves twitching. 'I won't wait.'

'He's not going anywhere. Now, another — what was that? A frappé?'

'I'm already late for school.' Mabor hissed and scooted out of the booth, but he stopped and leaned into the man's face. 'Adut shouldn't have got done, man.'

'Don't worry, I've got it now. Run along to school, and I'll be in touch.' The gangster pulled his phone from his pocket and started texting.

So. Adut Chol had been dealing — that much was obvious. But there was something else. *I had a little job for him and he refused.*

After a while, the gangster got up and dropped a twenty on the table. As he swaggered out of the café, I got a good look at the face.

A sudden impulse seized me and I ran outside and down

31

Racecourse Road towards the housing commission flats. Running, dodging the two women pushing prams, an elderly slow-coach with a walking-frame, I leapt the single chain slung between the posts and sprinted through the garden, past the playground and the skips and communal wheelie bins that were left strewn about after the garbage collectors had emptied them.

I ran into the foyer, and started stabbing at the *up* button. An age later, I pounded on Mrs Chol's door. She showed no surprise at seeing me, panting and leaning on my knees on her doorstep. She stepped back and allowed me to enter. 'You came for some coffee? I'll make coffee and I think perhaps you need a glass of water.'

'What? Oh yeah. Sure. Coffee. And can I use your bathroom?'

'Of course. You know where it is.'

I went down the hallway and straight into the room Mabor had shared with Adut. I dropped to my knees and felt around under the bed. There was no book. I stuck my head down under there. It was dark, too dark to see, so I slid right under and spread my arms. Something soft brushed my hand and I flicked it away.

'Here is your water.'

I crawled out. Mrs Chol was standing in the doorway, her expression unreadable.

'Thanks. I was just looking for a book of mine, er, that I dropped here.'

Mrs Chol blinked but her face didn't change. 'You have fluff all over your jumper.'

'Oh? Ha. Yeah. Not to worry.' I brushed my front and clumps of grey floated to the floor.

'Come with me, Stella.'

I followed her out to the lounge room. She put my water on a low table and sat on the sofa, and I sat on the armchair. 'Since the trouble with Adut I have not had the energy to clean.'

'Jeez, that's understandable — don't even, I mean, don't stress about that.'

Mrs Chol's eyes narrowed slightly. 'But after the police told me they had arrested Adut's killer, I cleaned all of his things out of his room. I did this for Mabor.'

I nodded. 'Right.' *All* of Adut's things. 'What did you do with his stuff?'

'I put it in the rubbish.'

My smile was a tight stretch of lips. 'Good.' The rubbish had been collected. The book was gone, landfill. Any sane person would leave it at that — I, however, was now planning to sort through the refuse of the entire city, if need be, for a book.

'The only things I kept were his books. Textbooks are so expensive. I gave them to Mabor.'

'What about exercise books? Used ones?'

'Even those, the books for writing, I gave them to Mabor. Adut's school books had only a little writing in them and Mabor could still use them.'

I was nodding furiously. 'Good, good.'

'But I did not find anything belonging to you.'

'No? You might have confused my book for one of Adut's. Can I go through them and check?'

'Mabor has them with him. At school.'

'He had some books on his desk. Maybe they're still there?'

'Let us go and see.'

'Let's.'

We stood. At the same time, a wall-phone in the kitchen started ringing. Mrs Chol held my gaze. 'Wait here for me, Stella.' She went to the kitchen.

'No need to trouble yourself,' I called from halfway down the hallway. 'I'll only be a moment.'

I ran to the bedroom and started sorting through the books on the desk. At the bottom of the pile was a stack of exercise books. I shuffled through them. Not there. I moved to the wardrobe; on one side, clothes were neatly folded on shelves, on the other, were some shirts on hangers. On the floor of the wardrobe were shoes lined up on top of some board games, Monopoly, chess. I pulled everything out onto the floor — and there it was, wedged between Scrabble and Cluedo. *Adut Chol, Year Ten, English*. I checked the back page. This was it.

I curled the thin book into a tube, shoved it in my handbag, and hurried back to the lounge. Mrs Chol was in the kitchen; without speaking, she hung up the receiver and came towards me.

'Got it,' I called breezily. As I made my way out, I turned back to Mrs Chol. 'See you round,' I said.

'Like a rissole,' she answered, a look of bewilderment on her face.

5

WITH THE book safely in my handbag, I jumped aboard a passing tram. It took off, speeding along Racecourse Road, the wheels screaming on the turn at the Showgrounds. It stopped at the lights on Bloomfield Road. I glanced around at my fellow passengers; none of them took any notice of me. Why would they, a sleep-deprived middle-aged woman in a tatty jumper, old jeans, and hair like a feral? No big deal, I'd looked worse. After a day of docking lamb tails, say, when a pile of tails stinking in the heat, bloody and covered in black flies, meant a good day's work. Or that one time during the school holidays when it was my job to ride my motorbike through mobs of sheep to find the flyblown ones. When I found one, I had a tin of foul-smelling chemicals that I poured over the fleece and watched the writhing maggots flee. After that, having fluff on my clothes and a few bags under the eyes were nothing.

Confident I was not being observed, I pulled the book from my bag, now curled and battered. I smoothed it across my knees and started to flip through it. Mrs Chol was right about one thing. It was mostly blank. There was a creative writing piece in the front about a boy with a flying skateboard who saves his family, and the world, from space monsters.

The centre pages were filled with a table of badly ruled lines, with a column of initials followed by several columns of numbers. I fanned out the pages, shook the book a few times, but nothing dropped out. I turned each page separately, the whole book, all forty-eight pages. Not one mention of me, other than my address. Nor was there any reference to an event at a certain commission flat six years earlier, nor the two junkies who lived there and the amount of money involved. I checked the list of initials to see if I recognised anyone: I didn't — nor did I see my own initials there.

I sat back, not knowing what to feel. Relief? Disappointment? I was a bit hungry, I could murder a bacon sandwich and — wait, why were we not moving? The lights had changed more than once and the tram hadn't moved. I craned my neck trying to see what the hold-up was. Cars had stopped at odd angles. Behind us another tram was backed up. I looked up at the sky, the low grey clouds, icy spit falling from them.

I flipped through the book again, slowly this time, studying each page. Then I noticed something on the page opposite the one with my address; it was the word: *Funsail.* It was circled and had arrows coming off it, leading around the page to my address.

Funsail?

An employee of the transport corporation began herding us from our tram, across the intersection and onto a packed tram in front. As I trudged along with everyone else, I heard quite a lot of whinging from the other passengers. Sure, it was raining again, and the temperature could freeze the tears in your eyes, but there were worse things that could happen. *Toughen the heck up, Melburnians,* I thought. *Toughen up yourself,* they said back to me, with their red, frozen eyeballs. *You know what you should do.*

Yes, I did.

I shunned the tram and kept on walking. Twenty minutes later I entered the grounds of Ascot Secondary College. I went directly to the office, where a harried woman slid open the reception window.

'Mabor Chol please, he's in year ten I believe.'

'What's your relationship to the boy?'

'Stella Hardy, I'm a social worker with WORMS.'

'Gee, sorry to hear that,' she chuckled.

'Look, can you please just page the student Mabor Chol?'

'Do you have clearance? Authorisation from a parent or teacher? We've had issues in the past.'

'How about the student counsellor, she in?' I asked.

Still chuckling to herself, she slid the window shut and turned on a staticky mic. 'Student counsellor to the office.'

The waiting area was directly opposite the principal's office. While I waited, I relived the trauma of high school, flashbacks of the hours of waiting for punishment, followed by my customary excuse: 'But it was all Shane Farquar's fault, sir!'

The counsellor bustled up to me, in a bright orange, over-sized jumper. I launched in like a woman on a mission, which I was. 'Mabor Chol. I need to see him.' I held up both my WORMS ID and my Department of Justice ID. She gave them a nod and started writing on a clipboard at the office window.

'Dear Mabor, such a good kid, you know? Really bright, hard working.'

'He's terrific, amazing. Look, this is urgent, can you hurry it up?'

'What's it about?'

'It's a confidential matter.'

'I'll keep it confidential.'

'It's about ... his brother. You are aware of his brother's death?'

'Yes. Tragic. Would you like me to be present?'

'No, thanks. It's all strictly ... confidential.' I was led to a room and told to wait again. Thirty seconds later, Mabor shuffled in. When he saw me, his eyes darkened with scorn. 'What?' he demanded.

He watched me as I closed the door — then we were alone. 'I'm not the enemy, you know,' I said.

A hint of a sneer. 'You? You're nothing.'

'Then who is?'

He shook his head and sat behind a desk. 'What is this? Huh? What do you want?'

'Are you in trouble?'

His face was deadpan, but his thumbnail was gouging at a crack in the desktop.

'Can you tell me what's going on with you? Who are you protecting?'

'You spying on me?'

'No.'

'I'm not protecting anyone.'

I considered my next move. 'A long time ago, when you were just a kid, there was an incident at the flats, same building as yours. There was a young couple living a few floors down from you, and they were junkies. One night they overdosed and they both died.'

He looked up, slightly bewildered. 'So?'

'I wondered if Adut ever told you about that.'

His puzzlement was clearly not an act. 'Adut? No, why would he?'

'You sure he never mentioned it?'

'What's this shit you're on about, huh? Junkies dying years ago — why would he care? Why would *I*? I've got enough problems to worry about.'

'Yes. Well. You were only about eight at the time, but gossip gets around. I thought you might have heard about it.'

'Can I go now?'

'Because there were lots of rumours at the time. People said there was money in the flat — drug money.'

'So of course you think me and Adut took it. If I was eight then he was ten; we were probably watching *The Simpsons* or some shit.'

'Of course you didn't take it.' This was not going well.

'I'm missing a science test for this garbage.'

'Just one last thing, Mabor. What is Funsail?'

'What?' He looked at me for a moment, then he closed his eyes and sighed. 'You don't know what you're talking about.' I watched him stand and head for the door. Before leaving, he turned to me. 'Stay out of things you don't understand.'

I don't understand? The nerve of him, the little juvenile delinquent. I understood all too well. I considered the events of the morning. I considered the book. The gangster type in the coffee shop. Then there was also the exchange of a bag, probably belonging to Adut, passed through the window of a four-wheel drive in the middle of the night. Clearly, it was time to swallow my pride and go see Phuong. Time to tell her everything I had heard. She could refer me to one of the detectives working on Adut Chol's murder. If that went well, maybe I could even show her the book, explain my reasons for taking it — after all, was it even a crime if the owner was himself a criminal? No, I could not tell her about the book. Never.

I pulled out my phone. There was a text from Boss, asking where the hell I was. I replied that he should calm down, and that I had been doing a home visit. Then I took a deep breath and rang the Footscray police station. Eventually, someone picked up. I said, 'Phuong Nguyen, please.'

'She got transferred. St Kilda Road.'

I hung up and checked my watch. Boss wouldn't miss me for another hour or so. It was time for a visit to the St Kilda Road police complex.

6

THE DESK sergeant was short, with a wrinkled-up face, grey hair in a basin cut. He was old-school — not the kind of man who might, say, photograph his food. I signed in and he issued me a visitor's pass. I was a little surprised that I was not required to reveal the contents of my handbag or walk through a metal detector. All that stood between me and about three hundred cops upstairs was a swinging metal gate, which opens when swiped with a security pass. Maybe they thought that, with so many cops around, no one would dare vault the gate and rampage around the building.

Bowl-cut phoned upstairs while I hung around the foyer, studying the cop miscellany in a trophy cabinet. After a while, I sat on a bench and read a copy of yesterday's *Herald Sun*. According to the weather forecast, it was rain and wind for Melbourne, with more snow expected on the mountains. Lake Mountain had opened its toboggan trails. Having scant feeling for snow, I turned to the celebrity news under the headline: *EYE ON THE GLITERATI*. My eye was drawn to a photo of a man and woman, arms around each other, both looking at a tall man with a moustache.

> ... Prominent Perth socialite Clayton Brodtmann and his wife, Crystal, with South African mining tycoon Merritt Van Zyl appreciating the champagne at last night's opening of the new Asian fusion restaurant at Crown, The Crouching Tiger ...

Mr Van Zyl was an odd fellow, judging from his outlandish, striped jacket and trilby. The moustache was circa 1970s Australian cricket team.

I didn't like the choice of name for the restaurant — *Crouching Tiger, Hidden Dragon* was in my list of top-five favourite movies; the *Lord of the Rings* trilogy, of course, took up the top three. I looked at Bowl-cut, he was staring at his computer screen. Just as I was considering leaving and trying my luck tomorrow, the security gate opened and she came strolling into the foyer. She wore a white shirt and navy slacks, and was kitted with her spray, cuffs, and revolver. I had to admit I was nervous to see her after all this time. She smiled and extended her hand. I nearly guffawed. Did she really expect us to shake hands?

'Chào bà,' I said. 'Chúc mừng năm mới.'

She blinked; a crinkle appeared in the serene forehead. 'It's July.'

'Is it? Dodgy bloody calendar.'

She snorted and dropped the cool act. 'Happy New Year to you, too,' she said, laughing. Not the gasping, desk-thumping, purple-faced fit of laughter my bad Vietnamese used to bring forth. Instead Phuong looked like she always did, like she lived on a diet of macrobiotic organic roughage and jogged ten kilometres a day. A complexion so radiant it made me physically ill.

'Coffee?' Phuong nodded towards the café across the road.

My headache tablets were wearing off; I was hungover, and buzzing, and lethargic all at the same time. There was a ringing in my ears and an odd tingling in my hands. More coffee would be ideal.

The café was the size of a walk-in wardrobe, with little kid tables and stools. Phuong ordered lattes and the guy flicked the switch on a coffee grinder. In the tiny space we waited, side-by-side, listening to the grinding. Probably the thing to do was to make some observation of the weather or the footy or the price of microdermabrasion these days, but my small talk was backed up like a dodgy sewerage system.

Phuong finally went with 'How's work?'

'Ah,' I closed my eyes — it felt nice, I was pretty tired. 'Okay.'

At last the guy put two glasses on the counter. I fished in my bag, but Phuong shelled out. 'We're taking these upstairs,' she said. 'I'll bring the glasses down later.'

'No worries, take your time.' The guy practically curtsied at her.

We went up in the lift, and I followed Phuong through a warren of partitioned workspaces to her cubicle. She patted the spare seat and I lowered my bottom onto it. By now, my vision was speckled, and either the air-conditioning was about to explode or I had developed tinnitus. 'Nice office, at least you get a window.'

'Building's already obsolete. We're moving to a mega cop-shop in the Docklands. So I'm told.'

'Why'd you transfer from Footscray?' I asked.

'Sat the test.' Phuong flashed her inscrutable smile. 'I'm with homicide.'

I hadn't seen it coming. Phuong, moving on. Moving up.

She picked up her pen, all business. 'So how can I help you?'

'Two years ago. Footscray. The Station Hotel.'

Phuong started to write, but stopped and looked at me. 'Stella, don't do this. Now is not the time —'

'Oh, yes. Now is. Very much.' I scooted my chair closer and lowered my voice. 'You sat there judging me like some B-grade celebrity on —'

'I really don't think —'

'I was simply trying to make a point about Australian men.'

Phuong mimicked me. 'It's culturally ingrained. Australian men think it's funny. Being a bastard.'

'Yes!' I hissed. 'But you took me completely out of context.'

'What was the context? Your abusive relationship?'

'No. I was speaking generally. But you go, "I don't think I can listen to this again." And I go, "What do you mean *this*?" And you go, "Endless complaining."' My face felt warm.

'Oh, I remember,' Phuong hissed back at me, pink spreading across her cheeks. 'Because you started going, "But Phuong, he's an arsehole. He laughs at me." So, you know. *Touché.*'

'But you got all moral about it.' Now I mimicked her. '"It's wrong, he's married."'

'God, I do not *believe* you. You think I was moralising? I was worried about you. What was I supposed to do?'

42

'You were my friend. You're supposed to validate the shit out of me. Instead of doing this one-woman intervention thing.'

'You were being emotionally abused. You said as much.'

'No. You objected because it was an affair. Because it was for sex. Jesus, the entire world does it. And you go all, "I can't pretend to tolerate it this time." And you go, "It's not just a bad relationship. He's not simply self-centred."'

Phuong sniffed, and squared off the papers on her desk.

'And you never said Jacob's name. What was he, Voldemort?'

'It was doomed from the start,' Phuong said, not looking up.

'Buddhists are supposed to be non-judgemental.'

Phuong leaned back in her chair, her eyes locked on mine. 'You know, there are a lot of women like you, intelligent, capable, confident, brought undone by scumbags. Men so beneath them —'

'Okay, okay.' How could I argue with that? I gave her an apologetic look, hoping I didn't have to give her a verbal one.

'Is Jacob the one? Does he make you happy?'

'No. He doesn't, actually, because it's over. For a while now. So, there you are. You were right.' That night, after Phuong left the pub and the door swung shut behind her, I watched as one of the few dependably heartening things in my life disappeared. 'I haven't been seeing anyone. It's the single life for me. All work and Thai takeaway.'

'Stella.' There was genuine sympathy in her eyes. 'He didn't deserve you.'

'By the way, you don't say *touché* about your own hit.'

Phuong raised a shoulder, a one-sided shrug, very French. 'I don't see why.'

I started to laugh. 'You say it when someone hits you. As in, *you got me.*'

She shook her head. Stubborn. Always was. 'Is there an actual police matter? Or did you just want to correct my English?'

'It's French.'

She rolled her eyes. 'Stella, come on, I'm busy.'

'Right, this is it,' I said. 'Adut Chol has a younger brother. I think he's in trouble.'

'African kids. There's always some crisis. You hear about the teenage prostitutes? They get driven around the western suburbs by a relative in a minivan.'

'Cop-culture got to you?'

'What?'

'Your fucking blasé racism.'

She turned to me, a look of surprise. 'No.'

'This kid, Mabor, I know him. I work with his mother.'

Phuong's gaze moved from me to the window. 'Adut Chol — who is he again?'

'He's the kid who was murdered last week. Clacker Pickering stabbed him —'

'Allegedly.'

'— Yes, whatever, and he died in hospital.'

Another cop peered over her cubicle. He wore a police-issue beanie and sported an enlarged upper lip, possibly from a fight. His name tag: *Constable Ashwood*.

'Tom,' said Phuong, with a sniff. 'What can I do for you?'

'Mind if I sit in on this one?' he said.

'That's not necessary,' Phuong said. 'I've got this.'

'Come on, Fang.' He came round and leapt up so his bum landed with a thud on her desk. 'Don't be selfish.' His indolent psycho-eyes began a slow sweep of my chest area. He looked stoned — maybe he was just tired. Then he picked up a small figurine from Phuong's desk, a deity of some kind, with flowing robes, and started to play with it.

I looked at Phuong. She sat back and closed her eyes. So I said, 'It's pronounced *foong*, dickhead, and get off her desk.'

Phuong opened her eyes, and I saw a flicker of light, as a silent understanding passed between us. Beanie-cop gave me a greasy eyeball. I smiled sweetly at him. He handed the statue to Phuong and moved, extra slow, off the desk. He pulled a notebook from his pocket and clicked his pen. The fluorescent lighting was unkind to his acne-scarred face. Phuong put the statue down. 'That's fine, Tom. I've taken care of the matter.'

'Matter? What *matter*?'

Phuong coughed.

'Going up the chain, is it? You seem to know how they like things done.' His words were full of barmy innuendo, like Phuong was in on some conspiracy. He pulled up a chair, turned it around and straddled it. 'Name?'

'Stella Hardy.' I spelled it, glancing at Phuong, who looked mildly amused. Frankly, I was frustrated with both of them.

'Address?'

'I've already got the details, thanks Tom,' she said.

Ashwood's fat lip curled. 'Of course you do.' He rose from his chair and swaggered back to his desk.

I knew his type. Where I came from, boys like him lived and breathed the same casual aggression. In my high school days, most of the boys were practised in the art of threat and humiliation, particularly Shane Farquar. Year eleven had been a difficult year for me — rumours circulated about me and some of the boys on the debating team. Farquar had cornered me in the gym and demanded to know the details. Every time I tried to get away, he blocked my path. He only let me go when the PE teacher came to get the croquet mallets. As for Ashwood, the dickhead remark probably didn't go down well.

Phuong tapped on her keyboard like Ashwood had never interrupted. 'Who is Adut Chol's brother then?'

'Mabor. Good kid. Smart, good at school.'

'And?'

'I overheard him in a conversation with a very dodgy-looking bloke, and they were saying stuff about *getting* someone inside.'

Phuong stopped typing, a hand went to her ear, moved the gold sleeper around. 'You overheard him?'

'Yes, I mean, it was clear. Very clear, and they were talking about making someone suffer.'

Phuong sighed. 'Stella, you do tend to get over-involved with your clients, emotionally. Sometimes it can be hard to see the facts clearly.'

I saw the facts clearly. 'You don't believe me.'

'I believe you heard something. Look, why don't you tell the Flemington police. They probably already know who Mabor's hanging around with.'

Tell Flemington? Tell Ross? Or that cop who referred to Ross as 'the Khaleesi' — that bully? 'It relates to Adut's murder. It's completely within your bailiwick,' I said.

'But I can't go to Copeland with something you think you heard. I need more evidence than a conversation with some guy — you don't even know who he is.'

'Show me some mug shots, I'll identify him. He seemed familiar, I bet he's a known drug dealer.'

'Evidence.'

Adut's book was somewhere in the bottom of my handbag. A drug dealer's client list. From it, the police could trace the dealer, connect the dots. I inhaled and drew myself up. 'Well, it was nice seeing you.'

'Oh come on, don't be like that. Got plans for lunch?'

I shrugged.

'I'm flat out here all morning but let's say I pick you up later at your place. We'll have lunch and you can tell me all about it.' Phuong ushered me to the lift. Before the doors closed, she started laughing: 'Did you see the look on his face?'

'Who?'

'Ashwood. Classic Stella.'

7

THE PLAN: go home, change out of my dirty clothes, and slip into a fabulous new outfit. Sitting on the tram, I regretted rushing to St Kilda Road in my usual shabby clothes. Phuong may have misinterpreted my attire as a sign that I was a depressed, barely-functional figure of misfortune. I intended to arrive at lunch looking confident, fresh, respectable — then give Phuong the book: *here's your damn evidence.* She would know what to do, how to keep me out of the picture. It was only my address after all, not some statement of guilt.

In the time it took to walk from the tram to my street, I'd changed my mind. The book was my secret. Why get the police involved? My god, what was I, crazy? I might inadvertently cause them to dig further, to investigate an event that happened six years ago; an event that was not really a crime, not a proper one.

In the *PineView* foyer, I found my letterbox stuffed full. I juggled the shopping and put the bundle of letters under one arm and bolted up the stairs. On the third-floor landing, a figure in a hoodie sat cross-legged on my doorstep. I released an involuntary shriek. It looked up from the newspaper it was reading. 'Hey Stella, it's me.'

My youngest brother, without a word, appeared and disappeared with the speed of a delinquent Harry Potter. 'Ben. Long time — no requests for money.'

'Good to see you, Stella. How's it going?'

I let myself into his embrace. It was not as comforting as I'd hoped. His body was cold and he was thin. 'I'm okay.'

He stepped back. 'You look different.' He studied my face in the poor light. 'You've got wrinkles.'

I let that go. 'When did you get out?'

He shrugged. 'A while ago, been living in Sunshine. Boarding house.'

'That sounds nice.' I unlocked the door. 'Eaten anything today?'

'No. Actually, I'm starving.'

I threw my bag on the sofa and had a good look at him. He was standing self-consciously in the middle of the room. He coughed. He frowned. He opened his mouth and closed it. Hard to believe that he'd once been a cheeky little hell-raiser, so advanced was his state of decay. The grey whiskers added ten years, and his number-one haircut made him look frail rather than tough. I was not a fan of the number-one. Why had every male in the country decided, overnight it seemed, to forgo hair? He coughed again. I twigged at last. 'No.'

'But you're family.'

'Mum's family. Stay with her.'

'Ha ha, very funny. Come on, Stella. My shit is together. Look, I'm clean.' He rolled up his sleeves and showed me his arms, twisting them round. I inspected them closely. Apart from his dodgy tatts, there were no track marks and none of those scratches the ice addicts do to themselves. 'I'm working,' he said, pushing his sleeves down. 'Going straight — and this time I mean it.'

I let my sigh go on till my lungs nearly collapsed. 'How long?'

'Only for a couple of weeks.'

'One week.'

He grinned and dropped his backpack. 'What's in the fridge? Fuck me, Stella. What do you live on?'

'Toast.'

'You can't live on toast. You need vegies. Five serves a day.'

'You want toast?'

'Sure.'

'One week, right? And that's it.' I dropped a couple of slices of Wonder White in the toaster. 'How did you know I wasn't at work?'

'I didn't. I was going to hang around until you got home.'

'You're pathetic.' I put margarine and Vegemite on the bench.

He stood guard over the toaster. 'Why *aren't* you at work?'

'Mind your own beeswax.' I left him to sort himself out, toast-wise. Heaven knew it was the only kind of sorting he could do.

In the bathroom, I opened the door of the medicine cabinet so I could see my wrinkles in the mirror — they were there. I turned to leave and whacked my forehead on the corner of the cabinet. I stood there cursing and holding my head. Then it occurred to me that Tania may have had an accident at home. If she had slipped in the bath and was lying there unconscious this whole time, I'd feel like a real dill. I found Ben in the kitchen sorting my mail. Perhaps this was what a personal assistant was like. I thought of Finchley, imagined the order and elegance of his daily routines.

'Who're Joyce and Frank?'

'Wrong letter box,' I said. 'I'll take it down later.'

'They're having the *best time*. Snorkelling and paragliding, and tomorrow they're taking a boat to Oarsman's Bay.'

'Ben?'

'S'up?'

'With all your unauthorised skills and talents, are you able to break into, say, a third-floor flat? Hypothetically?'

'Is the Pope an accessory to child abuse?' He munched his toast like a starved animal. '*Hypothetically?* What's the flat?' I gave him a truncated version of the particulars and a fib about lending Tania a DVD — *sure she wouldn't mind, must have it back.*

'You're sure she won't mind? I'm on parole, you know.'

'Yes. Totally sure.'

'Alright, let's do this shit.'

Apparently the paperclip-in-the-lock thing was bollocks. Ben told me that with a disdainful look. And with the words, 'Where'd you get that stupid idea?'

'*Terminator 2*,' I said. 'What, then?'

'Bathroom window.'

'On the third floor?'

'It'll be open. Everyone leaves their bathroom window open.' He was already bounding down the stairs, two at a time. I bolted after him and skirted round to the rear courtyard.

Ben was at the back of the flats pointing. 'See?'

I followed the line from his finger to a not-closed casement window roughly ten metres from the ground. He tested the downpipe; it seemed secure. He grabbed it with both hands and began climbing up the wall. He swung a leg round to rest a foot on a second-floor window ledge, and manoeuvred his weight across and up further. Then he grabbed Tania's window ledge and raised himself up. He flicked the metal arm, pulled the window back and squeezed in. Easy as you like. 'I'll open the front door,' he called, in a stage whisper. *Unnecessary*, I thought. *And a bit conceited.* I ran round and up the stairs. Tania's door was ajar.

Her flat was a mirror image of mine, only much, *much* better. The TV was the size of a boardroom table. A black leather Bauhaus chaise — a reproduction surely — stood in the corner. On the wall was a small, unframed painting that looked like an early John Blackman. It must have been a copy. Still. I was impressed by her taste. Or was that her business acumen? Art was considered a good investment. If I ever had money, I'd put it in art. I resolved to investigate some galleries just in case.

All this luxe made me wonder what a beauty therapist earned these days. Clearly, the community sector had some catching up to do. Of course, you didn't do it for the money. There was the opportunity to rub shoulders with grinding poverty and self-defeating behaviour. Unfortunately however, every now and then, you did come across some truly dreadful people: the bureaucrats and politicians passing through for photo ops. Truth be told, as far as my clients were concerned, money, or the lack of it, wasn't the number-one issue. The divisions were deepest in values, attitudes, clothes. The law courts were a good place to see that. The lawyers were all dark suits and business shoes and the accused was in his best hoodie. His friends and family showed up in trackpants — worn low — T-shirts with obscenities on them, football guernseys, a certain style of sports leisure-wear, the mere sight of which unnerved the more genteel middleclass. Only the deluded could say Australia was classless.

By now, Ben was going through her cupboards. 'Hey, this chick's loaded. Laptop, iPod, camera, phones —'

'Leave things alone, can't you?'

'An iPad.'

'Show me.' I poked my head in the cupboard. On a bottom shelf was a brand new iPad, still in the box. Next to it was a digital SLR camera, also new. I couldn't quite tally this place with Tania the naive, nervous Nellie.

Ben had moved on to some drawers. 'Wow.' He held up a bundle of envelopes. 'Someone likes writing letters.'

I rolled my eyes; he had the IQ of an amoeba.

'Fortynucks —'

'Give those to me.' Business-size envelopes — the top left-hand corner: *Faurtinaux Bath*, the address was a post-office box in Perth. The typed addressee on the front: *Miss Nina J. Brodtmann*, and some address in Cottesloe. I'd never been to WA and I didn't know much about the place, but I knew Cottesloe was the well-to-do part of Perth. Alan Bond lived there.

I checked the bathroom and the toilet. No unconscious Tania. I went to her bedroom, and found no one in there. Her wardrobe was equal in size to mine, built-in, and with two doors. But compared to my dull, monochrome work wear, Tania's wardrobe was a silky, glittering, sequinned, leopard-skinned, and shining gold mess. There was no dead body in among the sparkles though. I even checked under the bed. Nothing, no one.

Back in the lounge room, I noticed her coffee table had drawers, and one of the drawers was open and was empty. I checked the others: one had more bundles of letters, pens, small writing pads — all with the same Faurtinaux Bath swirl. There were a couple of business cards in there too: one for a security-door firm, a taxi service, and one for a *Vince McKechnie, Fairfax Media journalist*. In the another drawer, I found a packet of incense, nail clippers, a remote control, a USB drive, DVDs in plastic sleeves, and the WA licence of Nina Brodtmann with a photo of Tania's not-smiling face.

'Look,' I said, showing Ben the licence. 'That's her ... but her name's not Nina Brodtmann.'

'Interesting,' Ben said, flipping through a pile of CDs. 'Did you know she had all this gear?'

'No, I didn't.'

Brodtmann. I tried to remember where I'd heard that name before. I tried snapping my fingers, but it failed to jog my memory. Was it the name of a celebrity, perhaps? Then it came to me, someone with that name had been at the opening of the Crouching Tiger restaurant, in a photo with the South African bloke in the funny hat. *Prominent Perth socialite Clayton Brodtmann and his wife Crystal*. Could those people be Tania's parents? It would explain the money. I looked at the Blackman on the wall. It probably *was* an original.

Now Ben was into her kitchen cupboards, inspecting the pantry. 'Whoa, she's got scotch, tequila, vodka.' He showed me a bottle of French cognac. 'What does she do again?'

'Beauty therapist.'

'Jesus. Might take that up myself.'

'Let's go.'

'Do your nails, Mrs Hardy? Fancy a facial?'

'It's *Ms* Hardy and no, at least not from you. Now, let's go.'

'You going out the front door?'

'Yes. Why?'

'I'll make sure it's all clear.'

'Good one, Ben.' And for the first time ever, I was not being sarcastic. Brown Cardigan needed no encouragement to create rumours of my misdeeds. I waited while Ben looked through the peephole. On the sideboard by the door was Tania's handbag.

'All clear.'

'Just a sec.' I pulled the zip back. Phone. Make-up. Wallet. Keys.

'Come on, Stella.' Ben grabbed my arm and marched me out of there. Once inside my flat, Ben paced the room. Nothing like a little breaking and entering to get the juices flowing. 'She's been abducted,' he said.

I had reached a similar conclusion. I hadn't said the word, hadn't allowed myself to think it, but the idea was there, and it stirred dread in my heart like a sacred truth. 'That's bullshit. You have an excessive imagination.'

'She has a fake name. Why?' he demanded.

'Wants to get some distance from her family.' It was a choice I could relate to.

'So where is she?'

'Maybe she went to the wine bar on Union Road and met someone.'

'We both saw her handbag. Why would she go to a wine bar without her handbag?'

'Let's google the new name, real name, whatever — Nina Brodtmann.'

I set up my laptop at the kitchen table and Ben pulled up a chair. I started pressing keys, searching for an unsecured network. *Deathcult245, De-LINK888, Donteventhinkaboutit, Furphy.* Furphy aka Brown Cardigan had wireless, no password required. Network strength: very good.

Nina Brodtmann had made the papers. Celebrity news. She was the youngest child of Clayton and Juliana Brodtmann. Juliana died in 2002 and Clayton had married Crystal Watt in 2003. In the wedding photos, the new wife was a skank with a horsey face, dark around the eyes, fake-tanned the colour of baby poo, breasts that hung in mid-air, and eyelashes like a child's drawing. The gown cost more than I earned in a year. Three years.

'They're rich,' Ben said in awe.

I clicked on *Clayton* and followed the Brodtmann links. He went to Sydney University, was a member of the Castleburn Grammar old boys club … pro bono work for Sri Lankan refugees … had attended a fundraiser for the Cancer Council. One of the grainy photos had a familiar face. It was taken, judging from the foppish haircuts and pirate shirts, in the eighties. They both had goofy grins. Caption: *Clayton Brodtmann and Finchley Price in the Sydney University Law Review.* And he had been a senior partner at Faurtinaux Bath. Faurtinaux Bath was your average mid-sized law firm, based in Perth; specialising in corporate law, taxation, competition, and regulatory law. Offices in Singapore, Beijing, and Tokyo. Since leaving, he and Crystal had set up numerous enterprises including CC Prospecting, a mining company with assets over three billion dollars.

'I never thought I'd say this,' Ben said. 'But it's time to get the cops involved.'

I was thinking the same thing. 'You want to call? Anonymously?'

'What? No. Are you crazy? Tell that friend of yours. What's her name — Phuong?'

'Tell Phuong?' After she dismissed my concerns about Mabor? It was almost 1.00pm. Phuong was probably already downstairs. Damn, I didn't have time to change into something more professional-looking.

'Where's that copy of the *Herald Sun* you were reading?'

He pointed to the sofa. I flicked through to the *EYE ON THE GLITERATI* pages, found the article and tore it out. Then I put on my coat. 'I'm going to see Phuong.'

'Bout time,' Ben said.

As I opened the door, I noticed, with a heavy heart, a red blink on my landline phone. She must have called while we were in Tania's flat. I hit *play.*

It's Mum, love. Tyler's fortieth birthday's this weekend. I'm having a little get together for him here at the farm. Making that casserole you like, and a sponge. By the way, that Shane Farquar's been ringing up here leaving messages, saying things.

Ben was laughing. 'Dodged a bullet there, Stella.'

8

PHUONG ROCKED up in an unmarked Commodore she'd wangled from the Victoria Police maintenance garage. I hopped in and we fanged out of there. Soon, we were merging into the westbound traffic on the toll flyover and navigating the bewildering weave of highway ribbons. Make a wrong turn, hesitate for a nanosecond, and you could find yourself in Geelong or Bendigo, or back where you started. But Phuong was up to the task, and we threaded the concrete needle, an architectural hoax, unyielding and sculptural like a Playtex bra — for lifting and separating lanes — then she sped onto the bridge like those deep-fried spicy ribs would not wait.

As she passed a thundering P-plater in a ute — we had to be going over a hundred and thirty — she was chatting away. 'So Ben showed up, did he? How is he, what's he doing?' I held the side of my seat belt and concentrated on my breathing. At the Footscray Road turn-off, Phuong slowed to a hundred. I unclenched my every muscle and silently thanked whatever God it was that had allowed me to live to see another day.

In a lane off Hopkins Street, she parked, with two wheels on the footpath.

'Very narrow street; this is better,' Phuong said. 'Safer.'

'Pretty certain for a Buddhist. Where's the doubt? The reticence?'

She ignored me, and the many misdemeanours happening around us, like the enterprising teenager exchanging goods for money on the corner.

Footscray was busy — and deliciousness was in the air. That's when I twigged we were headed for Thien An, on Irving Avenue. As the aromas became stronger, I developed sudden, frenzied cravings: *must eat … sugarcane prawn … fried noodle … must have … shaken beef on rice.* We took a table and I studied the menu. The place was packed, and everyone was shouting to be heard over the cheesy love song on the PA and the industrial kitchen machinery being used at high revs out the back. When the guy came with the thermos of jasmine tea and the little cups, Phuong ordered in rapid Vietnamese without bothering to consult me. We were back, baby. *Old times.*

'I need to ask you about a police thing.'

'Another police thing?' She poured out the tea. 'What did you overhear now?'

I looked at her without speaking.

'What?'

I said, 'Well, just now I overheard my friend being a total bitch.'

Phuong had the decency to look chastened. 'I regret that remark.'

As apologies went, it was pathetic, but I moved on. 'It's about my neighbour, in the flat across the landing; a young woman living on her own. We were supposed to meet today and she didn't show. She didn't go to work. She's not answering her phone. She's not at home. I'm worried.'

'When was she last seen?'

'Last night — I left her place around midnight.'

She lowered her cup and put an elbow on the table, rested her chin on her thumb. 'Did you hear anything?'

'No. Look, I know it's too soon for an APB or whatever you do. But — and I only just found this out — she's been using a different name.'

She dug in her bag and pulled out an iPad. 'Give me all the details. Is she a client?'

'No.'

'An unofficial one, one of your rescue jobs?'

'Jesus, why does everyone keep saying that?'

'Who's "everyone"?'

'No one.'

'Ninety per cent of the time they turn up.'

'It's out of character.'

57

'Character is an illusion; at the centre of all beings is *shunyata*, the void. There is no abiding self.'

'I don't know when you became so supercilious, but that's twice now that you've dismissed my concerns. While you're making Zen jokes, Tania is God-knows-where.'

Phuong raised her eyebrows. 'Stella, I'm trying to take you seriously but you do have a tendency to overreact sometimes.'

'What? Is it too soon? How long does a person have to be missing, for fuck's sake?'

'There's no waiting period. You can report a missing person as soon as you think there's cause for concern.'

'There is.'

Phuong frowned. 'Was she in danger?'

'How would I know? Maybe.'

'Where's she from again?'

'Perth. And what about the name change? Her real name is Nina Brodtmann.'

Phuong pecked this information into the screen.

A waitress came from the kitchen with a plate held high. We eyed it reverently until it was in front of us, a pile of crispy, golden chicken pieces on a bed of lettuce and fried noodles, smothered in salt, oil, chilli — in short, the heroin of food. More plates arrived: broken rice with shredded pork, a platter of seafood, and assorted tasty morsels. We'd never eat it all — but we'd die trying. We transferred portions to our little bowls. I abandoned the chopsticks and used a fork, for improved face-stuffing results. Eventually, I came up for air and patted my lips with a napkin. I cleared my throat. 'This is confidential, okay?'

A crease appeared on the Phuong forehead. 'What?'

'I went into her apartment. Ben helped me break in.'

'Of course he did. When was this?'

'Before I spoke to you. Her handbag is in there.' I looked her in the eye, held her gaze.

'I agree,' she said. 'It's not good.'

'Her bag with her wallet, phone, everything; and her car is in the carport.'

Phuong expelled air with a small exasperated groan that told me I was taxing her loyalty, her patience, her Zen-ishness. 'How involved are you in this woman's life?'

I shrugged. 'Not much. I thought she was *Tania the blonde beauty therapist* until this morning.'

'Could she have gone back home? Did you ring her parents?'

'Not yet. Her dad is Clayton Brodtmann.'

'You say that like he's someone.'

'He's a director of a mining company that made a two-billion-dollar profit last year and didn't pay tax.'

Phuong stared at me, all seriousness, her chopsticks paused in mid-air. 'The parents are wealthy?'

'Top one per cent of oligarchs.'

'Shit, Stella. Fucking shitballs.' She whipped out her phone and started texting. 'Who are they?'

'Crystal Watt and Clayton Brodtmann. They have a mining company — more than one, actually. One is CC Prospecting, they're directors. Watt is her step-mother.' I took the newspaper article out of my bag and read: ... *Prominent Perth socialite Clayton Brodtmann and his wife Crystal ...*

Phuong took the article, barely glanced at it, and handed it back. Before I put it away, I studied the photo, carefully this time. Clayton Brodtmann was a handsome man in his fifties, work done round the eyes, distinguished grey hair at the temples. Crystal was somewhere between fifteen and sixty, blonde bun, thick black eyeliner, false lashes. From her bony frame, sheathed in gold lamé, sprouted improbably large breasts. Nature had not fashioned those, nor maternity neither. Old-school vulgar rather than fashion victim.

'Let's see what Bruce makes of it,' Phuong was saying.

'Bruce Copeland?'

'Yes.' She put the phone down and started a furious minute of typing on her tablet, finishing with a hard final tap. 'Is that it? You've told me everything now?'

'Yes. I only just found out about the Brodtmann thing myself.'

'She is estranged from the family?'

'Given she changed her name and moved interstate, that's a fair guess.'

Phuong seized another morsel and guided it to her mouth. 'She's worth God-knows-how-much but chooses to live in a tiny, nondescript flat on the other side of the country.'

'Hey. They're *nice* flats. Great location.'

'I've seen where you live,' said Phuong. She pushed her bowl away. 'Right. I've filed the missing persons. Bruce is in the loop, there'll be the leg work, cops going to her home, her work. They'll take it from there.'

She was on her feet, fished a twenty from her bag. 'You need a lift home?'

'No.'

She left and came back. 'Stella. It was Jacob, the man. The way he treated you. Not the fact that he was married. You know?'

'Right. I see that now,' I lied. How quaint her version of history was.

She gave me a quick hug. 'Let's catch up soon, okay?'

9

I SAT there while a waitress cleared the table. She worked briskly, getting on with it. I felt almost guilty, I had things I should have been getting on with too. I opened my bag to find my wallet and saw Adut's book. The idea of burning it was starting to seem wise.

I paid the cashier and asked for takeaway boxes and a plastic bag. Ben would get his damn vegetables tonight. Outside, the sun had come out and I wandered along Irving Street to the end of Nicholson Street. People were sitting outdoors in spite of the cold. Well-dressed men in suits: 'Do you have something for me in that bag, girl?' Tall, elegant women in printed dresses and headscarves walked in groups, some with babies in slings. Herds of school-aged girls were heading to the nail salon, others were hanging around the bakery. I turned right at Paisley Street and crashed into an A-frame signboard in the middle of the footpath. I cursed and clutched my knee. Public hazard, those signs. I dragged it to one side, reading the words: *The Narcissistic Slacker Art Gallery.* An arrow pointed up through a doorway between two shops, which was open and led to a wooden staircase.

Art gallery. That could mean anything: a pile of old junk, a grainy video, or stuffed dead animals. I thought of the Blackman in Tania's flat. I liked it. I liked paintings. But who was I kidding, I didn't have the money for art. I'd had money once, ill-gotten lucre, and I'd put it all on my mortgage. It would never happen again. Never would I let myself succumb to temptation like that again. And besides, dead junkies didn't just leave bags of money lying around every day of the week. The very idea induced a galloping heartbeat, shallow breathing, dizziness, trembling, and constriction in my muscles. *Drug money,* how could I have been so stupid? Whoever owned it, sooner or later, would come for it. For me. And I wouldn't see it coming.

Death, execution style. I looked around the street, to the rooftops, for an assassin.

The thing to do was run. Start a new life, maybe in Fiji. Live in the tropics, eat bananas, and become an artist, a modern-day Gauguin. I'd always had a vague ambition to be artistic. If I had only chosen that path back then, I'd be good at it by now and I wouldn't be a burnt-out social worker with real estate and a guilty conscience.

New plan: I would take the redundancy package from work and flee to Fiji — and live a humble, modest life in a tropical paradise. It was an excellent plan, and the first step was to visit this art gallery to get some inspiration.

Also, I imagined Ben's face when I told him I'd spent the afternoon in an art gallery: a look of soaring, credulous esteem.

In a sudden burst of elan, I bounded up the stairs. As I approached the gallery door, I heard a series of sneeze-explosions, five, six on the trot. At the top of the stairs a metal sliding door was open enough to squeeze through. Beyond, tinny music played through rough speakers, a female voice singing. I squeezed through the gap and found myself in a cavern with a high ceiling, concrete floor, white walls, and a wall of grimy windows at the far end. Standing by the windows, in front of an easel with a stretched canvas on it, was a dusty-looking dude with dark hair and grey stubble. He was blowing his ample beak into a manky hanky. I cleared my throat. He pocketed the handkerchief, picked up a paintbrush, and started tapping his foot and humming, oblivious to anything else. 'Hey,' I yelled.

'Jesus.' He clutched at his chest and staggered. 'You scared the crap out of me.'

'I saw the sign.'

He stared at me uncomprehendingly.

'Gallery?'

'Oh, right.' He dropped the brush into a tin on the floor and wiped his hands on his jeans. He had wary blue-grey eyes that watched me while he stooped and hit the stop button on the tape player. A genuine cassette tape player. Little towers of tapes beside it.

'Peter Brophy,' he said, hand extended.

I reached my hand through the handles of my plastic bag for a shake.

'Shopping?'

'Leftovers.'

'This way.' He got out a bunch of keys. 'Security conscious,' he said apologetically. The adjoining room was larger still, with afternoon sun filtered through cloudy windows. The canvases were arranged at even intervals along the wall, about fifteen or so. Repetition in the style: light central figures bordered by darker hues. I walked up to the nearest one for a closer inspection. A man, a business executive type, with multiple arms à la the Hindu pantheon. A fist full of dollars, a mobile, a flower, and a tea cup. A line of fish swimming nose-to-tail circled the man, and a kangaroo looked on from the side. The face, half in shadow, seemed skilled in the ways of absurdity — no smile, intelligent eyes. At once sad and beautiful. Strange emotions clashed within me; a fissure threaded along a weak seam.

The next painting had the same man in a different stance, dressed as a Shakespearean figure, with a rap-artist pose, encircled by seagulls. Sure, there was a naive quality, a surrealist idealism thing. But they were enthralling and pleasing and I liked these paintings, how uplifting they were. I was on the verge of laughing out loud. Not that there was anything cartoonish here; he was a serious guy.

'The opening is tonight.'

Whoa — he was behind me. I turned, a look of unabashed joy on my face.

'You're welcome to come, if you want. There'll be cheese. Some kind of cheese. On toothpicks.'

'Classy. Did you do these?'

Both fists went into his pockets. 'Mucking around with an idea.'

'I like them.'

'Buy one then.'

I laughed. 'How much?'

He blinked, smiled. 'Let me see. You a collector?'

'Absolutely. *All* my money is in art.'

'Really?'

'Oh, God yeah. DVDs mainly. Actual box sets of DVDs. Complete sets!'

A grin cracked under the stubble. 'You drink beer?'

'Is the Pope an accessory to — I mean, yes. I do.'

He stayed looking at me for a millisecond, then left.

Now I could continue at my leisure. I stopped at the last painting. A glimpse of lovers with languid arms entwined, plain and raw and magnificent.

'Here.' He pressed a stubby of VB into my palm.

I took a sip. The moisture triggered unrestrained thirst. I sipped at it again, then kept going, taking a long drink. It neutralised the saltiness but it wasn't enough. I upended it. It was good. Then it was gone. 'Thanks. So what time tonight?'

'What?' he asked, looking with astonishment from the empty stubby in my hand and back to me.

'The opening tonight, what time is it?'

'Oh, um. Nine-thirty,' he said. He picked up a flyer from a desk by the door. 'Official invitation.'

I stuffed it in my pocket. 'Great.' I handed him the empty. 'See you then.'

Trotting down the steps, I hit the pavement at a canter. The spring was back in my step. I walked to an idling tram and sat down just as my phone buzzed.

A Phuong text: *Brodtmann staying @ crown. You call?*

My phone battery was nearly flat. I replied: *Yes thnx.* While I was searching for the number of the Crown Casino Hotel, my phone rang.

'This is Clayton Brodtmann's assistant, Nigel Broad. Is this Stella Hardy?'

'Yes.'

'You are a friend of Nina Brodtmann?'

'How did you get this number?'

'You reported her missing. The police have been in touch with the family.'

'Right.' I was flustered for some reason. 'I told them that Nina didn't meet with me this morning as arranged, and she didn't show up for work. I'm worried about her.'

'And you're a friend of Nina?'

'Yes.' I fought the urge to say 'Sir'.

'Miss Hardy, Clay Brodtmann has instructed me to — just a minute.'

The tram moved with a sudden jerk and I almost slipped off the seat. Outside, two people came running alongside and banged on the doors. The driver stopped to let them on, telling them they should not bang on the tram. They told him to get fucked.

'Miss Hardy?'

'Who's this?'

'Clayton Brodtmann. My wife and I are very grateful for your concern about our daughter. We wondered if you might have time to talk to us, to tell us more about Nina. Would you mind coming to our hotel?'

'Sure, but I can't get there until —'

'I'm sending my car to your flat now.'

A car? Who were these people? When the tram was two blocks from my stop, I saw that the nearby high school had just unleashed its students on the world. It must have been sports day — teenagers in shorts wandered like Brown's cows all over the place, jamming the roads in every direction. I hopped off the tram and walked. There was no car waiting for me in Roxburgh Street.

As I neared my building, the stocky bloke in the shorts and the thongs, who I'd seen earlier, ambled out of the entrance and up Roxburgh Street. Maybe he'd moved into the neighbourhood.

Upstairs, I kicked off my boots, and plugged my phone into the charger and tried Mrs Chol while it was charging. Still no answer.

While I waited for Brodtmann's car to arrive, I opened the laptop and searched for images of Melbourne gangland identities. I scrolled and clicked for a while — then I found him. The man I'd seen talking to Mabor was Gaetano Cesarelli. He was a flamboyant man, Gaetano. In one picture, he was addressing reporters outside court in a Hawaiian shirt and striped shorts. In an *Age* photo, he had on aviator sunglasses and a black muscle T-shirt. An article mentioned his convictions for grievous bodily harm, illegal possession of firearms, his beating up an old man in a road rage incident.

There was still no sign of a limousine downstairs so I googled Constable Thomas Ashwood. There was a news item that named him as the first police officer on the scene of a suicide in a remote house in, of all places, Warracknabeal.

Nick Cave was from Warracknabeal.

I googled Nick Cave, chased a few random links, and found a great version of 'The Ship Song' by Amanda Palmer. I googled Amanda Palmer and found a YouTube video of her song about her 'Map of Tasmania', a clear winner for my new ringtone. Once I'd downloaded it to my phone, I googled Oarsman's Bay: a tropical paradise in the Fijian archipelago. Downmarket from Turtle Bay, upmarket from Suva. A place without a care. Little bungalows, all meals provided. My neighbours' friends Joyce and Frank were probably sipping cocktails as they swayed in their hammocks, the gentle lapping of the sea in their ears, the swish of palm leaves above them.

I closed the laptop, and checked out the window. A white limousine was just pulling up under the pine tree. A man in the chauffeur's uniform headed into my building. I hopped around the room trying to get my boot on, while brushing my hair and putting on my jacket. When I got downstairs, I found the driver studying the names on the intercom in the foyer. The remote locking system didn't work and the names were all incorrect but it did lend the

66

place a certain air of fear and suspicion that said *class*.

'You Stella?'

'Yes.'

'Nigel Broad. Mr Brodtmann sent me to pick you up.'

That was the extent of our conversation — after that, total silence, even the outside world was hushed, like being driven around in a sound-proof hotel suite — until the car pulled in at Crown Casino. Broad murmured into his phone then snapped it shut. 'Go wait in the foyer,' he told me. 'Ms Watt is coming to get you.'

10

CROWN CASINO, a cesspool of avarice, corruption, and thuggery, with fancy carpet and flashing lights — and the sound of money going down the drain. It was well known that Melbourne's criminal society used its rooms for their transactions, that urine gathered in pools under the blackjack tables, that highfliers were seduced while misbehaving low-rent punters were put in a wristlock and manhandled out the door. The ballroom hosted grandiose sports nights, replete with a televised red-carpet parade of tizzed-up WAGs.

I hung around the foyer wondering who, exactly, might be impressed by all this phoney razzle-dazzle when I saw a blonde bouffant weaving through the crowd. Crystal Watt wore a tan and white ensemble — leather skirt and jacket, white over-the-knee boots. Up close, her face was gaunt and pale, as though she was permanently exhausted; her nose was straight and probably cost a bomb, but she had left the eyes undoctored. The area around them was dark, the expression pure sorrow. Rather than a flaw, it had the effect of softening the beauty and making her extraordinary. I imagined that a lot of men, some women even, would very much like to make her smile.

'You're Stella?'

'Yes.'

She looked me over with a hint of dismay. 'You are friend of Nina?'

'Yes.'

'Come with me.' She hooked an arm around mine and I inhaled an expensive floral scent. 'We go in private entrance. Security-pass area.' She had a pass card on a lanyard. 'Suite is nice.' She took me out of Crown's casino and into its hotel via a covered walkway. I trotted to keep up with the clip of her boots on the polished marble.

'You will see my dogs. Did she tell you? I have two.'

'Er, no.' I assumed 'she' was Tania.

We stopped at doors marked *staff only*. Crystal opened them and walked to a goods lift. She swiped her card and gave me a sidelong look. 'She is Tania now.'

'Yes,' I answered, not sure if it was a question.

'Nina is nice name. After her grandmother.'

The doors opened; we stepped in and the lift raced skyward and then cruised to a stop. The doors opened again and a man in a tartan sports jacket stepped in. The moustache, spiffy bow tie, and waist coat — it had to be Merritt Van Zyl, the man I'd seen in the photo.

He backed up. 'Look who it is, the Polish Madame.'

'I told you, I'm Russian,' Crystal hissed at him as she passed. 'What are you doing here?'

'I had business with Clay,' he said.

'What business?'

'None of yours.' He looked me up and down. 'Who or what is this creature? Not one of the well-heeled, is she?' He turned to Crystal. 'Did one of your customers request an ageing lesbian cleaning woman?'

'Hey, Happy Hammond.' I pointed my finger at his face. 'None of those things is an insult.' I stepped into his personal space. 'But only a dick would say *well-heeled*.'

He shrank back into the lift, rapidly jabbing the *down* button.

Crystal laughed and put her arm around my shoulder. 'Don't take notice. He's fucking poofta.'

I didn't want to get into a homophobia thing with her so I said, 'How does he get away with insulting you like that?'

She did a demure lift of the shoulders. 'Because is true. I used to run brothel.'

I had no idea how to respond to that.

At an unmarked door, she waved her pass card. The room was open-plan and roughly half of the entire thirty-sixth floor. There was a bar, a dining table, and a sunken lounge, and several doors leading to other rooms. There was as a sudden movement from a basket in the corner and a pair of coffee-coloured pugs came shooting over the furniture towards us.

She scooped one up and kissed it on the mouth. 'Make yourself at home, while I find Clay. Always he's on fucking phone.'

I walked down a couple of steps to where three large sofas, upholstered in plush dove-grey velvet, were arranged around a curved floor-to-ceiling window. On a coffee table, there was a partly consumed fruit and cheese platter, two opened bottles of champagne, empty champagne glasses, a cheesecake with slices taken.

I glanced out the window. Grease-coloured clouds rolled over the towers of Melbourne, hurling ice water on the rooftop pools and tennis courts. A flock of birds banked over the Rialto then dispersed. Far below, trains rumbled beside the aquarium and under the rusted canopy of Flinders Street Station.

'Stella.' A man came striding into the room, grabbed my hand. 'Clayton Brodtmann. Good to meet you.'

It was like meeting a newsreader in the flesh — a familiar but unreal face, as though the years of public exposure had changed it to a synthetic veneer. Despite the healthy skin tone he looked like a man who had had many sleepless nights. He bared his dental work at me and pointed to a sofa. 'Please.'

I sat.

'Drink?'

I summoned my self-control. 'No, thank you.'

He nodded, studying me. From his look of mild irritation, I guessed I disappointed him in some way. *Get in line*, I thought. *Behind* me, *mainly.*

'Can't thank you enough,' he said. 'Alerting us about Nina. Your friendship and kindness.'

'My ... my ... yes. Thank you.'

Crystal sat beside her husband and both the dogs leapt into her lap. The sight of their pink, flat tongues was vaguely sickening.

'Cheesecake?' She held out a chunk on a plate. I declined.

'I like her, Clay,' she spoke like I wasn't in the room. 'She called that faggot ... what was it? Happy Hammond.' She broke off some cake for the dogs.

Brodtmann cleared his throat. 'I haven't seen my daughter for ... some time; not since she left Perth. I have no idea of her movements. You live next door to her, I believe?'

'I — yes.'

'She wants to be independent or some bloody thing. I send her money of course, and gifts —'

'You mollycoddle her.' Crystal poured herself some champagne. 'Let her be, if that's what she wants.'

Brodtmann's chin jutted forward. 'Sweetheart, please.'

Crystal sniffed and pulled an iPad out of her handbag.

'My daughter — would you say she seems happy to you?'

'Happy?'

'Happy Hammond,' Crystal said. 'Hosted kids TV show in the 60s. Did you watch it?'

Did I? My nose an inch from the screen: *Is everybody happy? Yeeeeessss!* And don't get me started on Zig and Zag. 'Yes,' I replied. 'I grew up in the country and they used to show the reruns in the 70s.'

Brodtmann glanced at me, and looked away. There was a buzz in his pocket and he pulled out his phone. 'Excuse me.'

'Sure.' I looked out the window.

'Yes?' He listened for a moment. 'About fucking time, Marcus. Someone will be down.' He put the phone away and called out. 'Broad?'

My driver came from a side door. He would have arrived after me, but I had not seen him enter. There must have been several entrances to the apartment. 'Sir?'

'The police minister. Downstairs.'

Broad nodded. 'Right.' He went out the front door.

Brodtmann started pacing. 'You notified the police today?'

71

'Yes,' I said. 'But they weren't that concerned at first —'

He cut me off. 'It doesn't matter. They're taking me seriously, by God.' He rubbed his jaw. 'In the meantime, please don't speak to anyone about my daughter's ... about Nina. Certainly not the media. It would not be helpful, and may possibly hinder the investigation.'

He thought I was an imbecile and I resented it. Talking to the media was the last thing I'd do. Still, I sensed police backsides were about to be kicked, so that was good. 'I understand,' I said.

The door opened and Broad walked in with — I couldn't believe my eyes — Marcus Pugh. Good old Mucous Pukus. We made eye contact but he didn't recognise me, or chose not to. A woman followed, short grey hair and dead eyes. If she wasn't in a police uniform she could be mistaken for an ageing lesbian cleaning woman.

We were a sombre bunch. With the cheesecake and the champagne still on the table, the gathering had the atmosphere of a baby shower full of guests who disliked each other. Brodtmann sensed it too, suddenly ordering us to move to the dining table.

Broad sat at one end and pulled out a notebook. Brodtmann was at the other end, and Pukus and the cop sat down opposite me. I had that uncomfortable job-interview feeling. Brodtmann did the introductions. Dead Eyes was introduced as Conway, the deputy chief commissioner, with loads of experience with kidnapping cases. She received a nod from Brodtmann and leaned in: 'Stella, what can you tell us?'

'I was with her last night at her flat. I left around midnight —'

'I mean, about her whereabouts?'

I was confused. 'I have no idea where she is.'

Brodtmann and Conway exchanged glances. 'You see,' Brodtmann said, 'she has done this kind of thing before. Run off.' His face creased at the edges. 'The name change, the move to Melbourne. She's always testing me.'

I almost felt sorry for him. He held his torment in check with sudden jerking movements, the squaring of his shoulders, the forward thrust of his chin. What a fucked up family. And I thought the Hardys were defective.

Conroy pulled out her notebook and started jotting. 'When did you last see her?'

'Last night, about midnight. We had plans to meet this morning but when I went to her apartment she wasn't home.'

'Did you go inside her apartment?' Conway said. 'Do you have a key?'

I coughed. 'No.'

'And her mobile, do you have the number?'

'Yes.' I looked in my bag for my phone. 'Oh shit, sorry. It's on the charger.'

'Do you know if she had more than one mobile?' Conway asked.

'Has,' said Brodtmann quietly.

Conway flushed to her grey roots.

'She might,' I said. 'I don't know.'

'Is there anything else you can think of — anything at all? Any friends she mentioned?'

'Not really.'

Pukus gave Brodtmann a look of regret, as though apologising for my inadequacies. Hateful man. Only I was allowed to do that. So I did. 'Look, I'm sorry but I really don't know her that well —'

Brodtmann mulled over that information by jutting his chin out further. 'I see.'

'She'll turn up,' Pukus said suddenly.

From the look of disgust on Brodtmann's face, I gathered he didn't appreciate such glib assurance.

Crystal went to Brodtmann and took his hands. 'She is getting attention.' He did a slow nod, apparently unconvinced.

Conway ripped a page from her notebook and passed it to me. 'If you think of anything or hear from Nina, this is my direct number.'

'Will do.'

Crystal stood. 'I regret you must all please excuse us. We get ready for tonight.'

Brodtmann walked me to the door. 'Minerals Council dinner,' he said. 'I'm giving a speech. Under the circumstances, I'd cancel, but I'm told it's better to carry on as normal.'

He came with me into the corridor. 'I am very grateful to you. If you hear from my daughter, I would appreciate you contacting me immediately, day or night. The number is on here.' He put a card in my hand. 'You don't need a pass to get to the foyer. The chauffeur is waiting for you. Goodbye, Miss Hardy.'

While I waited for the lift, I inspected Brodtmann's business card, which had a mobile number hand-written on the back.

I made my way back to the foyer and found the chauffeur leaning against a pillar reading a newspaper. 'All set?'

'Yes.'

'The limo's round the back.'

We walked through a mall of high-priced shops and restaurants. I paused at a chic bar and considered an alternative evening to one spent with Ben eating reheated Vietnamese leftovers, like reclining in one of those swanky lounges with a glass of something strong. My eye was drawn to a tall gentleman sitting by himself at a table in the corner. Uh oh, Finchley Price. I had not seen him outside court before and my brain was slow to make the connection. He seemed flustered, not the chill dude I'd seen during the trial. He sat on a low stool, his knees up near his chest, fidgeting with a napkin.

What was it about Price that fascinated me so much? He was a creepy butler of a man, with his permanent look of doom. Not ugly exactly, but funny-looking. Something to do with the rarefied air he breathed. Here was a man at the top of his game, respected, earning more than the prime minister, and yet who was at ease within the criminal milieu — and able to communicate with the likes of Clacker Pickering. Client confidentiality aside, Price was friendly with Melbourne gangland criminals, and he might know if they had learned which usually righteous social worker had deprived them of drug money six years ago.

Broad checked his watch and gave me a beseeching look.

I held up a hand. Could I just stroll up and say, 'What's up, Finchley'?

'Traffic's dire,' he said. 'Make up your mind.'

I brushed down the sleeves of my jacket and squared my shoulders, trying to think of a clever opening line. But before I could act, someone crossed the bar, hand extended, to greet Finchley Price. It was Gaetano Cesarelli, still in the purple velvet jacket and mirrored sunglasses. The barrister stood on his praying mantis legs and they shook hands, then they sat together and began a furtive *tête-à-tête*. I was tempted to saunter over and eavesdrop. Instead I tore myself away and told Broad to drop me on Union Road so I could pick up a box of refreshment on my way home.

The roads were clogged. As the car crawled north, the streetlights came on. Don't ask me why, but the change from day to night had always put me on edge. It was the feeling that time had run out, and I was forced to admit to failure somehow.

It had been, without a doubt, a horrible day. It was only once the wine cask was under my arm and I was walking home, that I started to feel better. It was pleasant to unwind, and be outside in the evening air. I passed the local wine bar and saw Amber and Jack, my neighbours from number 11, inside having a drink. Jack took a cracker, added some cheese, and showed it to Amber. She closed her eyes and opened her mouth. I averted my eyes and hurried home.

11

MY FLAT was Ben-less. Though the man-child was elsewhere, his presence was felt in the order and hygiene of the place. The flat was as clean as a hospital and as cold as a morgue. I turned on the heater, put the cask on the bench, and worked the tap out of the cardboard by feel, like a blindfolded SAS soldier assembling a rifle. In a matter of seconds I had a full glass in my hand and was contemplating recent developments. Cesarelli had morning coffee with Mabor Chol and late-afternoon drinks with Finchley Price. That didn't make sense — if Cesarelli was planning to have Clacker bumped off in prison, why would he partake of mojitos with the man who was representing Clacker?

You could also say it didn't make sense for a girl with a billionaire father to leave town, change her name, and work as a beautician. It was clear to me from our meeting that there was much that Brodtmann wasn't saying — but that I had sensed he wanted to.

I tipped the contents of my handbag on the kitchen counter. Wallet, keys, Adut's exercise book, the article about the opening of the Crouching Tiger, and Brodtmann's business card. The CC Prospecting Director wanted me to call him direct. I decided I would, but first I required a little more information about Mr Brodtmann, and the whole CC Prospecting situation.

As unlikely as it seemed, I already knew a few things about his mining business. I knew, for instance, that they were bidding for the Shine Point refinery. Also, the sketchy details from the article I'd read in *The Age* this morning were coming back to me. Tax avoidance, something about ASIC not enforcing the Corporations Act to the letter of the law, billionaires receiving special treatment. I searched *The Age* website and found it: *CC PROSPECTING FILED ACCOUNTS LATE* by Vince McKechnie.

That name was familiar, but I couldn't recall where I'd heard it before. Probably from reading *The Age*.

Vince McKechnie. *Wait.* The business card I found in Tania's apartment. It now seemed likely, not to mention fishy, that Tania had had contact with a journalist — and one that was concerned mainly with business and finance.

There was a link to an email address at the bottom of the article; I dashed off the following:

> Dear Mr McKechnie,
> I have information regarding CC Prospecting. Please reply to arrange a meeting at your earliest convenience.
> Stella Hardy

I had no actual new information on CC Prospecting, but I wanted to know what Tania had discussed with him and it seemed a good way to get his attention. Besides, it felt good lying to a journalist, selective truth was their lingua franca.

I closed the laptop and my eyes were confronted with the mess on the bench. Once, I could ignore mess, but with Ben now making things clean, it stood out as a chaotic slight on an otherwise ordered world. If he saw it he would have a conniption. Not that I cared — but I started picking up my stuff and putting it all back into the bag. I was sorting through it all when I came across the invitation to the exhibition opening at the Narcissistic Slacker gallery in Footscray. The room seemed mildly warmer, at least I certainly was, and when I thought of the paintings, and the grey-eyed artist, my pulse quickened. An idea took hold of me — why not go? Then an even more absurd idea hit me — why not dress up? — and I found myself in my room with my wardrobe flung open, and me, wanting to impress the arty crowd, grabbing at an assortment of tops and bottoms. A moment later I returned to the kitchen. Clothes were hell. Drinking made it better. I refilled my glass and flopped on my sofa. Only then did I see the red light blink on my answering machine.

'*It's me, love. Thought I'd let you know that Shane's not going to be here Sunday night. Reckons he's got an allergy. So you can relax about that side of things.*'

I hit *erase* and went back to look in my wardrobe. Deep in the back, I found an item I had bought in the throes of my Jacob insanity, that I had worn only once, on what had turned out to be our last date. I spread it out on the bed. Made from a floaty silky fabric in various hues of rose, it was bias-cut for a smooth fit. But even if the dress still fitted, there remained a serious problem: a lack of suitable shoes. My taste in footwear leaned towards the practical: chunky elastic-sided boots, sensible flats, and sandals you could run a marathon in. Then I remembered the ones Tania had given me. I opened the David Jones bag. They were things of beauty — high-heeled, with ivory straps, silver buckles. Very Tania.

I stopped dead in my tracks. Tania. I couldn't in good conscience wear these now, not with her missing, possibly abducted. What had happened to her? Whenever I thought about it I felt sick. Fear was taking root within me. Since this morning I had steadily become more anxious, but there was nothing I could do. It was up to the police now.

I needed to calm down, I needed numbness, I needed to stare mindlessly at a screen. I went looking for my glass of wine and found it in the bathroom. From my shelves, I picked one of the pirated DVDs Tania had given me: *The Blue Lagoon*. I took my laptop to the bedroom and took off my boots and jacket and got under the covers. I slotted the DVD and waited for the movie to start. There was a lot of computer noise but no movie. Then a folder appeared: *dcREPORTS_PRELIM_2008*. I clicked, it opened. Inside was a single PDF entitled *BLUE LAGOON*. I clicked again.

78

Report on the quality of alluvial samples in Mount Percy Sutton tenement area for Blue Lagoon Corp and Bailey Range Metals. August 2008.

Someone had erased the movie and used it to store their documents. I had no idea if this thing was important or confidential, or just the boring geological paperwork that it appeared to be. The parts I read were intractable guff. I scrolled speedily down a hundred and thirty-one pages — scientific waffle, with some graphs and tables and maps. I skipped to the conclusion.

... first assays, from deep drilling, were not encouraging ... shoots of zinc and iron rich sulphides ... limited trace amounts of gold ... GOLD MINING NOT RECOMMENDED.

It ended with contact details — email, phone, and fax — for an independent geological consultant.

Now the fear within me began to bloom like algae on a stagnant pond. This was not some mix up — it was the deliberate attempt to conceal a document on a DVD that had been disguised as a movie, bundled as it was with two other decoy DVDs.

Stella, please take them. As a favour to me.

Tania's request that I take the DVDs now appeared less than innocent. In fact, I was starting to believe it was calculated. Disguise the document and give it to your neighbour for safekeeping. From whom was I keeping it safe? A mining report might be of interest to a competitor. Perhaps CC Prospecting, Tania's father's company, had wanted to know what these Blue Lagoon Corp people were up to. One thing was certain, I had misjudged the young beautician.

I was deciding if I should go to the police with this when I heard footsteps on the landing outside. I closed the laptop and went into the kitchen. A key turned in the lock and Ben shuffled in, arms burdened with shopping bags, panting after the three flights.

'Hi,' I said, more sigh than greeting. 'You took a while.'

'I had to see a bloke,' he said, and dumped the spoils on the table.

'What's all this?'

'This lot is cleaning products. That bag is basic necessities: toilet paper, soap, air freshener. And that one is tonight's dinner, tea, whatever. Rice, tofu, broccoli, pickled ginger, a packet of Japanese curry.'

I opened one of the bags. 'Air freshener?'

'Believe me. A basic necessity. Put this in the fridge.' He handed me a bottle of wine and started putting away the groceries. In the last bag was a large cardboard box.

'What the flipping heck is this?' I demanded.

'An espresso maker. I like to have coffee in the morning. Drinkable coffee.'

'That's what Buffy's is for.'

'Waste of money.'

I put the wine away and saw the leftovers in the fridge. 'You don't have to cook,' I said. 'There's plenty of takeaway here.'

He snorted in disgust.

'Yes, but tofu? Really?'

'I happen to like the taste of tofu.'

I watched him move about the kitchen, enjoying the confidence he had with simple acts of peeling or chopping.

The image of Dad came to mind, and the memory of the coppery odour after the sheep bled out — and I stood there waiting, blood all over me. Dad had whistled but the dog was suspicious; he stayed where he was, tail wagging uncertainly. 'It's in the ute,' Dad called. I hesitated. 'Under the seat,' he added. 'Go on.'

'You had the shotgun with you the whole time? Why the hell didn't you do it — just bloody shoot her?' My voice sounded strained, the words strangled.

He frowned, serious but not angry. 'Stella, love ...'

But I didn't want to hear what he had to say. For a long time afterward, I regretted not simply walking the five kilometres back home. It would have been my first act of real defiance against him.

'Hey Ben, did Dad ever make you kill anything?'

He looked at me like I was an inmate with a shiv. 'What? No! Never. Why?'

'No reason.'

He had all four burners on the stove going, saucepans on each; I could have sworn I only owned one pot. Agreeable cooking aromas gathered in my nostrils. Chopped vegetables waited on the board.

'Where's your compost?' Ben asked.

'Don't have one.'

He made a noise of derision and poured me a glass of wine. Everyone I knew, it seemed, had better taste in fermented grapes than I did. It was a delight in my mouth and mellow in my throat.

'Have you been in prison or competing on *MasterChef*?'

'There's so much you don't know about me.' Ben stirred one of the pots, his back to me, though I sensed his satisfaction.

'Does the name Gaetano Cesarelli mean anything to you?'

'What is this, a test?'

'Yes. Your special subject is Melbourne's underworld criminals and your time starts now.'

He blew on some goo on the end of his wooden spoon, then tasted it. 'Yeah. I know him. Know *of* him. Bit of a poseur. Mafiosi wannabe. Plates or bowls?'

'Plates.' I took two plates from the cupboard and put them on the bench.

'He calls himself the Caesar of Sunbury. They reckon when he collects debts he says "render unto Caesar what is Caesar's" then he breaks your fingers. Why do you ask?'

'My client's son is —'

'Client's *son* is not a client.'

I nodded. 'Okay. Not officially a client. But she's already lost one boy to murder — and I'm pretty sure her other son works for Cesarelli.'

'Then he's probably a lost cause.'

I didn't think Mabor was irredeemable. People changed. Like Ben. The brother I used to know was always in fights, or drunk or stoned or worse, and now look at him: a more responsible human being you could never hope to meet. Perhaps he had had a revelation in jail, though that was not usually where people turned their lives around. He'd reformed all by himself. Magnanimity stirred within me. 'Doing anything tonight?'

'Yes,' he said. 'I'm having cocktails with the Queen.'

'Can you cancel? I've got an invitation to an art thing.'

'Art?' He eyed me suspiciously. 'Where?'

'What difference does it make? Footscray.'

'Not my thing, art,' he said and started to set the table.

'A favour to me.'

'No.'

'Fine.' I mooched to the sofa and flopped down on it. 'Ingrate.' I continued to mutter and drink wine in this passive-aggressive fashion for some time. I put the TV on for the seven o'clock news. After a few overseas stories there was a piece to camera from a court reporter:

There were sensational scenes in court today as Darren Pickering, 29, of Deer Park, had charges of murder against him dropped. Instead, Mr Pickering has pleaded guilty to one count of manslaughter. Mr Pickering was also charged with two counts of aggravated robbery, to which he pleaded guilty.

Asked by counsel why he attacked the victim, Mr Pickering replied, 'I had his phone and I was going home but he rushed me and I had to defend myself.'

After security footage of the incident was discovered to have been damaged, lawyer for Mr Pickering, Mr Finchley Price SC, successfully argued that there was no evidence that Mr Pickering had planned the attack on Mr Chol behind the Kensington restaurant.

Security was increased for the second committal hearing, with additional police and an additional metal detector placed outside the court.

Mr Pickering was charged after an alleged robbery that left Adut Chol, 16, dead. Mr Chol was stabbed through the heart with a knife.

Bail for the defendant was again refused.

The image cut to a shot of journalists firing questions at Finchley Price.

'Darren Pickering has cooperated fully ...' he was saying. 'My client protests his innocence and is not a flight risk. In light of the change to the charges against my client, we will therefore be appealing the decision to refuse bail. I will not be commenting further at this stage.'

I unplugged my phone from the charger and called Mrs Chol.

'Stella, hello, how are you?'

'I just heard.'

She sighed. 'The murder charge is dropped.'

'What happened?'

'The police told me they can't use the CCTV images from that restaurant. Now the case is not strong enough for the murder charge.'

'At least Clacker will go to jail for the crime.'

'Manslaughter. What is that? It is the same thing, murder.'

'In a way, yes,' I said. Those fine legal distinctions were not easily understood, especially not by me. I agreed the situation was rotten. 'And you?' I asked. 'Are you alright?'

'I don't know. I'm strong for the girls. I have my brothers to help me.'

'That's good.' Then I turned into the world's shittiest person and turned the conversation around. 'And Mabor? How's he?'

'He is not happy.'

'Because of the manslaughter charge? Or did you tell him about the book?'

'What? Your book? No, it is yours. Why would I do that?'

'No reason. Why is he not happy? I mean, is there another reason?'

'He is unhappy at school. He doesn't want to go anymore. I have tried to change his mind.'

'Is Mabor there at the moment? Is he at home?'

'No. What is wrong, Stella?'

'Nothing. Nothing. Not a thing. At all. Goodbye.'

There was food on the table. Ben had plated up with a swirl of sauce, a sprig of coriander placed just so, and the rice turned out in a perfect teacup shape. I mushed it all up together and the result tasted pretty good.

'Do you know Gaetano Cesarelli? Personally, I mean,' I asked.

'Stella, I barely know the guy.'

'What about Darren Pickering — know him?'

'Clacker? Yeah, I know him. A bit.'

'He murdered a boy called Adut Chol, for a mobile phone.'

I waited for a reaction. He coughed and stared at me. 'I saw Mabor Chol, the boy's brother, with Gaetano,' I continued.

Ben looked bewildered. 'So?'

'Mabor thought Gaetano was protecting Adut.'

'The boys were probably selling for him.'

'Yes. Clacker is involved with Cesarelli, isn't he?'

'Yeah. Clacker's in with the Flemington crew,' he said quietly.

I didn't like how serious he'd become. 'Why do they call him Clacker?'

'Don't ask.' Ben said, straightening up. 'They think he stabbed some African kid for a phone?'

'Yes.'

Ben shook his head. 'Clacker probably has three iPhones. He isn't some delinquent, he's a dealer with an organised set of connections.'

'Dealing in what?'

'Shakalak.'

84

'Just tell me, Ben, I'm not in the mood.'

'Crank, get go, shaboo, shard.'

'Shard? So you mean *ice*, why didn't you say so?'

Dealing ice was a dangerous occupation, and associating with vicious criminals like Clacker and Cesarelli was risky. What, I wondered, had Adut done to cross them?

Ben stood to gather the plates. I stopped him and took them to the sink myself. I turned on the taps and rinsed the plates, left them to dry. 'Dinner was excellent.'

He shrugged and poured more wine in my glass.

I sat down and took a big sip. 'Wine too. First class.'

'Fine. I'll see the art with you. But we're not staying long.'

12

I WANTED to leap over the table and give him a grateful squeeze. I went to my room to change, when my phone buzzed. It was Phuong. 'How'd it go with the billionaires?'

'Got a lift there and back home in a limo.'

'Good for you.'

'It's another planet — Planet Money.'

'Hungry ghosts.'

'Who?'

'Billionaires. When they die, they're too attached to their money. They come back as hungry ghosts. It's very low on the reincarnation scale.'

'Lower than a slug?'

'Yeah. Pretty much. So who was with them?'

'Oh, they had Marcus Pugh there.'

'The donor says "jump", the party says "how high?"'

'Pretty much. And that commissioner, Conrad.'

'Conway. She's very qualified, Harvard MBA or something.'

Here was the moment to tell Phuong about the mining report I found concealed on the DVD. It would be germane to the case, possibly send the police in a new direction, one potentially involving industrial espionage. My only hesitation was that I might inadvertently incriminate Tania. She'd asked me to keep the DVDs safe. I had to honour that commitment. Instead, I focused on the matter of Adut. 'What can you tell me about Gaetano Cesarelli?'

'He's a great big poonce.' Phuong laughed. 'No. Actually, he's a violent thug. Acts legit, coffee importer for a cover, but his KA's deal in ice, smack, ecstasy. Why?'

'It was Gaetano I saw Mabor Chol with today.' Phuong was quiet. I thought I heard tapping. 'Did you see Clacker's lawyer on TV tonight?'

'In up to his neck,' said Phuong.

'Who?'

'Finchley Price. And that's according to Ashwood.'

'Ah yes, he who likes to sit on people's desks. He'd know who was bent and who wasn't, I suppose.' I thought for a moment. 'Did I tell you I saw Price with Gaetano Cesarelli? They were having a drink together at some bar in Crown.'

'Figures. Ashwood says Price is way too close to the crooks he represents.'

'Yeah, but coming from Ashwood. I mean, the guy's a mindless thug. How can you stand to work with him?'

'Ashwood's not that bad. In a way, I feel sorry for him. Every time he gets a promotion, he does something stupid and gets busted back to constable,' she said, giggling.

'Stupid like what?'

'Bruce reckons he was reprimanded for an incident involving a prostitute.'

I feigned astonishment. 'Really?'

'Drug squad busted her unit but the evidence went missing. Charges dropped.'

'Ashwood stole the drugs?'

'Technically, he failed to secure the evidence. But everyone knew he was involved with her.'

'When was this?'

'Late nineties.'

'Wait. How old is he? He looks about twenty.'

'Baby face. He's in his thirties.'

A baby face, I thought, would be a nice problem to have. 'I wouldn't be feeling sorry for him, sounds like a total dick. I'd stay right away from him.'

'If I stayed away from every racist idiot in a police uniform, I'd never come to work.'

'That bad?'

'Some are. They're all friendly and welcoming, all the right anti-discrimination policies, meanwhile behind your back they say things to make a porn star blush.'

'Not Copeland.'

'Bruce? No. Got to go, Stella. I'll look into that African boy's information and get back to you.'

In all the years since I'd known Phuong, since we both dropped out of Arts at Melbourne University and I went into social work and she became a cop, she had never once offered to use her cop powers to help me with a client. Now, without me even asking, she looks into Mabor for me. What, I wondered, had come over her? And what was with the giggling and the silly joke? Maybe she was on drugs.

I put on the rose-coloured frock and, after some agonising, I put on Tania's shoes, after all, she had insisted I take them. I put my hair up in a twist, as I had seen Tania often do, and skewered it with a large bobby pin. Ben was sitting at the kitchen table. He'd done the dishes and changed into a clean pair of jeans and a long-sleeved shirt. Only a couple of neck tatts showed.

'You look awesome —'

'Shut up,' I said, pleased. I put on my coat. 'Looks like rain. You got a jacket?'

'No drama. We can go in my car,' he said, with a haughty sniff.

'What car?'

I followed him to the carpark under the flats. In my parking spot was a 1980 red two-door Mazda Rotary that smelled of stale motor oil and Fisherman's Friends. He gunned it and I nodded appreciatively. I jumped in, belted up, and the Mazda roared down Roxburgh Street. At the T-intersection, it backfired and then stalled. Without a word, he restarted it and we motored away down Union Road. As the Mazda conveyed us through the night, a light shower fell. We crossed the Maribyrnong and Ben flicked a lever — one wiper went flat-out and the other made a pitiable attempt to keep up. We made it to the Narcissistic Slacker gallery at the fashionably late hour of 10.15pm.

Ben drove by a couple of times to check the place out, and then parked a few blocks away. He made a great show of putting on the steering lock and checking that the doors were locked. I wanted to leap over the car and beat him to death with my handbag. 'Any chance of getting to this thing before Christmas?'

'Can't be too careful.'

'Yes, Ben. You can. You can be a complete tool for being too careful. Now come on before we die of old age.'

The Footscray streets were wet and empty, except for an elderly citizen inspecting the rubbish bins for treasure. We walked on until I stopped at the gallery entrance.

'Here?' Ben asked, apprehensive.

The door flew open; a girl rushed past us to vomit in the gutter.

'Yes,' I said, and moved my sandal away in the nick of time, avoiding a spray of carrot.

13

IT WAS not so much an elegant gathering of art-lovers as an old-fashioned punk party. The music was crazy loud. People lined the stairs and the corridors, and yelled in each other's ears. The main gallery space itself was packed with punters of all ages, dancing, drinking, and in some cases, pashing on. It was a bit early in the night for all this carry-on, I thought. And I was feeling way over-dressed. Most people were wearing clothes suitable for, say, mowing the lawn. But at least there was cheese — or there had been. An empty tray with vacant toothpicks was on a small table by the door.

I found a kitchen in which two people could comfortably stand; about fifteen people were in there. I squeezed past and added my beers to the ice in the sink. Grabbing two bottles, I squeezed out again. I found Ben in the hall and gave him a stubby. The heat was stifling and I reluctantly took off my coat; in my party dress and French twist I couldn't have been more overdressed if I was wearing a tiara.

'Where's the artist?' he asked.

'Don't know.' I'd been scanning every room we passed but so far had not located him.

Someone called out, 'Hey, Brophy!' Ben's eyes flicked behind me. I tried to pivot but a heel stuck in the carpet and I stumbled back, slamming into the wall. I looked up, dazed, into Peter's smiling face.

'Sold anything?' I asked.

'A few.'

'The seagull one?'

'Not sure. Let's go and see.'

I followed him into the exhibition space. Most of the works had red dots beside them. Labels put each one at $1500. The seagull one was sold. I could have cried. It felt personal. It was lost to me.

'Doesn't matter,' he slurred. 'I can do another one. Just for you.'

A charmer. My suspicion response kicked in.

'Hey, you want to see something?' he breathed into my ear. He ushered me out, along the corridor, in the direction of a ladder.

High-heels and ladders don't mix. 'You first,' I said.

I followed him as best I could, up through a manhole and into the roof. We crawled along a small cavity and out onto an open, junk-strewn rooftop. The rain had stopped, mist drifted in batches across the sky. I was freezing. I didn't care.

He attempted to erect a deckchair.

'Stella,' I said.

'What? Where?'

'Me. I'm Stella. Stella Hardy.'

'Stella Hardy.' He patted the wobbly chair. 'Here you go.'

The torn canvas was uninviting, and instead I took an Austen-esque turn about the rooftop. Brightly lit cranes were working on the docks. Further to the west, the curvature of the long bridge was bustling with white light flowing one way and a river of red going the other. A wind gust brought numbing cold, and the smell of rotting fruit from the street. A graceful tabby was picking its way along the wall. 'Whose cat?'

Peter was cross-legged on the floor beside the deckchair. He retrieved a beer from his pocket and waved it at the cat. 'That's Aragorn.'

'Aragorn? As in ...' my heart rate changed tempo, '... *Return of the King*?'

'Yeah.' He seemed slightly embarrassed.

I looked at him anew. Yes, that was a handsome profile. I watched the cat slinking, sleek paws and languid movements, to press its head against Peter's leg. 'He's not mine. He's Marigold's.' He stroked the cat's chin. 'Arn'cha, Aragorn?'

So. There was a Marigold. Of course there was a Marigold. She was probably my exact opposite. Beautiful. Creative. Her parents were probably gifted artists who'd never eaten meat or uttered a racist slur in their lives. I exhaled a sigh of white fog and wandered to the other side of the roof. 'Be nice up here in summer. Hot nights.'

'Yeah.' He looked around. 'Where are you? Come back.'

I walked around back to him. Everywhere was wet. No choice but to risk the deckchair. It held, just. He inched closer to me. 'Where're you from?'

'Ascot Vale.'

'Dangerous place. Bloke got shot.'

His hand was on my arm, nothing creepy in it. At that moment, my bobby pin pinged, the centre could not hold, and the hairdo fell apart. There was nothing to be done, and so I pretended not to care. At the same time, raised voices reached us from inside the building. A woman's hoarse accusation, and a male voice shouting a string of curses. I recognised Ben's unique turn of phrase.

'Sorry,' I said, 'I better see to this.'

I trotted down the ladder, slipped and fell for the last four rungs. A crowd had gathered around the kitchen. I couldn't see what was happening until I squeezed through. Ben stood with his back to the wall, cornered. A woman was pointing at him. 'Bullshit!' she screamed. The music stopped. I made my way to Ben. 'What's going on?'

'Tell your friend,' the woman growled, 'to keep his fucking hands off my phone.'

Before he could issue more abuse and denials, I took his arm. 'Time to go.' We drove home in silence. By now, Brophy would know that I was associated with a petty criminal, one who was unable to refrain from thievery for one evening. The weight of my despondency thrust me lower into the Mazda's bucket seat.

Ben pulled up outside my building.

I wasn't angry, I was numb. 'Ben —'

'I know,' he said. 'Back to the boarding house.'

It was pathetic, like he'd sent himself to the naughty corner. I had known many boarding houses over the years I worked with housing agencies. As a place to call home they were one step up from prison or rehab, which was where most of your fellow tenants there came from. A bunch of barely functional people forced to live in close proximity, with alcohol or drugs and the strain of poverty. It was not a recipe for happiness. I couldn't let him go back there, not in the middle of the night at any rate.

'Come on up. We'll see about getting you sorted in the morning.'

He parked the Mazda in my spot under my building and we trudged up the stairs.

On the second floor landing, a man in trackpants, a hood pulled up over his head, came bounding down the stairs. He ran too fast to take the turn and slammed into the wall before sprinting down the next flight. His stupid thongs going *slap-slap-slap* as he cantered down the steps. When I reached my front door, I saw some of the paint on the doorjamb had been scraped off, focusing around the lock, where chisel marks dented the woodwork.

'One of your ex-clients?' Ben asked. He inspected the damage. 'Rank amateur.'

I had stone cold sludge in my veins. The book. Cesarelli. The money. The execution-style hit. The deadness. 'I definitely think you should stay here tonight.'

Ben grinned. 'Good call. I'll protect you.'

14

IN THE bleary-eyed, semi-consciousness of morning, I staggered to the bathroom and did a quick wee. My head was heavy and I had chills. Virus season had taken its usual quota of victims, including, it seemed, me. *So be it*, I thought. If I was sick I could now indulge the raging self-pity that was welling up inside me. I sat on the toilet, idly pulling toilet paper from the roll. Only last night I'd had my moment on the roof with Brophy. That moment was a sweet centre in my world of shite. But any hope of seeing him again was irrevocably ruined. Sabotaged by the Hardy idiot gene. The main thing now was to let it disappear, to close the door and keep moving. I took the last sheet and groaned. Now I had to replace the toilet roll. The cupboard under the sink was empty. Thinking I would have to go without, I saw a stack of new rolls on the shelf above the toilet. I had to hand it to Ben, he was a domestic mastermind.

In the lounge room, his sleeping form snored softly under a pile of blankets on the sofa. Caffeine cravings led me to a packet of ground coffee in the fridge. I managed to assemble Ben's espresso pot, added a goodly dose of grounds, and set it on the stove. As I waited I noticed that something was different about the world outside, the noise level. Then it clicked: Saturday. The week was over. A blast of steam sputtered from the coffee machine. I poured the contents into a mug and had a cautious sip. It tasted — what was the word? — harmful. I tipped it down the sink and dressed for a Melbourne winter: jeans, thick socks, boots, spencer, shirt, jumper, second jumper, coat, beanie, scarf, and gloves.

At Buffy's, I ordered a double-strength flat white.

'Double? That's four shots.'

'Yep. Defibrillator in a cup. A coffee that could raise the dead.'

Lucas worked the machine. 'Got a plan?'

I looked at his face for signs of intelligence. I found only psoriasis. But then, oh right, *the dead*. 'Should they actually rise?'

Lucas tilted his head. Naturally that's what he had meant.

'I hadn't really thought about it,' I said airily. Oh, I had a plan all right. Who didn't? Who could watch a zombie apocalypse unfold on the screen without musing on the folly of the survivors and what they should have done instead? For me, it was the storing of tinned food, bottled water, spare batteries — and head for home. No zombie would be caught dead in Woolburn.

He looked alarmed. 'You should so make a plan. With, like, an upstairs safe room. They have trouble with stairs.'

Well, *der*. 'Right.'

'I don't say this to everyone, but you're welcome to hide out here.'

I had stairs of my own. Three flights. But it was the thought that warmed me. 'Thank you, Lucas. But I think you should know the juice has gone out of the zombie motif. It used to be a metaphor for dead-eyed consumerism and now it's just another fucking product. Soon there'll be a zombie Barbie, with little bite marks.'

Lucas winced. 'Yeah, maybe, but don't say it like that.'

I picked up a copy of *The Saturday Age* — a reconstituted forest — and flicked through its pages. No Finchley. No Clayton Brodtmann. On the back page, there was serious concern for St Kilda's newest recruit's anterior cruciate ligament. Scans were being conducted on the valuable knee. What was it with knees? There's an argument against 'intelligent design' right there.

I walked up the driveway to my apartment building replaying the Brophy moment in my head. The lovely offer of a painting, the touch of his hand on my arm, the heat inside me on the cold, cold night. I hadn't experienced heat like that for a very long time. I reminded myself that, thanks to Ben, I needed to forget about Brophy. The damage had been done. That didn't mean, however, that it wasn't opportune to lecture Ben — a reprimand was overdue. But the Mazda was not in the parking space, and when I got upstairs I saw the blankets were folded up on sofa, and the coffee mess had been cleared away. There was no note. Good riddance.

I made myself a breakfast of leftover tofu curry and scanned the paper, in a bored and disengaged fashion, until a headline caught my attention: *VELDT ART PRIZE ANNOUNCED.*

> Mrs Mathilde Van Zyl, wife of South African billionaire Merritt Van Zyl, is hosting a cocktail party tonight at the Dragon Bar to announce the launch of the Veldt Art Prize ...

Wife? So Crystal was wrong. Van Zyl was not a 'fucking poofta', just a snappy dresser. I read on.

> ... 'This prize is my way of giving something back,' she said today. The annual prize, which is valued at $100,000, will be awarded to an artist whose work best captures the Australian mood. Mathilde will be on the judging panel for the inaugural year. The Van Zyl's have agreed to fund the prize for the next ten years. Clayton Brodtmann, a long-time friend of the family, said that Mathilde and Merritt have a long-standing interest in modern Australian art. They opened the Albatross Gallery in 2011. Mathilde is reported to have once said 'I am completely comfortable about wealth. But one must be thankful to everybody who helped one get it.'

I had a momentary fantasy of Brophy and I showing up, arm in arm, schmoozing and sipping mojitos. I was taller, prettier, with nicer hair, and I was chatting to some insider and putting in a good word for Brophy. Oh, a girl could dream. A spasm of chills shook me. My headache was worse, my throat was sore, and my nose was running. I took a handful of analgesics and started the shower. Standing under the hot water, I allowed self-pity to descend into sobs.

An hour later I was on the couch in my pyjamas watching a DVD of *The Return of the King* on my defective television. *The Lord of the Rings* was my comfort food, my hot Milo. I needed to hear Howard Shore's soaring strains, witness Viggo's weary intensity. Halfway in, my ringtone interrupted everything — the ID was Mrs Chol so I relented and swiped the screen. 'Hey Mrs Chol, are you okay?'

'No. I am frightened … It is Mabor. He is mad.'

'Mad how?' I was alarmed by how alarmed *she* was.

'Crazy mad, looking through my kitchen for something to use as a weapon.'

'Have you called the police?'

'I cannot do that.'

'Would you like me to come over?'

'Please, thank you, Stella.'

A gale blew down Union Road. It cut through to my skin and I shivered involuntarily as I waited for a tram — but I didn't care. It was then I realised I had passed into virus euphoria. Though my head was filled with ick, my mind had vacated my diseased body. I stared like a glassy-eyed zombie, in an unblinking, almost pleasant trance.

When the tram arrived it was packed with schoolgirls being corralled, somewhat unsuccessfully, by a weary teacher. I wondered what event had required them to wear their uniforms on the weekend, and a long weekend at that, the opening of the ski season. They were the kind of schoolgirls with hundred-dollar hairdos, fake tan, perfect teeth. The kind who went skiing. In Europe. I felt sure that if I could read the motto on the breast pocket of their ugly green blazers, it would read *Pecuniosus Meretricus*. Sluts with money.

A text alert distracted me and I checked my phone: *Library items overdue*. One of the schoolgirls spied my phone and made a comment to her friend. Hysterics ensued. Teenage girls were the purest evil. They all got off, thankfully, and I watched them being herded towards the showgrounds.

I recalled that, at a similar age, my class had been taken on an excursion to Melbourne. When I think of it now, it was an exercise in teacher abuse, twenty-five high school students screaming, yelling, and laughing for four hours on a bus. It was the first time I saw *Anguish* in the National Gallery. A ewe standing in the snow, her lamb dead on the ground before her. Crows gathered, too numerous, hopelessly outnumbering her. Schenck clawed shamelessly at the viewer's heart, the white snow, the red blood from the mouth of the lamb. Those damn black crows.

While Mrs Chol made coffee, I stood at the window and watched a gigantic meccano giraffe loading containers onto a waiting ship in Swanson Dock. Assorted shipping vessels were paused in Port Philip Bay. She brought a tray to the low table and honked into a tissue. I tore myself away from the view and sat opposite her. 'What's up with Mabor?'

'He was out all night. When he came home this morning, he was so frightened. I had not ever seen him that way. Not even after Adut died. And this morning he was looking around in the kitchen for a knife. He said he needed to protect himself.'

'That's not good.'

'I ask him why. But he doesn't answer. He can't stop opening the cupboards and drawers. I say there are no knifes in the broom cupboard. And he started to shout at me.'

'That's not good.'

'Then he sees his sisters are upset. He sits down, his face is so sad, and his hands are shaking. And ...'

'Yes?'

'I say, "what are you afraid of?" And he says, "Mr Funsail."'

'He's afraid of Mr Funsail? Who is Mr Funsail?'

'He wouldn't say more than that. He said that everything was cool when Adut was selling some shards to the teenagers here, the neighbours' children.'

Not shards, *shard*. Ice. 'Go on.'

'But Mr Funsail wanted Adut to do a different kind of job for him.'

'Mabor told you this?'

'Yes. He said Adut didn't like that kind of job. So Adut and Mabor went to see that Darren Pickering. Mabor told me there was another man there with him. My boys told them that Adut was out of business. Mabor said everyone agreed, they even shook hands and Mabor came home. But Adut stayed out and he never came home.'

In another flat somewhere, a child was crying. Doors slammed. I felt jittery — and it wasn't the fever. I'd have to tell Phuong that Adut had been reporting to Clacker, who was probably dealing ice too. It was crystal bloody clear that the murder of Adut Chol was not an opportunistic robbery gone wrong. It was also clear that when Mabor was interviewed by the police, he left out some very important details. 'You have to convince Mabor to talk to the police.'

'No. I've tried. He won't. He says even they cannot protect him.'

'Where is he now?'

'I don't know. He left after I telephoned you.'

I put my hand under my jaw, touched the distended glands. 'I have a contact in the police — a very nice woman, completely trustworthy.'

Mrs Chol looked at the carpet. 'No.'

I wracked my brains for other options. 'You need legal advice. Go to Legal Aid and get some ...'

Mrs Chol folded her arms. I had seen this move before, determined, proud. It made me want to weep. I went to a sideboard that held sporting trophies and framed family photos. There were a few school portraits of the Chol children. One of Adut and Mabor together. Another of her girls, all with neat corn rows. One was a

99

group shot of an extended family, lots of children cross-legged in front, various women behind them, several tall men at the back.

'What about your brothers?'

'What can they do?'

'Tell Mabor to stay with one of his uncles, with the one in Shepparton, or Swan Hill or wherever. Let him stay there, hang out with his cousins.'

Mrs Chol was quiet for a moment. 'Yes. I will call them.'

I wrapped the scarf around my neck. 'I hope it works out.'

On the eleventh-floor landing, I stood for a moment in a little patch of light where the sun was trying to shine. Then I descended in the lift, with fuzz in my head, pain in my limbs, and considered the fact that Clacker was working for Cesarelli. Was Cesarelli calling himself Mr Funsail now? Adut was a loose end — he wanted out, he had incriminating information — so Cesarelli had Adut killed. That would mean his whole conversation with Mabor in the café had been a lie.

So why string Mabor along?

Because Cesarelli needed something from him. On the night Adut was killed, Mabor grabbed a bag of Adut's things and took it out to a waiting car, probably to Cesarelli. Why? Cesarelli knew about Adut's exercise book, filled with names and dates, and who knows what other highly incriminating information. But Mabor didn't know which book to look for. Cesarelli would need to keep Mabor on side until he could get hold of it. To Mabor's face, Cesarelli was pretending to want Clacker dead, and meanwhile he was best mates with the senior counsel for the defence, and probably footing the bill for Clacker's legal fees.

I crossed the playground, where children in puffy parkas were playing on the swings. A group of young people, boys and girls, were chatting near the skips and from their midst an airborne bottle flew past me, just missing my head. As real-estate went, the view was first-class, but it was a hell of a place to raise your kids.

On the tram ride home, I wondered how long Cesarelli had been selling drugs to the residents of those flats. The money I'd acquired that night six years ago could have been his.

Adut had discovered my secret, but I had no way of knowing if he had used that information. Perhaps Adut had been content to keep quiet until the right moment presented itself to use it for leverage. If he came to me, trying to blackmail me, that was one thing. By telling Cesarelli what I had done, Adut would have scored himself some major brownie points.

Either way, I was now on the radar of a dangerous criminal. He had sent one of his thugs to break into my flat last night. The man in the thongs, who'd been hanging around Roxburgh Street for the past week — he was probably working for Cesarelli.

The first time I fired a shotgun at a living thing was when I shot Dad's dog. The recoil jolted through my arm and shoulder. Dad, workmanlike, threw Marty in the back of the ute, with the ewe carcass and little bits of lamb. He was humming a tune but neither of us was fooled. When we got home, he took his time, butchered and bagged the ewe, chucked it in the big freezer in the small shed, the one next to the plane hangar. Food for the dogs. Then he buried Marty. And locked the rifle on a bracket in the shed. The dog had attacked a sheep, it couldn't be trusted. It was easily lost, trust.

I waited until I was home before I rang Phuong on my mobile.

'Sluts with money?' she said. 'That's not funny. Actually, I call that degrading.'

'You are very suited to your job, you know that? Police, that's perfect for you. Fine, I'll never mention it again. Now listen, I've just come from Mrs Chol's place. Mabor's been lying. The business with Clacker? It wasn't a robbery, it was a set up. I think there's a connection with Gaetano Cesarelli there.'

101

'Meet me out the front of your building in fifteen minutes.'

'Wait. What? No.'

'And bring your Department of Justice ID,' Phuong said, and hung up.

I stomped around my flat, annoyed with her, with everyone I had ever met, and with some I hadn't even met yet. And then I saw it: the red, winking eye. I hit *play* and flopped on the sofa, braced for the sounds of Gothic horror, the voice of Woolburn.

Stella. Hi. Er. Peter Brophy here. Narcissistic Slacker. I got your number out of the book. Not that many Hardys in Ascot Vale. Ha ha. This isn't stalking, I'm pretty sure. Um. So. I just was ringing to say 'hi'. And. I'm sorry I missed you at the party. I don't know what happened. You left in a hurry. But anyway ... if you want ... maybe we could —

The beep cut him off.

I leapt into the air, fumbled with the machine, nearly deleted it, replayed the message. 'Maybe we could —' And once more. 'Maybe we could —'

I was bouncing around the room now, not knowing what to do with myself. *Chill*, I told myself. I took a deep breath, and then put the kettle on. I got out a mug, found an ancient herbal teabag — then I played the message again. Several times. The kettle whistled. I turned it off, poured the water, and began to speculate. I said I liked his paintings. 'Maybe we could' might refer to an offer to purchase a painting. I did ask if he had sold any. So, it was a financial transaction he was interested in. But why the halting speech? Nerves? Nervous to ask me for money. It took effort to look me up. He didn't seem like the hard-sell type. So what type was he? Vision-impaired? But no, he had been drunk. And what of Marigold? God, what a total disaster. What was I getting mixed up in? It was a complete nightmare.

I stood in the middle of my lounge room with my tea. The DVD was paused. Aragorn's careworn face was frozen and purple. I knew the scene well, could almost recite the dialogue. In the mountain halls, having followed the Paths of the Dead — Aragorn was surrounded by the oathbreakers, the undead. They were closing in, yet he stood his ground. That measure of courage, I did not have.

I opened the laptop and googled Peter Brophy. Daggy photos of a long-haired Peter at the old Phillip Institute in Preston, circa 1983. A grainy photo of some inebriated people at the Tote, the caption: *Members of Pep Tide and the Chemical Compounds.* Peter played drums. Zero Google results for Marigold Brophy. I sipped the tea; it was like drinking hot toothpaste. This shit was never going to ease my suffering. It was time to kick the virus's arse. Whisky. I checked my watch, my fifteen minutes were up. I picked up my handbag and headed out the door, intending to tell Phuong to drop me at the local bottle shop.

15

I WAS standing in Roxburgh Street when a little blue toy car pulled up beside the pine tree. Phuong's ride sounded like a blender but was equipped with a powerful stereo and numerous drink holders. I hopped in. 'I'm sick. Take me to whisky.'

She squinted at me. 'You look well.'

I sniffed, hurt.

'Fine. I'll take you to a bottleshop. After.'

'After what? Where're we going?'

'Barwon Prison. I have an appointment with Darren Pickering.'

'Clacker's in remand, Spencer Street.'

'Remand is full. They moved him.' Phuong flicked the indicator. 'Now, what's this about Mabor lying?'

'On the night of the murder, Mabor went with Adut to a prearranged meeting with Clacker.'

'And how do you know this?'

'I've been talking to his mum. He's scared. He thinks his life is in danger — and it probably is.'

'Why?'

'Because there's a third party — someone they call Mr Funsail — and he asked Adut to do a job for him, but Adut wasn't keen. He was happy selling ice but he drew the line at whatever Mr Funsail wanted done.'

Phuong was listening, staring ahead, moving through the traffic.

'That's why they went to see Clacker,' I said. 'I'm guessing he's a middleman or something, and there's a connection with Gaetano Cesarelli there.'

'So Adut wanted to get out altogether, stop dealing?'

'Yes,'

'Did Mabor witness the murder?'

'No, he left.' For some reason I was gripping the seatbelt near my shoulder. We were on the only road to Geelong and a mad wrangle had developed for an imaginary front spot ahead. Trucks boxed in the little car, threatening to send us off to Hoppers Crossing, like it or not. Phuong held her course, able to drive and fiddle with her iPod simultaneously.

A gentle bit of acoustic guitar started. She put up the volume.

'Where is Mabor now?'

'I don't know.' I looked over at her. Her face was tight, the eyes strained as she glanced from the car stereo to the road ahead. I had the feeling she didn't want to look me in the eye. 'Are you going to put out the word to pick him up?'

Now she looked across at me. 'Stella, I'm working this case, we've got wire taps on everyone's phone. If there was a Mr Funsail I would have heard about it. We know Cesarelli's KAs, we know his little code words on the phone. He sure as shit wouldn't go around calling himself Mr Funsail. It's a creepy name, sounds more like a paedophile than a drug baron.'

'I didn't say Mr Funsail was Cesarelli, I said he might be — but he is *someone*. And Mabor is scared to death of him.'

'He clams up with the police,' she said. 'But I suppose it wouldn't hurt to try to talk to him again; we can bring him in, hold him for a few hours, keep him off the street.'

'Thank you,' I said, relieved. 'Now, can you please tell me why I'm coming with you to see Clacker?'

'Your presence is required because I plan to mislead him.'

I waited for her to explain further but she didn't. I could only guess at the arse-about logic of her decision-making lately. Perhaps it was a Buddhist thing, one of the three grandiose objectives, or the seven crazy thoughts, the four bizarre schemes. Say what you like, Buddha was fond of enumerating. Still, I was glad to be included in her ruse. Clacker gave me the shits.

'What is this? Cat Stevens?'

105

'Saw *Harold and Maude* last night,' Phuong said.

'Oh, I love that movie.'

'Me too. Whatever happened to Harold?'

'He's been in stuff.'

Out my window, the dull plains rushed by, ugly and treeless. In the distance an industrial complex of petro-chemical plants belched vapours into the atmosphere. I sang along with Yusuf, a simple ditty about letting people be who they wanted to be. I thought about how much Phuong had conformed to the will of her parents. I imagined it was because her parents had lived through a war. The only time Phuong defied them, apart from a brief goth period, was to drop out of uni and join the police. Actually, come to think of it, that was a major act of defiance. She was a complicated person.

I looked at her. 'A gamble, isn't it?'

'What? Interviewing Pickering? No. Good detective work. It's all about the one percenters. Bruce encourages it.'

'One percenters? You don't know what that means.'

'It's a football thing, isn't it?' She laughed.

'You're tense.'

The bony shoulders came down. 'This traffic —' She flicked a glance at me, then cranked up the volume on the iPod.

After a while I said, 'Any news on Tania?'

'I'm not in that loop.'

I looked at her until she looked back at me. 'If I hear anything I'll tell you straight away, but it's being handled at the top of the upper echelons.'

I sighed and looked out the window again.

At the prison, Phuong and I waited for Clacker in an interview room. I had my Justice ID on a lanyard around my neck and I put a manila folder, containing nothing but blank paper on the table in front of me. A couple of guards brought Clacker in and he slumped down opposite us. When the guards went away he yawned and picked his nose, wiping the findings on the tabletop. I maintained silence — and what I hoped was a suitably professional mien.

'Hello, Darren, I'm Detective Senior Constable Nguyen.'

'A gook? No fucking way will I talk to a gook,' Darren said.

Phuong ignored that and pointed to me. 'And this is Ms Hardy from the Justice Department. I have a few questions for you. Do you want to have your lawyer present?'

'Price? Nah. Fucking toffee-nose pansy, never listens to me.'

'That's your decision?'

He grinned and grabbed his groin. 'Give us a head job?'

'I wanted to see you today to ask you a couple of questions about some friends of yours. If you are cooperative, if your information is helpful, you may be able to negotiate with the DPP to reduce the charge.' She gestured at me. I did my best to look like I had that kind of power.

'I'm not guilty.'

'Right. Right.'

'I'm no dog.'

'Of course not. I'm not asking you to *inform* on your friends.'

He sniffed. 'Wasting your time.' He looked up. 'Unless youse are looking for a root. Then I might help youse out. If I had a couple of sacks to stick over your ugly heads.' He laughed and showed us his tooth decay.

'Mabor Chol. You know him? He's Adut's brother.'

He snorted. 'Fuck off.'

'How about Gaetano Cesarelli. Were you working for Gaetano?'

He adopted a good blank stare.

Phuong tried a few more times and Clacker kept on deflecting her questions.

'Don't usually root gooks but in your case I'll make an exception.'

I kept quiet. The only time I spoke was at the end when I whispered to Phuong about where we might have lunch. Phuong answered with a *shush* and a frown and then signalled for the guards to come. I shoved the folder into my bag and pulled the zip. Clacker was waiting by the door, rocking on his heels, his hands in his pockets. 'How's Mr Funsail?' I said.

He stopped still, facing the door.

I came up beside him, got a close-up view of the orange fuzz around his ears. The white under his freckles turning steadily pinker. 'He's your mate, isn't he? Mr Funsail. How is he these days?'

Clacker shook his head and clamped his mouth shut, a move toddlers used to evade an incoming spoon.

'What about Funsail? Any news? No? Not telling?'

'What the *fuck*?' He practically squealed at me. By now, the guards had the doors open, and he fell into their arms. 'Me lawyer,' he said to them. 'I demand me bloody lawyer. Get him down here pronto.'

We got back in the car and merged with the traffic heading to Melbourne.

'The Mr Funsail business, I'll send that up to Bruce,' Phuong said.

'You do that.' I looked out the window. My sinuses were full of concrete but my heart was trembling with fear at the prospect of being the target for a gangland hit. Clearly, Mr Funsail was one scary individual. And Phuong was right — he was not Cesarelli by another name. There was a creep out there so terrifying that the mention of his name made hard-arse felons flinch and cry for the protection of the law.

In the distance, the granite peaks of the You Yangs passed by, pale mauve and weirdly malevolent. I wondered what Brophy was doing. If he still played in a band. I wondered about his message. He said that he wasn't stalking me. Tania would say that, since the advent of Facebook, nothing was private. Everything was public. Everyone was stalking everyone. The car was warm and I leaned back in my seat, put my head against the glass and closed my eyes. 'He swears a bit, Clacker.'

'You think?' Phuong sounded shocked. 'Where do you want me to drop you off?'

'Footscray.'

'What for?'

'Alcohol, remember? Drugs, too, if I can get some.'

Phuong raised an eyebrow at me. 'So any street corner will do?'

She let me out at Footscray station and I headed to the supermarket on a mission to buy whisky. I walked around the corner and was approached by a boy in a flannelette shirt. 'You chasin'?'

'Me? Chasing? I mean, I'm flattered you would think that a woman in her forties might wish to buy your street-grade meth cut with baking soda, but no. Thank you.'

The boy said something unpleasant and I hurried away. I was at the supermarket entrance when I saw a familiar face manoeuvring a giant centipede of shopping trolleys. His hi-vis vest and employee cap might have been acceptable on a teenager, but Ben cut a wretched figure.

'So this is where you disappear to.'

He shrugged. 'It's a job.'

It must have been the bugs in my system, because I felt an overwhelming desire to give him a hug. 'Thanks for staying last night. You can stay a bit longer if you like. That boarding house must be a hellhole.'

He smiled. 'You know where you stand in a hellhole.'

I thought for a moment. *'Spinal Tap?'*

He raised a hand, the two middle fingers lowered: a rock salute. I nodded in appreciation. 'See you tonight. I might even cook.'

'Please. God. No.'

I punched his arm and walked away laughing. Instead of buying whisky or painkillers like I had intended, I walked towards the mall. Soon I was no more than fifty metres from a certain gallery. At the foot of the Narcissistic Slacker stairs my inner voice began to scream. *Abort! Now! Unless you want to experience humiliation on a massive scale.*

The voice won. I retreated.

'Idiot,' I said out loud, slouching away as fast as I could. Straight home was best, I thought. Who knew what stupid mistakes I might make if I was allowed out on the street any longer. I headed for the tram stop.

'Hardy?'

Whoa, sprung. I spun around.

Brophy caught up with me, his eyes crinkling pleasantly. 'I was getting some food.' He held up a plastic bag filled with takeaway containers. 'You want some? There's lots. Springees, rice paper rolls.'

'I'd love to but I'm coming down with something.'

'You don't look that great ... I mean ... You look sick.'

'I feel like death. I'm on my way home.'

'Where's your car?'

'I'm taking the tram.'

'Let me drive you.'

'No. It's fine. Really.'

'I'm driving you. Can't have you wandering about in the freezing cold when you've got the flu.'

A very persuasive argument, especially as my skull felt like an angry dentist was drilling small holes in it from inside. He led me down an alley to a lane, and out into a rear carpark. A battered white van was parked by some overflowing charity bins. He opened the passenger door. I climbed in and he got in the driver's side and started opening the takeaway containers. 'Come on, eat something. You'll feel better.' He handed me a spring roll. 'They're veg, if you're wondering. You veg?'

'Are you kidding, I had tofu for breakfast.' I ate one and settled back into my seat. He stuffed an entire spring roll in his mouth and swung the van out into the traffic. 'I got your message.'

'I found your number the old-fashioned way, an actual phone book. Not many Hardys in Ascot Vale.'

'Country folk mostly, my branch of the Hardys.'

110

'That right?' For some reason, he appeared to find that interesting. 'I got one painting left. I'm going to hang on to it. The last one.' He stuffed another spring roll in his mouth. 'Anyway, I was going to ask, there's this art prize announcement thing on tonight.'

'The Veldt Prize?'

He beamed at me. 'A hundred grand.'

'It's a pretty exclusive do, isn't it?'

'I got an invite. With a plus one.'

'I'd love to but —'

'But probably not, seeing as you're sick and all. Well, maybe we could go out for a bite one night? When you're feeling better?'

'Sure.' I started on another spring roll as the van powered over the Maribyrnong. A crew of rowers cut silently through water the colour of tarnished copper. They disappeared into the gathering fog, leaving barely a trace. Poor brave fools.

Brophy said, 'You left the party pretty sudden.'

'My brother. He's got ... mental issues.'

He glanced at me.

'Left!' I said suddenly. 'Here.'

I directed him to my street and I climbed out, brushing bits of spring roll from my coat. He came around to my side of the van. 'I'll walk you up.'

'No need.'

'Come on. You're not well. I'll get you settled with a cup of tea.' By this point he was in the stairwell. I sensed that he wasn't putting it on, he was one of those rare nice guys. Even so, I wasn't going to drink herbal tea for anyone.

Once inside, I began rapidly gathering up the pyjamas, undies, and blankets that littered the floor. Peter went to the kitchen.

'Oh please, don't bother. I really don't feel like tea.'

He shrugged and ambled over to the TV. The DVD was still paused. 'Me and Marigold love *The Lord of the Rings*.'

'Marigold?' I said, and closed the laptop.

'My daughter. She's with her mum this week.'

'How old?'

'Ten.'

'Nice age.' Nerds and ten-year-olds liked Tolkien. In a year or two, Marigold would probably rather die than watch wizards and orcs. She'd be Skyping and sexting and shopping and getting her nails done at Superlative Skin Sensations. She'd be asking for tatts and face piercings and tickets to Lady Gaga. Then God-knows-what. I dumped all the blankets in my room and went to the bathroom, took another dose of painkillers and grabbed a bunch of tissues. When I came back, he was sitting on the sofa. 'Colour's gone.'

'I know.'

'This bit's great. The ghosts close in. It looks hopeless — then he whips out the sword.'

'*Andúril,*' I said.

'Flame of the West,' he responded.

He looked me right in the eyes and the recognition of a deep accord passed between us. 'You should probably be in bed. That is — I'd better leave you to it. To get, you know, well.'

'Wait,' I said. 'Let me give you my mobile. I don't often answer my landline.' I wrote it down on a margin of newsprint. He put it in his shirt pocket and gave me a shy grin. I walked him to the door and we waved at each other. Despite the aches and pains, after he left I may have done a happy dance. No witnesses. May not have happened.

112

16

I WOULD have kept dancing if I hadn't pulled a muscle in my neck and had to stop. I stood in front of the TV, feeling bewildered. What now? Sit down, finish watching *The Return of the King*? No, I was filled with wonderful adrenalin that had pushed my illness to the background. I felt better than I had in a long time, neck strain aside. I craved change. I wanted to throw the TV out the window and do something radically different. What could I do that was new, fresh, and utterly out of character? I rinsed some plates, tidied up, and decided to find the overdue library book. It was a racy read about a stripper who solves crimes, recommended by a work colleague. I had finished it in a day and put it down somewhere. I found the book under a stack of newspapers by the door and then, after tying the newspapers with string, I carried the bundle downstairs to the recycle bin.

I sprinted back upstairs and took a banana from a bowl that Ben had filled with fruit. I liked this new positive me. My illness now seemed like a normal part of winter — to be borne with good humour, rather than as a punishment inflicted on me alone by a cruel, vindictive universe. Tania would turn up, I felt sure. Mabor was out of harm's way. He would settle down now — become a model citizen — having learned his lesson. Ben was going to make it to the final three on *MasterChef*.

There was a knock on my door. I scoffed the rest of the banana — it was probably good news — and flung open the door. I beamed at the man on my doorstep.

'Hi,' I said. 'What can I do for you?'

The hollow cheeks in his grey face were separated by a nose the texture and colour of rhubarb. The eyes were beads of disquiet. He leaned a hand on the doorjamb and breathed hard. 'Stella Hardy?' he wheezed. 'Vince McKechnie.'

'I don't think so.' My memory was not fully functional at this point. I started to close the door.

He wedged a toe in the doorway. 'Miss Hardy,' he said. 'Stella Hardy? Is that right?'

'What's this about?'

He fished in his coat. 'Vince McKechnie.' He flipped out a card, same as the one he had given to Tania.

I peered at it, stalling for time, trying to think. 'Ummm.'

'You're the one who contacted me, Miss Hardy. Remember? *Dear Mr McKechnie, I have information regarding CC Prospecting. Please reply to arrange a meeting at your earliest convenience.* So, now would be convenient.'

'I said *reply*, didn't I? By email? How did you find out where I lived?'

'You're in the book.'

That I was — I'd checked the book myself. 'Vince, it's Saturday afternoon. There isn't a person alive for whom this could possibly be considered a convenient time.'

'It is for me,' he said, panting like an over-heated dog.

'You okay?'

'Stairs. Crook lungs. Me own fault.'

'Smoking?'

He ignored the question.

'Bloke downstairs tells me you're friendly with the young woman who disappeared.'

Curse you, Brown Cardigan.

'The media are not supposed to be involved.'

He sniffed. 'She calls herself Tania.' He checked a notebook. 'Tania Bradman.'

'Bradshaw, she's Tania Bradshaw now.'

He nodded. 'That's her. Not seen since Thursday night.'

'Come in and sit, before you drop dead.'

McKechnie sat at my table. 'So,' he said. 'CC Prospecting. What have you got?'

'The question is, Mr McKechnie, what have *you* got?'

'Sorry?'

'Don't act dumb with me. Tania had been in contact with you. Hadn't she?'

His face puckered like a slapdash Year-Eight sewing sample. 'Maybe.'

'What did she tell you?'

McKechnie looked puzzled for just a second and then folded his arms. 'Nothing. We never met. She said she had something of interest, and I wanted to meet up but I never heard back.'

Damn. A dead end. Surely, though, the 'something of interest' was the DVD, the mining report.

'So, Miss Hardy, what is this information you have for me?'

I stood up and paced. 'The Shine Point refinery Brodtmann is bidding for? He has real competition now; foreign companies are allowed to bid for the project.'

His nose wrinkled contemptuously. 'Matter of public record.'

'Yes. Okay. Fine. Well, now tell me this, why would Brodtmann fail to report his earnings to the ATO?'

He sat back and popped out his lower lip like a disappointed child. 'You don't have shit, do you?'

Oh, I had shit. I had some proper shit. But I had to protect it, for Tania's sake. 'Only what I've read in the paper,' I lied.

He sniffed again. 'I've come all the way from Perth. Got on the first plane.'

I was stunned. 'But why? Why not email, or ring me first?'

He coughed, turning a shade of beetroot, and then recovered. 'I'm researching a book on their whole shady empire — an unauthorised biography. The Brodtmann family are very private. Wall of silence among their friends and business associates. I tried to contact Nina, Tania, whatever. I thought she might be more cooperative, seeing as she was estranged from Clayton and she's dirty on the step-mother. But she was hard to find. There were rumours she'd moved to Melbourne and changed her name. Then, out of the blue, she called.'

'She called?'

'Rang the paper, yes. But she wouldn't say anything on the phone. So I posted her a good old-fashioned letter, a list of questions with me card. But she's a skittish little thing, didn't want to go that way. So we arranged to meet. I came to Melbourne about a week ago, but she didn't show. I got suss and spoke to a mate in the force; he told me she's a missing person.'

The police, I was coming to understand, could be very indiscreet. 'I see.'

McKechnie stood up. '*Anywho*, you don't know shit. Another wasted trip.' He started to walk away.

'What's so shady about the Brodtmanns?' I said, before he made it to the door.

'Brutal lot, the Brodtmanns — hardcore political clout. Litigious. But they always settle out of court, everything confidential.'

'What kind of cases?'

He thought for a moment. 'I think maybe you do have something for me. Did she tell you something? Confide in you?'

I shook my head so vigorously I got a little off-balance. 'Tania knows about good skin hydration, pigmentation. Microdermabrasion. I doubt she knows anything about corporate malfeasance.'

'If you say so.' He looked at me expectantly, as though we were already conspirators.

I smiled coolly, like we were already adversaries.

Then McKechnie cleared this throat. 'She ever mention a company called Blue Lagoon?'

My heartbeat jazzed. The report. 'No. Why?'

McKechnie moved his head, popping a bone in his neck. 'Do me a favour?' He put his card on the table, a gesture laden with negative expectations. 'Get in touch if she turns up.'

'Will do, Vince,' I said, and walked him to the door. As I watched him go, listening to his footsteps echo down the stairs, I realised that I was shivering. My fever was back, my nose blocked, my head heavy. I was not better afterall — I was worse, much worse.

A moment later, Ben came through the door carrying his customary quantity of grocery bags, looking like a man who'd spent the best part of the day taming recalcitrant shopping trolleys. We nodded to each other for greeting. After dropping the bags on the kitchen counter, he went to the stove and put his head in the oven.

I took the laptop to the sofa and started frantically googling 'Nina Brodtmann' and 'mining company' — and got a gazillion stupid and irrelevant hits.

'When was the last time you cleaned your oven?'

'My what? No idea.' I looked up and saw Ben was wearing rubber gloves, spraying a toxic substance into the oven. Fumes reached my nose and my lungs spasmed. I opened the window and stuck my head outside for some fresh air. Ben unrolled some paper towel, which I did not know I possessed, and wiped out the oven. Then he pulled the gloves from each hand with a *thwack* and opened the fridge, taking out vegetables and something wrapped in white paper.

The problem, apart from my near asphyxiation, was that I didn't know how significant this mining report was. What did it mean that there was little gold to be found on Mount Percy? And what kind of companies were Blue Lagoon Corp and Bailey Ranges Limited?

I needed to talk to an expert on mining, someone who could untangle the various threads of businesses, companies and ownership. I knew Brodtmann now, but I felt certain that Tania had not wanted her father to know about the existence of the DVD. So who else? There was one other person in the industry that I knew of — and I was wary of him. But Merritt Van Zyl was an experienced mining

117

magnate, and so he knew his onions. And tonight his wife was hosting a cocktail party to announce an art prize.

Ben was putting a chicken in a roasting pan. 'You eat chicken?'

I leapt up and grabbed him by the shoulders. 'Put it back; put it all back in the fridge. Dinner tonight is my shout.'

'What? Aren't you sick?'

'I was — I feel much better now.' This was a lie, but I figured a couple of hours of schmoozing, and the odd cocktail, wouldn't kill me.

17

THE TOP floors of the Tallis Tower, an office block in the heart of the legal district, were reserved for a couple of high-end restaurants, a reception room, and a fashionable cocktail lounge called the Dragon Bar. Ben and I drove to the station and took the train to Southern Cross Station, then walked for about ten minutes. Once inside the building, we had to wait around in the foyer before a woman, seated at a desk, allowed us into the lift. The bar was on a 'hidden floor' and the lift buttons stopped at the fifty-fourth floor. 'It's a hidden Dragon,' I said to Ben.

My reward for this droll observation was a look loaded with accusation. 'You sure there's food at this thing?'

'Quite sure,' I lied. 'Lots of food.'

The interior was in shadow, save for the economical glow of little candles dotted around here and there. The crowd was large; I could sense bodies everywhere — extravagant-looking silhouettes seated in cliques or standing in clusters. When my eyes adjusted, I searched the room for Brophy. But I found only shiny people who smelled good and purred with chitchat, issuing the occasional high laugh. The waiters in long, white aprons transported trays of flutes, and I took two. A small stage with a lectern had been set up in the corner of the room, behind it the dizzying city lights. I ventured over for a look. At this height, the city was almost unrecognisable.

The noise level dropped suddenly and I turned to see Mathilde Van Zyl bustling through the crush. Shorter than I imagined, her face was smooth, and the dark hair twisted in long tresses over her bare shoulders. The dress was a Crunchie-bar wrapper that finished well above the knee, and she wore four-inch stilettos. The crowd closed in, and she was forced to stop when shanghaied by a determined art lover. She graciously air-kissed and smooched her way out of their grasp, and continued.

Ben had gone to the bar, where wooden trays of sushi and canapés were lined up. I sat beside him and offered him a champagne. 'This isn't going to fill me up,' he whinged.

'I'll buy you a hamburger on the way home.'

He sneered at that, and shoved in his third sushi piece, covered in bright orange fish eggs.

Mathilde tapped the microphone — time for me to get some fresh air on the balcony. The shock of cold and the rush of wind caught my breath and set my hair whooshing around my face. Set up a couple of turbines in this gale and you could power a small city. A few brave smokers passed me, heading inside to listen to the announcement. 'Bit fresh,' said a voice. On a bench seat, back to the wind, sat Merritt Van Zyl, smoking a cigar and holding a glass of whisky that looked like a triple.

'Exhilarating.' I pulled my coat around me.

'Have we met?' Van Zyl turned to inspect me.

I wasn't going to fall for that old put-down. 'I don't think so.'

'Yes.' He peered at me and nodded. 'Crystal's friend. From the elevator.'

'We say "lift" in this country,' I said.

Van Zyl baulked slightly.

'And yes, that was me you insulted.'

His smile was almost apologetic. 'I assure you it's nothing personal. It's … that woman, she gets under my skin.'

'She does seem —'

'Nasty is the word. I've been friends with Clay for years. He and Finch and I go back years. "Bow-Tie Club" we called ourselves, out on the tear — Perth nightlife, which isn't much but we made the best of it.' His words ran together, and even sitting down he seemed unsteady.

'Finch — do you mean Finchley Price?'

'Top bloke, Finch. Put me onto the bliss of the Islay whiskies.'

He held the glass to his nose. 'And Clay, he was a joker. But then his wife died and he married that harlot. Sorry, but that's what she is. A harpy.'

'Actually, I'm no friend of Crystal, I'm Nina's friend.'

That shut him up for a couple of seconds. 'You do get around. Rub shoulders with money. What was that phrase that so upset you … the *well-heeled*?'

From inside, Mathilde's amplified South African accent was exulting her audience to realise more ambitious projects. 'The goal of the prize is to enrich the Australian cultural landscape by supporting ingenuity in the arts.'

'I didn't know Nina had money,' I said.

'No, of course not,' he said, all seriousness. 'So how *do* you know Nina?'

'I live right next door,' I said, now shivering violently.

After a pensive puff of smoke, he said, 'You feel you know her without the barrier of money.'

At last he was making sense. 'Definitely,' I said. 'I think there's more that connects us than divides us.'

He nodded. 'Our common humanity.'

'Exactly,' I said, and sat beside him.

He puffed on the cigar and allowed the wind to steal the smoke from his open mouth. 'And what is your interest in art prizes? An artist, are you? A woman of many sides?'

'My boyfriend is a painter,' I said. The concept of 'boyfriend' was a malleable one and open to interpretation.

He put his head on the side and studied me from behind his whisky glass. 'Any good, is he?'

'Excellent.'

'Like me to put in a good word with the wife?'

I inhaled sharply and a speck of something caught in my throat. 'Peter Brophy,' I coughed. 'The Narcissistic Slacker Gallery, Footscray.' A second later, I regretted it.

'There, now.' He turned calm eyes on me. 'I think you're learning.'

As easy as that, I'd succumbed to corruption.

'I see you're still here, so tell me, you're not freezing your tits off out here for the pleasure of my company — what do you want?'

'Advice. Help. I have a technical document, mining industry-related, and I don't know who else to ask.'

'What kind of document?'

'It relates to soil samples, that kind of thing. Nina gave it to me for safekeeping.'

'Safekeeping? Why would she do that?' His voice was even, his face emersed in shadow.

'That's what I need to understand. I assume it's significant. It concerns gold deposits at Mount Percy Sutton.'

He sipped his drink. 'I'm not familiar with that location.'

'What about the companies then: Blue Lagoon Corp or Bailey Range Metals?'

'Sorry,' he said. 'Never heard of them.' Then he sat up and seemed rather more sober. 'They might be one of those flight-by-night ventures, set up to close down the next year. There's a plethora of small-time operators. You might want to check the business register or the Minerals Council list of member companies, just to see if they still exist.'

I leaned back and bit my lip.

'Probably just paperwork from an abandoned project.' He dropped the stub of cigar in his drink. What a waste. That inch of whisky was what I needed right now.

'I'm not sure what to do,' I said, more to myself.

He smiled at me. 'Want my advice? Toss it. The mining caper is drowning in reports of one kind or another. I doubt this one is relevant to anything.' He made an apologetic bow. 'Would you excuse me? I have a phone call to make.'

A shudder shook my entire body. I'd get pneumonia at this rate.

It was time I started taking better care of myself. And definitely time I gave up on this foolish business. I needed to be home in bed, not fifty floors up in the freezing wind.

I found Ben still at the bar. His shirt was covered in fish eggs, and he had consumed a great deal of champagne. 'But I'm enjoying myself,' he slurred. I had to physically drag him off the stool and out to the lift. The lift doors opened and Brophy stepped out. 'Hardy, you feeling better?'

'No. Big mistake — dying. Sorry. See you.'

As the doors closed, the sight of a bewildered and slightly hurt Brophy bore into my retina, leaving a permanent impression. And all the way home on the train, I was thinking that I should have stayed, if only for long enough to explain myself. I imagined Brophy now thought I was a capricious liar.

18

BEN'S MAZDA was still parked in the train station's carpark, so there was that to be thankful for. He drove us down Roxburgh Street and parked near the pine tree.

'Look,' he said, with sudden alarm.

I followed his pointed finger to the top floor of my building, where a light flickered in my lounge room window. The light swept the windows and moved to my bedroom; I had left the curtains open and I could see shadows creeping up the walls.

I was out of the car, and sprinting across the road into my building. Ben was shouting at me to stop. I ignored him and took the stairs two at a time. I reached the top landing before I realised that my front door was shut and my key was in my bag, which was still in the car with Ben. Adrenalin had hiked up my heart rate. I was shaking with rage and pounded on the door, screaming words that made no sense. Brown Cardigan's front door opened. 'Call the police,' I shouted. His door slammed shut. I turned back. My door had opened, but I couldn't see anyone.

I stepped in to hit the light switch — and my head snapped back, white hot pain searing the side of my face. I staggered, and a dark figure came forward and shoved me backwards; I landed hard on my arse and both elbows. Shockwaves reverberated to my shoulders. At least my head didn't hit the deck. The figure leapt over my writhing body, and I heard feet galloping down the stairs.

Brown Cardigan opened his door. 'I called them. They said they'd be a while.'

For an answer, I held my face and rolled around in pain.

'I'll get you a bag of peas,' he said, and left me again.

There were more footsteps on the stairs. Ben crouched down beside me. 'Bloody hell, Stella. You okay?'

He tried to lift my arm but I flinched and shrugged him off. 'Never better.' I rolled onto my knees and sat on my haunches. 'Did you see who it was?'

'No,' Ben said. 'I tried to take a photo with your phone but —'

'But what?'

Brown came back and thwacked an icy plastic bag on my face. 'Hold that there.'

I did as ordered, and realised I was still shaking.

'The fucker saw me. He reached right in the window and pulled the phone out of my hand.'

'Ben,' I said, 'where's my phone?'

'I'm trying to tell you. He chucked it somewhere.'

'Where?'

'It was dark. I didn't see.'

I drew breath. 'Go. And. Get. It.'

He fled downstairs.

Brown Cardigan made a *tut-tut* sound that I found intensely irritating. 'You don't think it will happen here,' he was saying. 'Not on the third floor.'

I was sitting up now — and everything hurt: my elbows, my arse, my face. Then Brown raised a finger to his lips and nodded towards Tania's.

'In there,' he whispered, and he dashed inside his flat.

I braced myself. The door opened and Ben walked out carrying a bottle of Glenfiddich.

'What do you think you are doing?'

'It's an emergency,' Ben said. 'Medicinal. I'm sure Tania won't mind.' A good point, and I felt especially entitled to the whisky, since I had tried for the entire day to get my hands on some. The fact that Ben *stole* it from Tania was the least of my concerns. In the landing light, I saw the blood drip from his nose.

'Let's get you inside,' I said, and dropped the packet of peas on Brown's doormat.

The place had been trashed. Every shelf cleared, every cupboard door opened. Books were strewn over the floor, papers tossed in every direction. In the middle of the lounge room was a pile of DVD covers — all opened, and every disc smashed and broken. I went into the bedroom. My mattress had been upended. I went back to the kitchen, where Ben was pouring three fingers into two jars. I leaned against a wall.

'Get this down. It'll help.'

I drank half the jar and rubbed my sore bottom, fearing it may never be fit for sitting on again.

'I'll look for your phone in the morning. You can't see a thing now. It's probably in someone's garden. He kind of frisbeed it.'

A loud knocking scared the living Buddha out of both of us. Ben opened the door, with the chain on. 'Only me,' Phuong said. He let her in. She was in uniform.

'Jesus, look at you.' She came over for a closer look at my face.

'I disturbed him. He gave me a whack and took off.'

'Take anything?'

'I can't tell yet. Turned it over pretty good.'

She looked at the destruction on the floor. 'Looks like he wanted to break things.'

Ben had been inspecting the doorframe. 'Lock's intact, wood's not splintered.' He stepped over the debris and started picking up bits of broken plastic.

'You should go to Casualty,' Phuong said.

'Nah.'

'On the safe —'

'Nope.'

Phuong looked at Ben, exasperated. 'And what happened to you?'

'Same guy,' he said.

'Go wash your face.'

Immediately impelled by some impulse to obey Phuong, he shuffled along the wall to the bathroom. Phuong took out her phone

126

and started taking photos. 'You should make a report, when you feel up to it.'

'I need to show you something.' I took Adut's exercise book from my handbag and handed it to her.

'What's this?'

'It's a list of drug deals. Adut Chol kept a record of his customers — my guess is, to satisfy Cesarelli's paranoia. Make sure he wasn't keeping a stash of his own.'

'Stella, this is evidence, part of a major murder investigation. Do you have any idea how many laws you've broken by knowingly holding on to this?'

'I know. But just hear me out. I'm involved in this. Look.' I rolled back the curling cardboard cover and revealed the last page. 'My address.'

Phuong looked at it and frowned. 'That's not your number. That's a two, not a zero. It's flat twelve.'

'Wait, what? No, that's not possible.' I inspected it closely. The zero vanished, the two was real: a half loop, the circle never joined, the little tail at the bottom. It was obvious now, like perceiving a *Magic Eye* image. It was impossible now to un-see it. 'It's Tania's address.'

Sweet relief sent me into a convulsion of laughter. I'd lost sleep, and countless waking hours imagining hypothetical scenarios in which I was led handcuffed to a waiting police car. But Adut hadn't found me out — the address he had written down was Tania's. I stopped laughing. If I hadn't been so paranoid, so self-obsessed, I would have read that address correctly. I would have handed the stupid book straight to the cops.

Phuong took the book and started flicking the pages. 'We have to talk to Cesarelli,' she was saying. 'Bring him in tonight.'

'You think Adut was selling drugs to Tania?'

She scratched her part, and smoothed the hair back down. 'Not drugs. This is about money.' She had her phone out, her thumb flicking across the screen. 'Maybe he's gone beyond drug dealing, diversified, expanded his operation.' The phone at her ear: 'Bruce? Yes. There's a development with Brodtmann.' She walked outside onto the landing, speaking rapidly into the phone.

Expanded beyond drug dealing to what, kidnapping? Adut was a silly delinquent, not a kidnapper. It seemed wildly unlikely. Phuong came back and put a hand on my shoulder. 'Pack a bag, okay?'

There was a pause. I realised Ben was in the room; he was going around with a garbage bag, picking up DVDs.

'They might come back, maybe even tonight. They've searched your place for something. Who knows, maybe it's this book they're after.' She waved it in my face like she was scolding a puppy. 'Who knows you have it?'

Mabor? Mrs Chol? 'No one.'

'Well, you're not safe here,' Phuong said.

'I'm not leaving.'

'Ben, talk sense into her.'

Ben frowned at Phuong, like an Aztec virgin might look at a priest holding a knife. 'Yes, I suppose. We ... we can go to Woolburn.'

'Out of the question.' I folded my arms.

Phuong walked through the mess. 'Stella, you should listen to Ben.'

'I don't believe anyone has ever uttered that sentence before.'

'Take some advice for once and stay with your mother. At least for the long weekend. Get some pampering?'

I laughed. 'If by *pampering* you mean scorn, then my mother's it is.' The adrenalin was waning, leaving me teary-eyed. It was a violation, the flat, the damage — not just the smack on the face.

Phuong took my arm. 'I'll help you pack.'

'Fine. I'll go. But it's not pampering. Just saying.'

We went to my room, and together we pushed the mattress back on the frame. The doona was in a heap on the floor. I found the corners, ready to fling it out over the bed, when my laptop dropped to the floor. It had been hidden among the bedclothes. A little luck at last. Phuong pulled a sports bag down from the wardrobe and I threw some clothes in it. I put the laptop in a satchel and put the overnight bag on my shoulder. Ben was already packed. The whisky bottle stuck out of his backpack.

We walked out together, and Ben pulled the door shut behind us.

At street level, Phuong held me by the shoulders. 'Go and be safe,' she said. 'And when you get back and things settle down, you are going to tell me everything — why you held on to that evidence. And whatever possessed you to think this was in any way about you.'

'Yes, of course, we'll have a long talk about things,' I lied. And I followed Ben, who had walked up the street to where the Mazda was parked. My legs, all of a sudden, were unfit for the task of coordinated movement. He reached the car ahead of me and threw his backpack in the boot. He put the bottle on the passenger seat. I dumped the satchel and bag in the car.

Out the back window, the street was dark and still.

'You all right?'

'You owe me a phone,' I said, and tipped some whisky into my mouth, felt the burn, its cleansing goodness. Ben gunned it, and we fishtailed up Roxburgh Street. For a while I watched the sleeping suburbs go by. I wondered if I'd ever see Tania alive again.

19

A PALE yellow sunrise, a rural location. An open landscape with hills in the distance. I saw Ben drop my laptop satchel on the ground and drive away. My brain struggled to understand what was happening; neurons were firing all over, to no avail. A conniption of small dogs leapt and yelped around my feet. A terrible confirmation. I turned around and saw the farmhouse. Now I knew my exact whereabouts and could, therefore, confidently identify the senior citizen in a soiled pink dressing gown coming down the path towards me.

Delia Hardy's gaze swept over me. Her rheumy eyes lingered on my hair, and moved on to my clothes. 'Bedraggled, as usual.'

'Hi, Mum.' I put my arms out and saw the whisky bottle still in my hand. My mother sniffed impassively, the spectacle not unprecedented.

'Can't wear a dress? Just once? Do your hair?'

For Delia, the idea of live-and-let-live was for the weak.

'Nice to see you too, Ma.'

She gave me a brisk pat on the shoulder and shuffled back to the house. The dogs followed her. I followed the dogs.

Inside the old farmhouse, the Hardy family home for over sixty years, a familiar aroma forced its way into my nostrils. I'd never come across it anywhere else. Its composition was a mystery, but it included Ajax and boiled chook, thickened with ennui. I poked my head in a couple of rooms: the same furniture in the same positions. Renovation was not in my mother's vocabulary. The stubborn, unapologetic monotony of it closed in on me. Memories ran like blood from a cut.

I found Delia in the kitchen, where some concessions to progress had been made — in 1970. An electric stove had been installed next to the old wood stove, and a two-door electric fridge droned in the corner. The room was cosy-ish, though, and a fire glowed in the wood stove.

'Long drive,' I said. 'I'm a bit tired — mind if I have a lie down?'

'Of course not,' said my mother. 'Have a rest. We'll talk later.'

Talk? *Good God*, I thought, *will the torture never end?* I headed for my old room.

'Tyler's pec-deck's in there.'

'Pardon?'

'In your room. His gym equipment's in there. And his weights. You can have Kylie's bed, if you don't mind the birdhouses.'

'I don't mind.'

'She can't work on them at home because of the twins. They're that wild. No control. Can't tell her. Knows everything.'

I went to Kylie's room, then changed my mind and opened the door to my old room. A pectoral-declinator was jammed up against it but I managed to squeeze past — other than that, the room was untouched. One of my first proper paintings was framed and hung above the bed. The perspective was terrible and the subject, a desert landscape, was a cringe-worthy cliché. But the use of colour, I had to admit, was tolerably imaginative.

I went back to sit among the birdhouses in Kylie's room, and then collapsed on the bed. Assorted pieces of wood at various stages of construction surrounded me. In high school, Kylie had received praise for a birdhouse constructed in woodwork. That moment of success kicked off a tumult of backyard entrepreneurship that had never slowed. Year after year, Kylie pumped them out, selling them on consignment to ye-olde-worlde joints in Warrack and Ouyen that offered vintage items, the odd genuine antique, and an assortment of crass shite. The birdhouses walked out the door.

I lay between the musty, striped flannelette sheets on my sister's old bed and heard screeching from the kitchen. It was my mother. 'Where's Ben?' That's how we did things around here — you simply stayed where you were and yelled.

'He's putting the car in the shed,' I yelled back. It was a guess.

'In the shed? But your father's —'

'He knows, Mum.'

'I better go and see what he's up to.'

'He's not up to anything.'

I groaned and got up. I found Delia outside, putting on her gumboots. She stamped them on and set off for the sheds. The chooks were out and they darted around her, little brown bantams that *bok-bokked* amiably. I trotted along after her with the terriers, another dog in the pack.

The sheds, five in all, were built by Dad and a mate, and each had a separate purpose. They had thick, redwood posts and stood in a row at the back of the house. The largest was padlocked. It was big enough to house a Cessna — which it had, until my father's plane slammed into the Mallee dirt one summer evening in 1983. Now it housed the wreckage. After his ill-advised crop-dusting attempt, the pieces had been sent to the aviation people as part of their investigation. When they finished, it was returned on the back of a flat-bed truck, and my mother locked it in its hanger, where it has remained, untouched, ever since. My mother undid the lock, and I helped drag back the wooden door. It was dark inside, but I could see the plane, coated in dust and bird shit; one wing broken, the other sheared off. The nose was crumpled, the fuselage burnt.

'See Mum? Safe and sound.' A rat ran out from under the door and the dogs gave chase.

'Ben's car's over here.' I pointed to the shed next door. Delia ignored me. Nothing new under the sun. She reached up and put her hand on the wing. I looked for signs of Ben. He was nowhere to be seen.

'I'm going to bed,' I said and went inside the house.

Sometime later, I woke to the sound of repetitious thumping. I opened an eye. Standing by my bed were two young boys with identical faces; the taller one was bouncing a football on the lino.

'What are you doing in Mum's old bed?' said one.

'It is nearly lunchtime,' said the other.

'Hello.' I frowned, but their names were lost. 'Boys.'

They stared at me. The one with the ball kept bouncing it. 'Mum's talking to Nana.'

'Is she? That's nice.' I prayed for some magical guardian angel to come and jam the football down his throat. 'Hey, does your mum keep headache pills in her handbag?'

'Yeah.'

'I'll give you five dollars if you go and pinch some for me.'

'Ten,' said the taller one. 'Each.'

'Get lost.'

Chair and Blad, or Blair and Chad, or something like that — the little bastards — ran laughing out of the room. I rolled over, bedsprings creaking, and stared at the wall. My heart was a lump of cold lead; if I had the energy I would have cried. There was a tap on the door, and a hand with a cup of tea was extended like a white flag. Ben's head appeared.

'Not tea,' I said.

'Do you good.'

'Coffee,' I said. 'Double shot.'

'Ha ha, very funny.' He looked at me for a moment then frowned. 'There might be some instant somewhere.'

I groaned — something I had been doing way too much of lately.

'Outside,' Ben said, and put the tea on the dressing table. 'When you're ready.'

I put on my jeans, and an old jumper I found in the chest of drawers — a purple hand-knitted sack — and went to inspect the bathroom cabinet. Powders. Ointments. Nothing bought this century. I found a box of Bex, emptied four packets into my mouth, and then put my lips to the running tap and drank for several minutes. I looked at my face in the mirror: frightening. I waited a moment to see if it would all stay down. Some therapeutic dry swallowing seemed to help. I snuck out, avoiding Kylie and Delia in the kitchen, and found Ben behind the sheds.

'Let's walk down to the creek.' He set off across the paddocks without waiting for an answer. He walked away, down the track beside the fence. I went after him. These hills, usually brown, were a glossy English green after the rainy autumn. I lost sight of him, and the thick brush slowed my progress. I found him by the creek sitting on the embankment. I sat beside him.

'Creek's full,' Ben said. He kicked a small rock; it tumbled into the water with a *plop*.

I watched the current divert round the new obstacle. 'The guy who broke into my flat, what'd he look like? Was he short, stocky, wearing a hoodie?'

'I didn't get a good look at him. He snatched your phone and was gone. But he wasn't short — more medium. Why?'

'There's been a bloke hanging around the flats, short, wears thongs. Thought it might be him.'

'What is it you're not telling me?' Ben asked. 'The person who broke into your flat was looking for something, a *particular* thing. What have you got that's so valuable?'

Not a school-boy's exercise book — I now saw how preposterous that idea was. It was a teenage bookkeeping system, a means for Adut to keep track of his deals. After he was murdered, Cesarelli asked Marbor for it. The book's existence was inconvenient, but I doubted Cesarelli had managed to trace it to my flat let alone send a goon to break in to get it.

'Well?' Ben demanded.

'A DVD Tania gave me.'

He tilted his head. 'Not *The Blue Lagoon*?'

'That is what the label says, but it's not a movie. It's a report about mining.'

Ben pulled a bent cigarette from of his top pocket. 'Where is it now, the DVD?'

'Still in the laptop. The one place the burglar didn't look.'

'Bloody amateur.' The same pocket yielded a matchbook. He lit the smoke, and piffed the burnt match into the grass.

'A mining report?' He scratched an eyebrow with his thumb. 'What if we offer to sell it to him?' He blew smoke at me with the words.

'Who?'

'The guy, the burglar.'

I rolled my eyes. 'It belongs to Tania.'

After a thoughtful drag on the cigarette, Ben said, 'Stella, listen. It must be worth something. Otherwise, why did he want it? Why did he break into your flat, demolish your movie collection, and take nothing?'

'Mum must have dropped you on your head. More than once. We both know the guy is working for Cesarelli, and he doesn't want to *buy* the damn DVD. He wants to *destroy* it.'

Ben crushed his butt under his heel and put his arm around me. 'You seem upset. Sometimes I worry about you, Stella.'

I shrugged him off. 'Worry about yourself.' I went to the edge of the creek and stared into the flowing stream.

A raucous bellowing drifted down from the paddocks. Lunch was the general gist. 'I'll feed it to the dogs in one minute,' Delia Hardy was screeching.

When I reached the house, I was relieved to find that Kylie and the twins had left. Ted Newstead, however, having returned from mass, was sitting at the table in a brown suit and tie, reading the paper. I saw him look up at the two adult Hardy children, the criminal and the social misfit, and then wipe his moustache with a napkin. A plate of cold roast lamb sandwiches was on the table, near an industrial-sized teapot under the industrial-sized tea cosy I had knitted in high school.

'Tell us, Ted, what's new in the world?'

'Lamb prices down,' he said, not looking at me. 'Wheat's gone up.

Come summer, property prices are going through the roof. Dams full, creeks flowing. Good for morale.'

'Terrific,' I said. 'Isn't it, Ben?'

Ben was chewing pensively. 'What?'

I poured tea into a mug and remembered the smell of Brophy's hair. He said he'd phone. Meanwhile, my mobile was lying in a garden somewhere in Roxburgh Street, Ascot Vale, covered in snails. If my phone sang 'Map of Tasmania' no one would answer. I couldn't use the landline here, not with Delia and Ted listening.

I went outside for some fresh air, and Ben followed. 'God, I wish I had a phone.'

He put his hand in his pocket, retrieved a phone and flipped it open. 'Use mine.'

'What the —? Give me that.' I yanked the phone from his hand. Directory told me there was a P. Brophy in Footscray. *Would I like to be put through?* 'Yes, please.'

'*This is Peter — and Marigold — we can't get to the phone so leave us a message …*'

'It's Stella. My mobile's out of action. Just letting you know I'm visiting my mum in the country for … a day or two.'

Ben put his hand out for the phone. 'Happy?'

I snapped it shut. 'Thank you, yes.'

I spent the afternoon in Kylie's room studying the Report on the quality of Mount Percy Sutton alluvial samples for Blue Lagoon Corp and Bailey Range Metals. August 2008.

It was an analysis of mineral composition, full of very dry language. The conclusions were unequivocal: the gold deposits at Mount Percy Sutton were not worth the cost of extraction. There were several pages of tables and maps and indices. I stayed in my room until I heard the first guests arrive for Tyler's fortieth.

Ted was opening cans of Victoria Bitter. I joined my family, and miscellaneous locals and, thanks be to beer, their forgotten nicknames returned. I was bear hugged by Ledge and Ox and Froggy. The company was warm, and the vibe friendly. After a while, I resolved to go home more often. My memories of cruelty and dust and mourning were a collection of half-truths. These whackers would give you the shirt off their backs.

Kylie's husband, Tyler, was delighted with his birthday gifts. 'Car polish? Grouse. Good brand that.'

When Kylie married the newly arrived Baptist minister, Delia worried, often out loud, that her youngest — and a local beauty of considerable status — would be consigned to a life of preaching and pastoral care. But between Sundays, Tyler enjoyed shooting and fishing and drinking. The arrival of twins settled the matter: Tyler was 'the best'.

'I always use it on the Mazda,' Ben said sincerely. 'Duco comes up beautiful.'

Ben had bought it at the supermarket. To the best of my knowledge, he'd never used that or any other brand of car polish before.

'Awesome. A spotlight!' Tyler had us believe that his night could hardly be improved.

'For spotlighting,' said Delia Hardy.

'Thanks, Mrs Hardy.'

We dined on casserole in the big kitchen. A pavlova, replete with a topping of tinned passionfruit pulp, coins of fresh banana, and tinned crushed pineapple, awaited in all its magnificence on the bench. We were singing 'Happy Birthday' and Ted, who'd had a few beverages, was conducting by waving his stubby holder at us, when the phone rang.

'I'll get it,' screamed Blair.

Chad grabbed the receiver and they started wrestling, until Chad smacked Blair on the head with it.

'Give it to me,' Kylie said, and gave them both a shove. 'Hello?' A pause, her eyes travelled to me. 'Yes, she's here.' She held out the phone. 'It's a man.'

All eyes on me now. I took the receiver. 'Hello?'

Brophy's voice sounded a long way off. 'That you, Hardy? Got your message ...' He may have imbibed a drink or two himself. 'Your mum's in the book, too. Too easy.'

'That's very ... resourceful of you.'

Every person in the room was listening. I made a carry-on-having-a-party gesture with my elbow.

'Who's having pav?' Delia said in a loud voice.

I pressed the phone harder against my ear. 'Sorry, what was that?'

'Have dinner with me when you get back.'

'Love to.' There was no possibility of private conversation. I had no choice but to cut it short. 'I'll call you when I get back.'

'Goodbye, Stella Hardy,' he slurred.

At the end of the evening, I shoved the birdhouses aside and collapsed. Before sleep took me, Peter Brophy's words looped in my head. It didn't matter that somewhere in Melbourne a crazy person was hunting down a DVD in my possession, I needed to hear that voice, in person, one more time.

20

THIN CURTAINS, no blinds. Morning light kicked me in the eyeballs — no sleep-ins at the Hardy's. No central heating either. After a sub-zero night, the lino was like a frozen lake. My bare feet were appalled.

The dip in the old mattress had rigidified my lower back. I walked like someone recently brought back to life by a jolt of electricity, staggering towards the grey-haired woman seated at the kitchen table, clothed in a robe of pink chenille. The radio was on, muttering about rams and rain gauges. On the table, an open broadsheet, a plate with a crust on it, a mug; and a coffee-plunger, half-full. According to the old kitchen clock, it was nearly eight.

'You want some of this?' Delia pointed to the coffee plunger. 'Ben made it. It's not bad,' she admitted.

I did want some. And a Panadol with the circumference of a family-sized pizza. I found a mug in the cupboard — a relic from my childhood that would now probably fetch a large sum on eBay as a 'vintage' item — and filled it. I observed the enigmatic Delia from the crook of one eye. She hummed, smiling at some private joke, and turned a sheet of newspaper. That was odd. I walked around the room, pulled out a chair opposite her. I considered the course of my mother's life: harsh childhood, abbreviated education, manual labour, sacrifice, grief and loss, the disappointing offspring. When she didn't annoy me, when she didn't speak, I loved her. And I admired her, too. No one could accuse Delia of not being authentic. Besides, she'd decided to carry on living. Her decision to marry Ted was starting to seem less immoral, not as mistaken. A third-age reward, if you fancy a big dag in a tweed jacket — which I didn't, but *horses for courses.*

I went to her, put my arm around her fluffy shoulder, and planted a kiss on her silvery bob. Delia allowed it. I settled down at the table beside her just as the ABC News fanfare announced it was eight o'clock.

> Notorious gangland figure Gaetano Cesarelli was found dead outside his Keilor Heights home this morning. Police are door-knocking the area and are appealing for anyone with information to come forward. Detectives are tight-lipped but it is believed the murder weapon was a kitchen knife, found near the body.

Free at last, I was free at last. It was time to go back to Melbourne. There was no reason to stay in Woolburn any longer.

Delia, unaware of the importance of this development, was still reading the paper. 'The Highland Fling packs up soon. You going?'

Returning to Melbourne was at the very top of my list, but I had fond memories of the fling, and a quick look wouldn't kill me. 'Yeah, I might head down with Ben.'

'Ben's gone.'

Her words were lead sinkers that hit the bottom of my brain with a clang. Words of my own answered back: *Stuck. Here. Hellhole. Suicide.* A flicker of hope remained, perhaps I was wrong to assume the worst. 'Gone where? The shops?'

'Back to Melbourne, he just left.'

'The dirty little rat!'

Delia *tut-tutted*. 'Language.'

I tried to fathom the breathtaking temerity of my so-called brother. The loving, loyal younger sibling, the one who made Japanese tofu dinners and cleaned my flat, was a mirage. The real Ben was a treacherous, conniving tip rat. 'It's not for long, right?' I asked. 'He'll be back soon. Because he is my lift. My only means of ...'

Delia shrugged. She had started writing in the margin of the paper with a pencil. 'I'm thinking of having Kylie's fortieth here.'

'But. But. But.'

'I'll do that nice pudding everyone likes.'

'I can't stay here.'

'Salads. Meat on the Webber. You like that, Stella, don't you?'

'I'm vegetarian,' I screamed.

That amused her. 'Since when? Lamb casserole last night, scoffed it like it was your last meal.'

'Melbourne things. I need. To do.' I needed to do Peter Brophy. If I didn't get out of here, I might kill them all, including Ted. Happened all the time on remote farms. People went crazy. 'Mum, listen, I *cannot* stay another day in Woolburn.'

Delia scratched her arm and frowned, as though the itch and I were the same problem. 'Why not?'

Outside, a deep booming rocked the foundations of the house. A large bomb had been dropped at the rear of the property.

Delia slapped down the steps in her slippers and darted around the house. I followed her. As we turned the corner, huge clouds of black smoke bulged from the far shed and billowed up where the wind caught it and sent it east. The doors had been blown off, and I could see the flames engulfing the plane. I looked at Delia, who was yelling for me to find the twins. I had the fire extinguisher but Delia ran for the garden hose.

Another explosion. A ball of orange heat rolled out the opened door and the windows, and any gap it could find, bending the iron sheets. A corrugated rectangle ripped free and flew across the paddocks. Delia came, pulling the hose, the water pressure a pitiful trickle. I ran inside and phoned emergency services.

'What is the nature of the emergency?'

Apocalyptic. Cataclysmic. Armageddon-esque. 'The shed's on fire. Some flammable materials.' From the kitchen window, I saw the twins skulk along the side of the house. I hurried out to collar them — and had put a foot on the back step when another explosion showered the yard in debris. Through the smoke, I saw Delia running with the hose, spraying spot fires. I yelled at her to move back. I put an arm out, like a midfielder trying to land a tackle, and we collided, entwined, and fell to the ground.

Flames lapped the sides of the next shed. There was a screech, and the roof shuddered and collapsed, and fire feasted on the entire structure. Delia was on her knees, covering her face in her hands. I closed my eyes. Nothing that had mattered still did — not my dismay at being stuck here, not my bitterness toward Ben — only the slow-motion horror of this moment. I heard a crisp *clack*, like an old Bakelite record being snapped in half. It was either a rafter in the shed breaking apart, or my heart.

Five CFA volunteers spent their Monday morning pouring water on a smouldering mess. They worked casually, seemed happy, cracked jokes. How was that possible?

I rang Ted, who was out inspecting one of his properties, and then Kylie, and made cups of tea for the fireys. The twins were later found walking on the road, halfway to the highway. They denied everything, of course.

Delia, meanwhile, had changed into a blue velour tracksuit and retreated to the plastic outdoor table and chairs on the side veranda, and was staring into space. The twins sat together, cross-legged on the pine boards, red-faced and teary. Desperate for something to do, I walked around assessing the damage. The chooks were penned and seemed unfazed. Mercifully, Delia's car was safe. Ben had parked it on the front lawn the day before. It was a small miracle that he had not 'borrowed' it — preferring to use his shitbox to abandon me instead.

They arrived simultaneously, Kylie and Ted, and they walked through the house with barely a nod to me. I watched through the window now as Kylie, Mum, and the twins sat in solemn silence around the plastic table. Something prevented me from joining them, a self-preservation thing.

Light rain started to fall from dark clouds. I went back inside.

Ted was doing the breakfast dishes, shirt sleeves rolled to the elbow.

'Your mother's had a shock but she's okay.' He said this with a soupçon of emotional grievance, as though I needed reminding of Delia's trauma. Ted, I realised, didn't like me much.

'Thanks for taking care of her,' I said pointedly.

He stopped scouring the tines of a fork and eyeballed me. 'You seem to find this hard to understand, but I love your mother.'

Were we naked, this conversation could not have been more awkward. 'I guess.' I deadpanned like a stroppy adolescent.

'She is my wife. I've been taking care of her for the past twenty years.'

Twenty years. That was longer than Delia's marriage to Russell. And my longest relationship was a couple of anxious years, more like wolves circling each other than human commitment. Did it damage my feminist credentials to admit I wanted someone, just once, to take care of me?

'Ted, I need to get back to Melbourne.'

He shrugged. 'So go.'

'I can't. No transport.'

'There's a bus.'

My nods were more a repeated lowering of the head.

'You should get yourself a car, Stella.'

I almost told him: one evening five years ago, I blew one long continuous breath into the plastic tube and they disqualified me from driving for twelve months. My licence was cancelled and I never bothered to get it back again. In the city, a licence wasn't necessary.

'Would you mind taking me to the bus stop?'

'Not now. Maybe in a couple of hours — I'm taking your mother to Ouyen.' He put the last plate in the rack and went out of the room.

I looked at the clock: 11.30am. Time in this place was nasty. I gathered some provisions — an apple, a bottle of water, two butter-and-Vegemite Saladas placed butter-side together and cling-wrapped — into a bag, and put on my coat. On my way out, I grabbed a handful of dog biscuits to bribe the dogs into joining me, and marched.

In my nothing-to-do youth, dragging your feet along the unsealed road was what you did when 'going for a walk' was the only privacy on offer. This road was the site of my initiation into teenage society: first cigarette, first kiss, first drink and spew. Rites of passage. After a long while, I recognised a track that veered off into the bush. The dogs watched me for a while before trotting away home.

Some of the landscape was familiar. Some not. Since Ted had started selling off bits of the farm, there were new subdivisions. Where I had once ridden the motorcycle in search of flyblown sheep, there were now houses, on one-acre blocks encased in wire fences. They were squat, thin-clad dwellings with flat-ceilings, surrounded by scrub, yards strewn with semi-functional swing-sets, and the occasional above-ground pool or trampoline — a weird transplanted suburbia.

Distant thunder made me stop. It grew louder. It was low, on the ground, a rolling rumble, not mechanical but heavy and persistent, coming closer towards me. Dust rose in the air, then they came into view: kangaroos. Thirty-five, maybe forty substantial eastern greys moving in a loose mob across my path. They scaled the fences, leaping straight through the backyards, and carried on, with smaller roos bringing up the rear.

The last joey couldn't clear a fence. He tried and fell short. By now, the mob had moved on. Again and again he jumped, but fell back each time. I wondered if I should intervene. Then the tough little bugger tried again. This time he cleared the height and jumped away.

When the dust settled, silence returned. I lingered, revelling in that brief psychological respite, when ecstatic wonder displaces monotonous self-concern.

If I were fifteen, I'd have rushed home to tell my father. He'd act amazed or surprised, or disbelieving. In my father's company, I would stretch out in laughter, or perhaps lean into an embrace of rock-hard arms and shoulders, and inhale his signature scent, a blend of diesel, Solvol, sporting club. That rich aroma that had soaked into every flannelette shirt that had hung in his wardrobe. So old and soft, the cloth had felt weightless in my hands as I took them from their hangers. The folding and packing had taken an entire day. And, at the end of the process, we gave those treasures to a charity shop.

I walked to the end of the track. Soon, I was in an open field, where granite rocks rose up out of the flatness, grey-white against the ochre-brown. Large as houses, they were rounded by years of wind and rain. I sat down and ate my Saladas. Only the far-off buzzing drone of a line-trimmer cut the inertia of the countryside.

Delia's car was gone when I got home; she and Ted had gone to Ouyen. I headed to Kylie's room, for another look at the report. There had to be something I was missing, some vital clue in the text that could explain everything. I opened the satchel and found it empty. The laptop was gone.

Now it became clear. The fire had been a distraction. Ben knew it would take all day before I realised he'd stolen it. He probably intended to offer the DVD to Cesarelli; problem was, Cesarelli was dead. I wondered if Ben had heard that news yet. What would he do if there were no one alive to sell the DVD to?

I grabbed my bag and started shoving my stuff in it. I wrote a quick note to Mum and ran out onto the road. It was four kilometres to the highway. It would take me over an hour, with the damn empty laptop satchel bouncing on my hip. After a gruelling twenty minutes schlepping over the pitted road, a car heading in the opposite direction slowed. A black V8 Commodore with fat tyres. It stopped and I hurried over. A tinted window lowered.

'Get in, Stella.' Shane Farquar.

I backed up. 'Fuck off.'

'Come on. Where you headed?'

'Bus stop. Melbourne bus.'

He grinned. 'No worries. Get in.'

I was desperate. I opened a door and threw my bags onto the backseat, beside a child's car seat. Dear God, he'd procreated. I pitied the poor woman who'd joined her DNA with this specimen. He accelerated to an alarming speed and skidded to a halt at the highway. He turned left and drove like a lunatic towards Woolburn.

'So, going back to Melbourne, hang out with your arty mates.'

I ignored him.

'Bloke in town tells me your mum's been checking out units in Ouyen. To live in.'

Delia would never leave the farm, let alone live in a unit. 'I think you've been sniffing the sheep-dip fumes again.'

Shane rolled his eyes. 'Grow up, Hardy. I'm trying to discuss business. He reckons she's been talking about putting the farm on the market, what's left of it.'

Could Delia really leave the farm? Ted had a lot of influence over her, and he was the kind of man who called a shed a studio, or a unit a townhouse. He sold lifestyles; perhaps he'd sold one to my mother. There was Delia's odd humming at breakfast, like she was up to something. It was a horrible idea but I began to think Shane Farquar was right.

Mortified, I turned away to hide the angry tears filling my eyes. I was not ashamed of my justifiable sorrow at the property changing hands; the real betrayal was the secrecy.

Was it too much to ask? A little honest, open communication in the family? But no, I had to hear the news from a Farquar.

'Well, even if she is, what do you care?'

'I'm interested.'

Oh, boy! My nemesis, my tormentor, swanning about in my childhood home, touching the door knobs with his meaty hands, walking on the floors with his cloven feet. The moment called for fury, revenge, cursing his family unto eternity. Instead, another part

146

of me, stubborn and disgustingly *reasonable*, refused to cooperate with this descent into hate. The farm was a mausoleum, a monument to catastrophe. Let the Farquar have it. 'So ask her.'

'Every time I try to, she says she's busy.'

I chortled. The woman did lead an active life.

He grabbed my arm. 'You've been telling her not to sell to me,' he said, with a flush rising from his neck. 'Haven't you?'

'What? That's silly.'

'Bit of harmless teasing in school. You're all uptight about it still, arn'cha? On your high-fucking-horse.'

'Don't know what you're on about.'

He stopped near a row of abandoned shops on the main street, where a thin pole had been erected with a V/Line sign stuck to it. I was surprised to be still alive.

'You take the bus to Ballarat,' he said. 'Then the train to Melbourne.'

'Thanks,' I said stiffly. I unclicked my belt, but didn't get out. 'Shane, if you're so keen to buy why don't you talk to Delia? Make a time — let's call it an appointment — and go see her. Make an offer.'

He faced me, suspicion and hope in his eyes.

'And just so we're clear, I have never said a word to Mum about not selling to you. I had no idea you were even interested. You're feeling guilty about the crap you did in your past. Stuff that I've completely forgotten about, and I don't give a shit about now.' I pointed at my chest, feeling teary again. 'I've left that all behind. Right? I don't hold on to shit that happened twenty years ago.'

He held my gaze and didn't reply, but the menace in his eyes was gone. I stepped out, and he did a burn-out and roared away.

I waited beside my satchel and bag. Time. Moved. Slowly. A quiet town, Woolburn. Dead almost. There was the odd ute. Distant trucks on the highway. An epoch passed. I aged, and yet I was no wiser, nor more mature. God help you if you lived around here and didn't drive. It was late afternoon when a woman pulled up and yelled across the road to me. 'If you're waiting for the bus, you've missed it.'

147

'When's the next one?'

'Tomorrow morning. Seven-thirty.'

'No. Seriously. When's the next one.'

'There's only one a day. Leaves at seven-thirty in the morning.' The woman laughed. Then she got out of her car and came over. 'Are you okay?'

I kicked a veranda post. 'Utter, utter, utter bastard.'

Both her hands went up, palms out, 'Calm down.'

'Gah!'

'Just take it easy.'

'*Grrrrraaaagh*!'

She backed away slowly, got in her car, and sped off.

As her car receded into the distance, the place returned to its torpor. I stood in the middle of the road, my hands balled into fists, desperately conjuring an alternative getaway plan. There was one possibility, but it called for a last desperate effort. I wiped my nose on my sleeve and trudged towards the pub.

21

HALF THE town was in Woolburn's Victoria Hotel, playing pool, reading the paper, sitting at the bar making jokes. It was a small, single-storey pub that had remained unchanged for years. The place had never been lovely, but now it was exhausted; the walls had yellowed, and the furnishings and fittings were elderly. Framed photos of footy teams covered the wall. I went looking and found the team portrait from the famous 1968 grand final. Woolburn lost the game but it had been a noble failure, with tales of blokes spitting out teeth, of a punctured lung, broken ribs, of blokes manfully staying on the field and playing on but missing set shots — and in the end, they lost by two points. In the back row, second from the left was Russell Hardy. His arms were folded and he had the sneer that he used for a smile. I had to get out of here.

I stood in the middle of the public bar and, in a loud voice, said, 'Who do you have to sleep with around here to get a lift to Melbourne?'

All activity stopped, the farmers hushed, the boys rested their cue sticks. The barmaid leaned both elbows on the soggy mats. 'You're Delia Hardy's eldest, aren't you? That poor woman. How is she?'

'Mum? She's good, thanks. Considering.'

'Terrible shock for her though, your dad's plane and all.'

'It was only the sheds.'

'Made of titanium that one,' the barmaid said. Everyone present agreed my mother was tough.

'I hear she and Ted are selling up, moving to Ouyen.'

'Yep. Apparently. That's what they're doing.'

An old bloke folded his paper. Hair shot out in wiry clumps from above his eyes, and from his ears and even from the top of his whiskey nose but there was none on his head. He nodded and said to me. 'A Hardy, eh? Well, I'm about to head off to Melbourne. Got me truck outside. And no funny business,' he added with a wink.

I suppressed a squeal and gave him a short nod instead. 'Thanks, mate.'

He put on his hat — not an old cockie's felt hat, but a truckie's cap advertising a brand of tractor — and went out.

I followed him outside to a vehicle for which 'truck' was too strong a word. It could transport five sheep at the most. But it would do, and soon we were on the highway. In fact the doughty little engine seemed capable of driving all day, carrying on to Queensland if required — a thought that crossed my mind. But for now, the brown smudge on the horizon, a city of four million people, beckoned — and, at last, I was headed there. At last I was, as an old state slogan had it, *on the move.*

A strange mood took hold of me, bitter, aggrieved. I grizzled internally about how the old catchphrase *Victoria: on the move* applied to a place that was so often not. Not the capital anyway, with its choked heart, its hardened arterials. And there was not much fluid movement in the social fabric either, with its postcode apartheid, organised crime, disorganised crime. Its cold-blooded politicking and its hot-headed sports lust. A city whose idea of sophistication began and ended with caffeine.

Still, Melbourne did have its attractions. Specifically, Brophy. And towards it I gravitated with grim determination, reluctant to stop. But after a couple of hours the truckie wanted a piss and pulled in at a lonely service station, a vast concrete bauble in the middle of nowhere. I found a working public phone and inserted some change. The police-complex reception put me through to Phuong. 'Stella? How's the countryside?'

'Countryside? This isn't fucking England.'

'You're having a nice time then,' Phuong said dryly.

'Any news?'

'Cesarelli's dead.'

'I know, I'm on my way back to Melbourne now. Listen, Ben stole my laptop. Set up a manhunt, a BOTLO, send cars to all the junkie dens and pawnshops.'

'Stella …'

'I messed up. Everything is my fault. I didn't understand the danger Tania was in, I could have helped her.'

'You're not at fault here. Tania wasn't a drug user, that's what you said. This isn't some gangland hit. It's probably about ransom.'

She had a point. Yet there *had* to be a connection between Adut and Tania. 'All the time, I thought that address in the book was mine. I was paranoid and stupid. If I'd realised Adut had written down Tania's flat rather than mine … I don't know, maybe I could have done *something*, acted sooner. I'd give the book to you and —'

'What have you got to be paranoid about?'

I didn't answer.

'Stella? What have you done?'

I couldn't tell her, I couldn't speak.

'Why didn't you tell me about the book straight away?'

'I stuffed everything up,' I wailed. 'I have to fix this. Tania's life is in danger, and it's all on me.'

'Wait, go back. Tell me what you —'

I hung up on her. I looked to see if my truck-driving son of a gun was ready to go. He was still in the gents. There was a dollar in twenties left in my hand. What the heck. I prepared a soliloquy for Brophy's machine, but he picked up. The words flew away.

'Still in the sticks?' He made it sound exotic.

'I'm on my way home now.'

'Can't wait.'

I put the phone down and beamed at the world. The service station was bathed in the light of a hundred fluorescent battens, illuminating the lovely industrial-sized waste bins and revealing the beauty of the litter that collected in the weed-choked shrubbery. A truck swept past; the back-draft showered me in a rain of warm dirt. If there was a more beautiful purveyor of petroleum products, I would like to see it.

I stood, smiling stupidly until a fellow in shorts, with a gut the size of an exercise ball, approached me. His body odour arrived a second later, a sour, rotten stench that snapped me out of my reverie.

'Finished with the phone, love?' he asked, breath like a half-full wheelie bin.

'Yes,' I muttered, and hurried away.

The truck came in to town on the Princes Highway and had just passed Flemington Racecourse. 'This'll do,' I said and my mate pulled over. I thanked him and walked the rest of the way, along Epsom Road. Somewhere, a siren wailed. Overhead, a jumbo whined as it cruised low enough for me to read the numbers on the tailfin. Every toxic greenhouse fume, every grating noise, was a greeting for me, an urban welcome-home party. I muttered an apology. It was a city of wonders in a handsome corner of the country.

Half an hour later, I was home at last, standing in front of *Pine View*, about to climb the steps to my building, when I remembered. Behind me, across the street, it lay. I estimated the trajectory of the arc.

The garden was neat, one of those little-old-lady gardens with a square of clipped lawn and a row of standard roses behind the picket fence. No one seemed to be at home. I lifted the latch on the gate and a security light came on. I walked along the front perimeter, peering into freshly spread mulch.

'Can I help you?'

An elderly woman was coming down the driveway towards me, in an elegant blue wool-crêpe pantsuit, stooped from the mid-back, with a superb head of lavender hair.

'Yes. I've lost my phone. I think it's in your yard.'

'Ay?'

'My. Phone.' I shouted.

'Ay?'

'My. Mobile. Phone.' I opened my palm and pressed invisible buttons then put my hand to my ear. 'Phone.' I studied the ground, slowly walking, searching. The old woman must have shovelled tons of mulch since Saturday.

'Now you listen to me. If you don't leave this instant I'm calling my son —'

There, near the tap, an odd shape. I dropped to my knees and dug the phone out of the pile of sticks. Back in my possession at last, it seemed pleased to see me, too. It blinked courageously, made a pathetic beep, and died.

'There!' I waved it at her. 'See? I found it.'

The senior mouth opened.

'Now, excuse me,' I said. 'I've got stuff to do.'

22

I RAN up the steps to my flat, two at a time. Once inside I turned on the heater and found my phone charger. I plugged in the phone and stood with my back to the heater. Now what? Ben had my laptop *and* the report and he was probably trying to sell it to the highest bidder. I had no idea who that might be now that Cesarelli was dead. In order to work it out, I needed to think like Ben — in other words, like an imbecile. I tried for a while, but it was useless. All I could think about was Brophy. I picked up my landline and called him.

'S'up?' A young voice.

'Is Peter there?'

'Who's asking?'

'Stella.'

'Yo, Stella, it's Marigold. Dad briefed me about you.'

Briefed? One side of my face twitched. First impressions counted for a lot. Ted's mistake, coming over all parental from day one, had strained relations, and he had never recovered. 'Yo, he told me about you, too. Is he at home?'

'He's meditating. For reals. Does it every day. Seriously.'

'Can you tell him I'm back in Melbourne?'

'S'up, shorty? You sound upset.'

Shorty? Did Peter tell her I was short? I was five-five in my socks. That's not short. Of course, nowadays young girls were towering giants, raised on a diet of chicken hormones and chemically enhanced infant formulae. 'I've had a tough few days.'

'True that. Bad thing happen ev'y day. You chillax, now, aiight?'

'Um, okay.'

'I'll tell him. Take care, aiight?'

'Bye, Marigold.'

'Lates, yo.'

I put the phone down and bit both lips. My frown could not have been deeper if my eyebrows had crossed sides. Peter's daughter had clearly watched one too many episodes of *The Wire*. Did ten year olds even watch *The Wire*? Perhaps — with the subtitles on. Innocence only lasts about five minutes now. Once you're weened, you're exposed to every dodgy human behaviour the imagination can muster, real and cyber. For the first time, I had a sense of the awful day-to-day dilemmas of the modern parent. The internet, Facebook, reality TV, porn, celebrity culture — a potpourri of moral predicaments. Poor, mixed-up kid. I was feeling appreciative of my sheltered upbringing.

There was no knowing how long I might be waiting for Brophy. I turned on the TV in time for the late edition news. The usual guff: factory closures, a celebrity marriage break-up, a Collingwood president hits out. Then:

Police Minister Marcus Pugh said today that police were close to solving the murder of notorious gangland figure Gaetano Cesarelli.

PUGH: Public safety is a matter of the highest priority for this government. I have every faith in the hardworking men and women of the homicide squad. There are several leads being followed and I trust the matter will be resolved soon.

I held a glass under the cask in the fridge and worked the tap. A single drop trembled and refused to fall. No wine left — things were worse than I had imagined. Time to visit my local bottleshop. I put one arm up a coat sleeve and before the other arm found its place, there were three raps on my door. It reminded me of the way Tania knocked: soft, almost apologetic. I took the coat off, slotted the chain across the door and opened it a crack.

'Wondered if I might have a word?'

I spied a portion of Brodtmann in a buttoned-up double-breasted coat, fur collar turned up. 'Of course.' I undid the chain and stepped back.

Chin jutting, shoulders twitching, he stood in the middle of the room. It didn't feel big enough to contain him.

'Take your coat?'

'No, thank you.'

I pointed to the kitchen table, but he looked confused. I sat there myself, a demonstration. He frowned, hesitated, and looked around like he couldn't believe the place could support human habitation. I drummed my fingers. I was late for wine. I was upset. I missed Brophy. My guest perched on my hardwood chair as one might a befouled public lavatory.

'Are you all right, Mr Brodtmann?'

He coughed and said, 'Well enough.'

'Any developments?'

He shook his head, glanced up at me, and I understood that he couldn't or wouldn't have told me if there were.

'Would you like a drink?'

The chin came out. 'Scotch. Thank you.'

Ah. Now I'd done it. I was thinking of tap water. 'I've just run out.'

There was a tiny quiver at the corner of his eye. 'I see.'

'We could to go to the pub. Okay with you?'

He sniffed but I could see he was warming to the idea. 'Which pub?'

This struck me as an odd question, and it forced me to think carefully, since the answer might change his mind. 'Not far from here, the Screaming Goat.' It was a trendy place that served craft beer, superfood salads and, best of all, was carpeted, so we could hear each other not speaking.

He shrugged, and I took that as a *yes* and put on my coat.

'I wanted to thank you again for calling about Nina,' he said as we headed down the stairs. 'Might not have known for days, weeks otherwise.'

'No problem.'

Downstairs, Broad was waiting by the limousine. He spotted us coming down the path and opened the door for us.

'The Screaming Goat, Broad. Heard of it?'

'Sir?'

I told him where it was and we cruised through the streets of my neighbourhood in grim silence, until Brodtmann turned to me and cleared his throat. 'We were close once, Nina and I. Did she tell you that?'

His need to be believed was palpable. 'Yes,' I lied.

'I wondered.'

I did the smile-without-teeth, the one that looks like a grimace. Mercifully, a small television, mounted on the rear of the driver's seat, was on and it suddenly caught his eye. Brodtmann used a remote to turn up the volume: '*And in finance news, Veldt Minerals signed a deal today with the federal government worth over two billion dollars to take over the Shine Point refinery.*'

Some distant memory involving the Shine Point project made me bolt upright. I knew little of the detail, but I knew CC Prospecting had been bidding for the deal. And I knew that Veldt Minerals was Merritt Van Zyl's company. So the two were friends *and* competitors. Brodtmann raised the remote and turned off the TV.

'The Screaming Goat, Sir,' Broad announced. Brodtmann and I walked inside and found a half-dozen hipsters sitting on sofas arranged around an open fire, they were nursing spirits and playing a card game. At the bar a fellow with a number-one haircut sat with his back to us, hunched over a beer.

We took a small table by the window and Brodtmann removed his coat. I was willing to bet the charcoal-grey suit he was wearing cost north of four figures. A young woman, inked to the whites of her eyeballs, suggested the Western Australian gin and we agreed. When she'd gone, he asked me: 'Do you know of a journalist by the name of McKechnie?'

157

'Let me think ... No.'

He put his fingers to his temples, rubbed circles beside his closed eyes.

'Who is he?'

'A troublemaker. He speaks to anyone who's had the slightest involvement with my family. Tries to get them to betray us.'

'Sounds like an arsehole,' I said, and felt bad about it. I thought for a moment and said, 'Wait. Is he the bloke who wrote that article about CC Prospecting not paying any tax?'

'That's him.'

'Mr Brodtmann, can I ask you something? Why don't you pay the right amount of tax?'

He frowned.

'I mean why don't you just pay up? I pay tax, the woman serving drinks over there pays tax.'

He raised his eyes to mine. 'Anybody in this country who doesn't minimise their tax, wants their heads read ... Kerry Packer said that, or something like it.'

'Yes, but leaving the Goanna out of this for now — you don't even pay what you are obliged to. It seems to me that you're sponging and you're proud of it.'

He coughed. 'I invest millions in this country. Create thousands of jobs.'

'But the minerals belong to everyone and the tax goes back into —'

'You *have* been speaking to McKechnie, haven't you?'

I shrugged. 'That's not the point.'

The woman brought our drinks, served in highball glasses and garnished with a thin slice of raw capsicum.

'He interviewed me once.' He held the glass in both hands but didn't drink. 'I had no idea he was, well ... It's the whole profession; they can't be trusted.'

I drank half my gin in one swallow. 'What happened?'

He looked up. 'My wife had died. He asked me all about that.

I thought we would discuss the jobs I've created, the wealth I've brought to the state, the entire nation.' He took a big drink and put the glass down. 'More of a gossip columnist than a financial reporter. Only interested in my relationship with my second wife, the family dynamic. All very tawdry stuff.'

As he spoke, I glanced about the room. The man sitting at the bar — something looked familiar. I turned back to Brodtmann. 'Is that why Nina came to Melbourne?'

He stroked the corners of his opened mouth. 'Frankly, I don't know.'

I chewed my capsicum, thinking he must have known. Everyone I spoke to knew Crystal and Tania hated each other.

'How would I know? I tried to talk to her ...' He put down the glass. 'Miss Hardy, if anything happens to Nina I'll never forgive myself —'

I held up my hand and he stopped speaking. I could see the man at the bar in profile now, as he spoke to the barmaid. He picked up his backpack, rifled through it — then he lifted out a laptop and showed it to her.

'Excuse me a moment,' I said to Brodtmann. I stood up and walked to the bar. I made a fist and, pulling my arm back and as hard as I could, punched the man on the side of the head. He howled in pain and nearly fell off the stool. The hipsters all looked up. I could see Brodtmann was on his feet. The inked barmaid came tearing over the bar to restrain me. But Ben did nothing to stop me. 'Stella, how'd you find me?'

'Relax,' I said to the barmaid. 'The laptop's mine.'

She'd worked this out for herself. 'Get out, both of you.'

'I don't want any trouble, I just want my damn laptop and I'll be on my way.'

'Guess I can't stay at your place tonight then?'

For an answer, I hissed at him. When I went back to the table, Brodtmann was gone. I put the laptop in my bag and both arms in the sleeves of my coat, and headed outside. I walked home, surprised by the pity I felt for Brodtmann.

With the DVD now back in my possession, I decided it would be prudent to make a copy — maybe several copies — of the report, in case I ever lost it again. Besides, I didn't want to be the only one who had access to the report, given the startlingly real possibility that I might die or something. I set up my laptop on the table and opened *The Blue Lagoon*. I attempted a simple drag and drop onto my desktop but the file bounced back to its original folder, as if held off by an invisible, repellent force. The document file would not attach to the email. I tried again. Each time, the icon skittered back to the DVD folder.

Out on the third floor landing of *Pine View*, music was playing at a volume that could peel the skin from your face. If I had to guess, I'd say it was Slayer. I was pretty sure Brown Cardigan did not favour thrash metal. It was coming from Jack and Amber's. I put the DVD in the case, and went and pounded on their door. Jack opened the door in a highly stroppy state, bespectacled, bearded, and beanied. 'What?'

I entered and turned the music down.

'Wait. Stella. You can't do that.'

'Need to use your printer.'

'Get your own fucking printer.'

'I *really* need to use your printer.' Perhaps it was the emotion in my voice. He jumped up and turned the music off completely.

'What for?'

'This.'

He shook his head. 'A movie?'

'Not movie.'

'I don't have a disc drive.'

I held out my laptop. He took it from me and started to fiddle at the back with the cables. 'Amber doesn't like metal. I can only listen

160

when she goes to her sister's,' he said, not looking at me.

'No need to explain.'

'This thing's ancient. Gotta install print drivers off the internet.'

'Install away, Jack.'

He tapped the keys and the printer began a frenzied mechanical response. I watched as he opened the file, the disc whirring in the drive. He hit the *print* command and a message box appeared. *Password.* He tried to save it in a different format. *Function not available.* He ejected it and handed it back to me.

'I tried to email it but it won't attach. Something blocks it.'

'It's set up with a layer of security, password protection. All copying or printing functions, stuff like that, you need the password.'

I thanked him and left. Immediately, the Slayer volume went back up.

Back in my flat, I checked my phone: no message; my landline: no message. I was looking longingly out the window when I saw a white van drive down Roxburgh Street and park opposite my building. I inspected it from a distance — flecks of paint all over it. I dared to hope. The driver's door opened and out he stepped, in a clean shirt and jeans, the face stubble a sheen of silver. His hair was combed into an extravagant rockabilly arrangement. It was a sight of unutterable magnificence. I ran downstairs and he clocked me as I sprang across the road. He held his arms out and I let him wrap them around me.

'You eaten?'

'Not since last century,' I said.

23

VYVY'S WAS on Racecourse Road. Brophy and I both spotted the one empty table, second from the back, simultaneously, and we ran for it. As if there was a chance it might be taken from us, we started placing bags, jackets, and scarves over the chairs to stake our claim. A waiter brought menus, jasmine tea in a thermos, and two small cups. Brophy ordered vegetarian laksa. Extra tofu.

I said, 'Two.'

Brophy said, 'There are Laksa King enthusiasts out there, poor misguided fools. Right here, best laksa in Melbourne.'

I looked at him, amused. 'What am I, a blow-in?'

He lifted his chin in query.

'I practically *live* in this establishment. I work down the road.'

Brophy acted chastened. 'Forgive me. It's a bloke thing. We like to appear knowledgeable.'

The remark had charm. 'This once.'

He nodded, keeping steady eye contact. He looked away. 'Your brother —'

'Jesus, look at this. The soy sauce and the chilli sauce are in the same kind of bottle.' I made a careful study of them. 'Those two you do *not* want to mix up.'

He smiled. 'Right.' But the crease in his brow deepened.

'Just saying.'

He rested his hands on the laminex and pushed back in the chair. Possibly preparing for departure. I had blown it.

'I spoke to your daughter on the phone,' I said. 'Very bright. Socially aware.'

'Marigold? I suppose so. Sometimes.' He pulled at his ear.

'She was interested in my welfare. At her age, I didn't know other people existed.'

162

'Oh yeah.' Relief in his voice. 'She can be caring.'

'And the language, the way she speaks.'

'Ah. That's her mother's influence. Well, the boyfriend. He's into rap.'

I nodded. A tangle of discordant family relations. Yay!

He did an imitation of a rap artist, with a hand-flicking gesture. 'Keepin' it real.'

'Yo.' I countered. There was silence. I tried to think of something to say; came up blank.

He leaned forward, sipped some tea. 'So, you like Peter Jackson.'

'I do?'

'*The Lord of the Rings*. The director.'

'Oh, *that* Peter Jackson.'

He leaned over the table. 'I like the movies but I prefer the books.'

'You say that like it was heresy. I like the books but prefer the movies. That *is* heresy.'

He laughed. 'Go on then, what do you like about them?'

Tell him? I wanted to. I had quite a lot to say on the subject actually. But how could I answer without revealing something of me? The haunted, lonely individual who found solace and meaning in the actions of characters in a movie, and who was brought to tears by the bravery of imaginary people. Admissions like that hinted at too much secret suffering; made me appear emotional, weird — more red flags than a May Day parade.

'The final scene in Moria,' I said, keeping my tone cool. 'Gandalf falling. Those battles, when they're outnumbered. The humans versus Sauron thing. The odds are so small. Impossible really.'

'Yes. And the sword, of course; layers of symbolic meaning there.' His blue-grey eyes had a pleasant intensity.

The arrival of bucket-sized bowls of soup put an end to that wistful moment. Scary slices of red chilli floated in it. The lemony aromas made me want to close my eyes and swoon. Brophy launched in, spoon digging up noodles, vegies, and broth. I watched him: loud slurping, unreserved — a good eater. I raised the china spoon to my lips and the world became quiet. There was only tang and heat.

Halfway through, he wiped his mouth. 'Arwen. When she chooses a mortal life.'

'Yes?' Perspiration on my face; I could feel it. I put down the spoon, patted my chin with the napkin.

He looked at me, serious. 'Why become mortal?' A rhetorical question.

I answered anyway. 'Love?'

'You can love in the Undying Lands.'

'Right.'

'Immortals can love.'

'Right.' I liked this Peter Brophy.

'Mortals die, don't they?'

'Yep.' I was drinking in the arch of his eyebrows. 'Pretty much what the word means.'

'And facing death. That's the ultimate fear. We all have to do it.'

I posed, philosophical, hands together, fingers steepled. 'Go on.'

'Immortals can never know what that's like.'

I considered that idea. 'They can't die, so they can't experience fear. They exist in a fear-free zone.'

He lowered his eyes. I gazed at his mouth — a crooked smile. 'They're missing out.'

I guffawed. 'On what? The joys of terror?'

'A test of courage.'

I had to wonder if he had been reading my mail, going through my rubbish.

He drank the last of his soup straight from the bowl. He lowered it. 'Or something like that.'

'You are familiar with *Crouching Tiger, Hidden Dragon*?'

'I've seen it.'

'At the end, when Mu Bai is dying from Jade Fox's poison dart and he finally tells Shu Lien with his dying breath —'

'She says he must use it to meditate, so that his soul rises to eternity.'

'Yes! But he doesn't,' I said, breathlessly. 'He tells her he's wasted his whole life!'

His eyes shone. 'He lived on the mountain, in peace and tranquillity.'

'Yes, but it was a form of cowardice. He never admitted his love for Shu Lien. Only at the very end he tells her that he loves her and has always loved her and that he would rather give up enlightenment and drift as a ghost by her side as a condemned soul.'

'Because of her love, his spirit would never be lonely.'

'And Shu Lien kisses him, and then he dies.'

On the walk back to his van, Brophy's hand slipped into mine. It had rained. The wet footpath reflected the city lights. I said, 'If Arwen really wanted to test her bravery she could always become a St Kilda supporter.'

We were at the van now and he unlocked the door. When he turned, I stood on my toes and he bent his head, and my mouth was on his, and I was pushing him against the van. I pressed my hips against him and put my arms around him, breathing in the warmth of him rising up through his clothes.

24

A RUBBISH-TRUCK, working the hydraulics, lifting bins, dumping them. Then daylight. Brophy's soft breath. I closed my eyes, drifted back to sleep. Light filled the room from high, bare windows. My eyes were closed but I was awake. I moved my hand around his bare chest, along his arm. I turned to meet his face, and kissed his mouth.

'Tigers,' he said, a lingering, ridiculous smooch on my cheek.

'What about them?'

'Braver. A Tigers supporter.'

'You poor sap.'

'Hereditary. My old man, his father.'

'Born like that then. Unfortunate.'

There was a persistent meowing at the bedroom door. Brophy went to let him in. Then he went to the kitchen, and I could see the cat fold itself around his legs while he fossicked in cupboards for cat food. I raised myself up on an elbow.

'Have you heard of Oarsman's Bay?' I called through the open door. 'Fiji. Wonderful this time of year, so I hear. Paragliding, snorkelling.'

He looked at me over his shoulder; one eyebrow rose.

He made toast and tea, and I was feeling content. Then my phone sang 'Map of Tasmania'. I retrieved my bag from under our clothes on the floor.

Mrs Chol. 'Stella. Are you in Melbourne? Can you come now?'

I'd forgotten. 'Now?'

'Yes. Please.'

Brophy was kissing my shoulder.

'I'll come ... today. Soon.' I ended the call. 'I have to go.'

'Can I drop you off somewhere?'

Too soon, we were outside the commission flats on Flemington Road.

'Can I see you later?' I asked.

'Today. Soon.'

Brophy tooted as he drove away in his clapped-out van.

Mrs Chol opened the door, wearing an apron over her dress. 'Come, come.'

I followed her to the kitchen. The gas stove was busy: a stockpot was on the front burner while another frying pan sizzled with chopped onions and parsley. A coffee pot steamed at the back.

'Excuse me while I finish here.' I watched with some unease as Mrs Chol slammed some lamb bones to pieces with a meat cleaver and slid them off the chopping board into the pot.

'What're you making?' I inhaled spicy aromas.

'*Shorba*. For my neighbour. Yesterday she was at home with her children and someone threw a bucket of petrol at her front door and threw a match on it. And the fire came right inside her flat. Did you ever hear of such a thing?'

Bored, destructive delinquents who attack their neighbours for fun? Yes. That particular act of arson? No.

Mrs Chol washed her hands and took out a tray. 'She is so upset, she can't leave the flat. Can't go outside.' She carried the tray to the lounge. 'Come. Sit down and have coffee. Have you eaten?'

'I'm fine, thanks.' The smell of meat made me woozy. I sat on the couch and watched her pour coffee into two small cups. 'What was it you wanted to tell me?

'Stella, you are my friend.'

'Yes, of course. Is it about Mabor?'

She adjusted her scarf. 'My brother from Shepparton — he came to take Mabor.'

'Did he go with him?' I sipped the coffee, bitter and sweet in extremes.

'Yes. But before he left, I was helping him pack his bag, and he suddenly held my hands. He had tears in his eyes. He said to me, "I must tell you something."'

'What something?'

'That Adut had been selling drugs for a man. Cesare ...'

'Cesarelli.' I put down my cup, waiting for her to say that Mabor killed him.

'This man, he makes the drugs. He has some men and they cook this thing up in a laboratory.'

'A meth lab.'

Mrs Chol stood. 'You know what it is?'

I gave her a grim affirmation.

She went to the kitchen and took a long metal spoon, started moving the stew around. 'I love both my sons. Adut was a difficult boy — in trouble at school, drinking, running away. But Mabor, he is quiet. He does his homework. Up very late, reading.'

She looked at me, and I was nodding emphatically. It was true — at one time, Mabor had been studious.

'Adut introduced him to some bad people and he changed.'

'He's still ...' I tried to think of something helpful to say. 'Mabor.'

Mrs Chol shook her head. 'Adut is gone, and I don't want to say bad things about him, but I am ...' her voice dropped '... very angry with him.'

'It's understandable.'

She waved the spoon at me. 'I think Mabor wants me to tell you.' She looked at me with that direct, clear expression of hers. Her face had an ageless quality. Like most refugees, Nyahol Chol did not know her date of birth. She put the first of January on her documentation. Even the year was a guess. She bore five children — was maybe sixteen when Adut was born.

'To tell me? Why?'

She turned down the gas and wiped her hands on her apron. 'He said to me, someone must know this things. Someone must be told.

He won't go to the police. I'm sure he meant you.'

I was confused. Mabor wouldn't want me to know he murdered Cesarelli. 'And is that it? Adut worked for Cesarelli.'

'No. Mabor said that after he heard that Mister Cesar was killed, he went to this laboratory.'

'How did he know where it was?'

'Adut told him.'

'And why did he go there?'

'I don't know.'

A door slammed in the flat next door. I jumped. Then there was a knock on Mrs Chol's door. She opened it to a tall African man with one milky eye. He shook her hand, said something in soft Arabic. She thanked him and came back to the sofa.

'My neighbour. Some of the people here are kind. But, in this place, also there are many bad people.'

'I know.' I hoped it was better in Shepparton.

'Now listen, Stella. This is important. Mabor said that a bad thing happen there.'

'At the meth lab? What bad thing?'

She shook her head. 'He won't tell me. He was very upset and said that I must tell someone. He said someone must go to the house to see.'

I realised that my hands were clenched. I made myself breathe more slowly. 'Mabor — where is he now?'

She closed her eyes. 'Shepparton, with his uncle.'

'Mrs Chol, what did Mabor find?'

'I don't know what he found. Mabor wouldn't say. I think he was too afraid to say, even to me. But what can I do? I don't want Mabor to get into trouble.'

'Where is this place? Is it in a house?'

She grabbed my hand. 'Promise me, Stella. Promise you won't tell the police.'

If I had a dollar for every time a client said that to me. Most times, I would say, 'sorry, mandatory for the profession, I can't

169

withhold information from the authorities,' but with Mrs Chol holding my hand, I heard myself saying, 'Trust me. I'd never do that.'

She stood up. 'He wrote it down for me.' From a drawer under the family photos on the sideboard, she took a writing pad.

Adut's murder was only the tip of an iceberg — literally, a mountain of ice. The police, going on what I'd heard at Darren Pickering's trial, were clueless about a resurgent drug market in this area. A meth lab was not in the memo either.

She tore off a piece of paper. 'Here, it is in a Diggers Rest. You know this place?'

'I'm afraid so. For now, it would be best if Mabor stayed where he is,' I said.

As soon as the door was shut, I heard the lock turn and a chain go across.

I looked at the scrawled directions on the paper in my hand. Of course something was amiss at Cesarelli's meth lab. It was a meth lab. Obviously, I should now go immediately to the nearest police station with this information. On the other hand, there was client confidentiality, a professional requirement for discretion, and my burning need to know what exactly the bad thing going down at Diggers Rest was. I stood on the walkway on the thirty-sixth floor, where an icy squall messed with my hair. Mrs Chol had said nothing about the actual murder of Gaetano Cesarelli. I remembered Mabor in the café — his nervousness and Gaetano's cool indifference. I wondered if Cesarelli had underestimated the quiet, scholarly younger brother.

Cesarelli was dead, but what of his crew? At least, in Shepparton, Mabor was safe for now.

It was after eleven; the morning was disappearing. I put the directions in my wallet and sent a text to Phuong — *Call me* — and headed home. Almost at once, Amanda Palmer was singing in my handbag.

Boss: 'Where are you?'

'Um, I'm back in Melbourne.'

'That's terrific, Stella, but why aren't you *here*?'

'Oh, I was doing a client visit, seeing Mrs Chol ...' This time, my excuse was true.

'You've forgotten, haven't you? Bloody Pukus will be here in one hour.'

The big announcement — the partnership thingy between justice and community services — I had *completely* forgotten. 'Relax, will you? I remembered, I was about to buy some biscuits and orange juice, or would you prefer more posh refreshments? Cocktail onions? Cheese sticks?'

'I've already organised catering, got a large packet of Family Assorted. So get your arse here pronto.'

I ended the call and started to jog up Racecourse Road, towards Wellington Street and WORMS.

25

'AND NOW the minister will say a few words.'

There was a smattering of applause, and The Right Honourable Marcus Pugh smiled benignly at his audience. His sizable entourage of staff and advisers and PR people made up most of the numbers — then there was Boss, Shaninder, and me. A Burmese refugee with her three children, who happened to be in the waiting room, were ushered inside as a hasty rent-a-crowd. One commercial station had sent a crew of one underage journalist, currently mesmerised by her phone, and one camera operator. Pukus glanced inquiringly at the camera to see if everything was ready and received a thumbs up.

'It is with great pleasure and personal satisfaction that I announce today the launch of the new partnership between justice and community services, a program we call Justice Uniting Neighbourhood Knowledge with Inter-agency Expertise — or JUNKIE.'

The minister frowned and paused to make a closer study of his notes. He glanced at one of his advisers but she only shrugged and made a *keep going* gesture.

'Yes. Er ... um ... I ...' Pukus stammered, looking into the camera lens.

A thin PR woman in a lavender pantsuit was taking photos. The flashing lights delighted the Burmese children.

'I believe JUNKIE will make a significant contribution to the lives of people living in Flemington.'

'Yay!' said the children.

'It is my hope that the people of Flemington will embrace JUNKIE, that they will trust JUNKIE, and that they will turn to JUNKIE for aid. I want the people of Flemington to understand that JUNKIE is here to help.'

'Yay!' they called, and clapped their hands.

One of the advisers was sent to quieten them down.

At that moment, my phone started to wail. I fished in my handbag, but it was right at the bottom. The song was getting louder and louder and still I couldn't find the damn thing. At last I had it — but now I couldn't turn it off. Pukus had stopped speaking and was glaring at me.

I went outside. It was Phuong. 'You rang?'

'Got a good one for you. One percenter.'

'Go on.'

'We have to break into a house,' I said.

If this request surprised her, Phuong didn't show it. I heard only a chortle. 'I'm busy all day. Can it wait until after work?'

'That would be best — under cover of dark,' I said. If Cesarelli's place had already been taken over, we'd need to be careful. 'Okey dokey, I'll meet you at the Station Hotel.'

I went back inside just as things were wrapping up. The Pukus retinue was packing up. Boss was schmoozing the shit out of Pukus, so I went and started inhaling the biscuits before the kids finished them all. When I looked up, Boss was back in his office, looking greatly dejected — some further loss of WORMS funding, I imagined. I stuffed a couple more Anzacs in my mouth and turned to go to my desk, but Pukus was beside me, grinning weirdly. 'Hi,' I said.

'You were at Brodtmann's apartment in Crown the other day,' he said, as though he could hardly believe it himself. 'You two seemed rather chummy.'

Chummy? 'Not really.'

'It's just that he seemed taken by you.'

I thought of the night before — my assault on Ben, Brodtmann fleeing. 'I don't think so.'

'Listen, I'd appreciate a good word, if you can manage it.'

'A good word about what?'

His smile was as real as a botoxed android. 'A long-time, faithful servant of the community.'

'You?'

He appeared crestfallen. 'Donors expect certain favours. Sometimes these favours are not in my power to give. This makes them unhappy.'

'You mean the police have failed to find Nina,' I said.

'Failed is a strong word. Every effort is being made. But ...' He glanced around the office, 'it's another matter I'm talking about. Party colleagues in WA have taken a decision that is against our mutual friend's interests.'

'Shine Point?'

I thought Pukus might actually puke. 'How did you ... I mean, it's hush-hush. But you're his friend, so he must have told you. Yes, I see that.'

The poor man was completely delusional. 'Mr Pugh —'

'Marcus.'

'Marcus, listen, the only concern Clayton Brodtmann has right now is for the welfare of his daughter.'

'I'm looking for a win-win here. Give and take, eh? Let's sweeten this arrangement, shall we?'

Yep, delusional and pretty far gone, too. I looked over my shoulder at Boss. 'Tell you what, WORMS is rather fiscally challenged right now. Things being different, a girl could pile on the praise about a certain faithful servant to a certain mutual friend.'

Pukus's eyes shone with evil comprehension. 'Right. Impecuniousness readjustment. I'll see what I can do, Hardy.'

It was a huge relief when he gathered his followers into the government car and left; I was exhausted.

I figured this conversation qualified as work, and decided to call it a day. I went home to the empty flat, did some washing in the empty laundry, hung it out on the communal clothesline. I was about to have a shower, but thoughts of Brophy made me pause and look longingly at the phone. An age had passed since this morning, when we'd shared tea and Vegemite toast and each other. It wasn't healthy to spend too much time alone — this was legitimate grounds for a phone call. Not some flimsy pretext.

'Hello?' He sounded sleepy.

'Busy?'

'Nope.' He sounded happy.

'Meet you somewhere?'

'You want to come here?'

Did I? I'd teleport there in an instant if I could, but a shower first was essential. 'See you in an hour.'

Though the drawbacks of my humble flat were many — the low ceilings, the cramped space — the water pressure was first class, and the hot water unfailing. I stood under its soothing force for a long while, as I considered Mabor's information. When things settled down a bit, I would arrange some decent legal advice for him. As I patted myself with a towel, the landline trilled. Thinking it might be Peter, I ran, dripping, to the lounge room. 'Hello?'

A long delay, distant static. 'Hello Mrs Hardy? I am John, and I am calling from the Computer Watchdog Violation Centre, how is your computer doing today?'

I slammed down the phone, went to my room and started to dress; it rang again. I hopped over to the phone, one leg in my jeans. 'Hey,' I yelled. 'Why don't you just fuck off?'

'Stella? Vince McKechnie.'

'Vince. Sorry. Caught me at a bad time. I was just —'

'Some tourists, a German family, went off-road near Laverton. Got a bit lost.'

'Lost in Hoppers Crossing?'

'No, sweetheart — Laverton, Western Australia. Pronounced *Lay*-ver-ton, as in Rod Laver. Back of nowhere.'

I didn't like where this was going. 'Germans got lost, you say? That can't be right.'

'Well, it happens. Gits drove the Winnebago the wrong way for hours. They come across a little billabong, an unreliable water source that they call a 'soak' around there.'

'Vince, I'm in a hurry.' Steam rose from my still-damp skin.

'The wife goes to fill the billy, finds a car up to its axles in the mud, with a body inside.'

'Who was it?'

'Don't know yet.'

'Male or female?'

'Male. That's all I know. The area is restricted, off-limits except to mining company personal.'

'What company?'

'CC Prospecting. The area is known as Mount Percy Sutton.'

My blood turned anaesthetic-cold in my veins. 'Why are you telling me this?'

'Because this is serious shit — a woman is missing, people are dying. Isn't it time you told me what you know?'

'I have to go.'

'Give us your mobile.'

I recited the number and hung up. In a daze, I finished dressing and ran a comb through my hair. My mobile rang.

Vince. 'I know it's a shock, but we need to talk. It concerns Tania.'

'How does this have anything to do with her?'

Vince's breath was a wet crackle. 'What are you hearing at your end — anything concrete?'

'Nothing. You want information, why don't you ask your mate in the force?' I could hear him tapping on what sounded like a typewriter.

'Don't want to push my luck,' he said pointedly.

'Well, I'm sorry, but the media are not supposed to know anything right now.'

'You must have something.'

Was it time to tell him about the report? The one Tania gave to me to keep safe? The one that was password protected from copying, printing, or attaching?

No. I couldn't trust him. Brodtmann was right. It was all part of the profession; journalists were duplicitous bastards. But I did have one thing I could tell him. And maybe McKechnie could be of use to me.

'Tania has a friend called Jimmy. That's all I know. No last name. He worked for Faurtinaux Bath apparently, and he might still live in Perth.'

'Jimmy? Never heard of him. But thanks, Hardy. I'll do a bit of digging at my end.'

I ended the call and thought about his request for a progress report. Even with Phuong as my BFF, I was told nothing. I desperately wanted to believe that Mucous Pukus and Deputy Commissioner Conway, and every cop in the state, were busy following leads, combing the state for Tania.

I put my mobile in my bag and took the tram to Footscray. When I reached the steps of the Narcissistic Slacker, I paused to remind myself that this was a short visit. I was meeting with Phuong later and planned to go to Cesarelli's hideout after dark.

There was the usual music coming from inside. Before I reached the studio's top step, Brophy slid the metal door open. He pulled me inside and pashed me senseless.

'Cup of tea?' he asked when we came up for air.

'Mind reader.'

He put the kettle on. 'How's your client?'

I didn't want to go into the whole Chol business. And the news about the dead body in the WA desert was too depressing to share with my new ... with Brophy. Best to say as little as possible. 'Okay.'

'And you?'

'Fine.'

A girl of about ten came up the steps and flounced into the room: blonde bob, freckles. She threw her bag on the floor — a satchel decorated in skulls — and slouched into a chair beside Brophy. 'What it do, boo?'

'Okay,' said Peter. 'How was Mum's?'

"K.'

'Hi Marigold,' I said. Oh no, I had used the wrong voice. I intended to sound neutral but it came out in a high-pitched singsong — the I-want-you-to-like-me-so-badly-I'll-demean-myself voice.

'Yo,' said the child.

My phone started singing: Phuong. I waved to Brophy and his daughter and went out onto the stair. 'What it do, boo?'

'I have no idea what you're talking about,' Phuong said. 'Now, bit of goss for you: Ashwood got the sack.'

''Bout time. Fondle the work experience student?'

'No — humorous email. Pictures with a stupid caption.'

'They never learn.'

'No, they don't. Escorted from the building. He reckons top brass have no sense of humour.'

'Escorted, you say? I'd say they probably do.'

Phuong laughed. 'See you at the Station for a happy-hour debrief.'

I went back inside and sat on Brophy's couch, a relic the Salvos would have chucked. Meanwhile, Marigold swivelled on an old office chair, playing a hand-held device that emitted a jaunty, repetitive tune and the occasional tinny beep. 'Looks like you guys are getting pretty serious,' she said.

Peter sighed, 'Whatever it is, Marigold, knock it off.'

'What?' Playing the angelic child, her eyes on the game.

Peter handed me a matching cup and saucer. 'Too cold for the roof today.'

'Shame,' I said, eyes on the swivelling girl.

'I'm just saying, if you're serious then you should tell her.' She made a half-hearted attempt to suppress a grin.

I stirred my tea; there was a small chip in the cup, and a crack that probably went all the way to the bottom. 'Tell her what?' I asked Peter.

Colour rose in Peter's face; he looked like someone cornered.

Marigold snorted. 'Oh. My. *God*. This shit is going to be good.'

Peter took the computer game from her. 'Go and watch TV in your room or something.'

She turned to me. 'Ten thousand junkies can't be wrong, you feel me?'

I was having trouble understanding my native tongue. I turned to Peter, bewildered. 'What is she talking about?'

Marigold sighed condescendingly, closed her eyes and said, 'I'm talking about *methadone*. Have you heard of it? It's this drug for people —'

'I know what methadone is, thank you, Professor Smarty Pants.' I wondered why no one had put this child to work in a mine somewhere. They don't mine like that anymore, that's why. It's all open-cut: dynamite and big trucks. They should go back to digging underground with picks and shovels, little lights on their hats — with children like Marigold loading coal into bins. 'What's ten thousand junkies got to do with it?'

'Ten thousand registered methadone users in the state of Victoria.' Smart little bugger gave me a smug look. 'Aren't there, Dad?'

Time slowed, my perception sharpened. There was my cup on the coffee table, with blue flowers on a white background, and the unhurried thought: I didn't have one sip.

'Go.' Peter was standing over Marigold. '*Now*! Go to your room.'

The child baulked. Discipline was evidently a new experience — an affront.

'Now,' said Peter again, soft but resolute.

'Fine.' She slid off the chair. 'But you should have told her.' She ran from the room.

Peter coughed. 'Ah, you will probably —'

I addressed a spot on the linoleum. 'Don't tell me what *I will probably*. You have no idea what *I will probably*.'

He waited, silent.

The evil spawn had a point. Status: junkie. That's probably something he should have told me sooner. Much sooner. Like at 'hello'. I gathered my belongings, made some progress at the laborious business of walking. At the door, I pulled my shoulders back. 'Lates, yo.'

179

The stairs appeared obscured by cloud. I stumbled down and out into the street. In a panic, I turned right. The eastern end of Paisley Street was bus-stop central — buses all over the place, pulling in and trying to pull out. Car horns beeped. And the crowds. What time was it? A surge of humanity churned along the footpaths, spilling onto the road — groups of men laughing together, herds of school kids, big kids like giants in school uniform, mothers with children in strollers, hipsters, junkies, office workers, people with ten shopping bags on each arm or pulling two-wheeled shopping carts — all trying to squeeze around each other.

I moved among them, was absorbed, going nowhere. I changed my mind and did a one-eighty, aiming now for a café at the far western end. I passed by The Narcissistic Slacker in a rush, not looking up. I kept going, passing the medical centre on the corner. Around the café entrance, a group of locals had stopped to discuss important matters of the day.

I pushed through the crowd and practically fell through the doors. The café was an old-fashioned coffee shop that made cheese-and-tomato toasted sandwiches on plain white bread, with butter on the outside. Here quinoa or kale were unheard of. I ordered a pot of tea — and like I always did when my heart was broken, I pretended it wasn't.

I took a table by the window and watched the crowds. It wasn't so bad. Things had not really progressed so very far. It wasn't like I had to sift through the bookshelf or record collection. All we'd really shared was one night and some crazy ideas. A nice lady brought the tea and called me 'love'. I held the little stainless steel pot over my cup and poured; tea went everywhere, some made it in the cup.

The problem, as I saw it, was that I was always doing things for other people. In the process, I'd been hung out to dry. It was time to focus on myself. On my own affairs. Not men. Not smart-arse little girls. Not sick bastards with tins of petrol wondering the halls of the Flemington Housing Commission with nothing better to do. Not craven politicians. Not crazy-arse billionaires.

I drank my tea and focused on myself. The overwhelming sensation I felt was the heaviness of my body in the chair.

Better to focus on Tania. The last time we spoke she had promised me the mythical Golden Trifecta — gorgeousness, in fact — at her salon in Knifepoint. If I went to her salon, I could freshen up *and* ask her colleagues about Jimmy. I stood to go. Onwards, I thought, to Knifepoint — and into the fires of Mount Doom.

26

I ENTERED the muzak-filled acres of consumption-land and located Tania's salon on the touch-screen map at the entrance. On the way there, I passed Peppermint Sherbet, a hairdressing salon decorated with enough mirror balls to double as a discotheque after-hours, where I made an appointment for a trim, and continued on my way. Superlative Skin Sensations was fitted out with crystal chandeliers and swathes of black tulle. A series of curtained-off cubicles at the back were where, I supposed, the miracles happened. I surveyed the young beauticians as they stood around chatting among themselves, all made-up and shiny in their medical-looking white jackets. I approached a girl sitting behind a glass desk. She looked me over dismissively.

'Any chance of a triple golden?' I asked.

'A gold triple,' she corrected me and paused for the duration of a disdainful sigh. 'We're fully booked.' She was the one I'd spoken to on the phone. Another girl, who had been looking into a mirror and tweezering stray hairs from her eyebrow, came over. 'I have half an hour before my next client.'

The girl behind the desk looked doubtful. 'You sure, Sophie?'

Sophie looked at me and nodded. 'A mini-facial. No worries.' She guided me towards one of the rooms. 'It's not the gold, but you'll love it.'

I climbed onto the narrow massage table and under a pre-warmed doona — that part was kind of nice. I was about to doze off, when Sophie said, 'Where did you hear about our famous gold triple?'

'From Tania. I had an appointment for Friday but she didn't show. Where do you think she's got to?'

'Honestly, when she didn't come to work, we all just thought she was sick. But now everyone's saying she's, like, missing.'

'Do you think she's gone back to WA?'

Sophie put a hairnet over my hair and started slathering cream on my face. 'Doubt it.'

'Why?'

'Because of her work, and because her family are there.'

'Her family are ... difficult?'

'Very. That's why she came to Melbourne all on her own. Her family are so mean to her. She had to get away. You know her stepmother came in here last week?' She wiped the cream off me with a damp sponge.

'No, Tania's never mentioned her.'

'It was, like, totally random,' she said. 'And she was such a bitch.'

'Really?' More cream on.

'Right in front of a client — calling her a scheming so-and-so.'

'Tania? Scheming?'

'I know! As if, right? And she was, like, "whatevs!"' Cream off.

'Good for her,' I said.

'Totally. And her step-mum's hair was so dry. All that money and she hadn't had a treatment in, like, forever.' Different cream on.

'But what about her friends,' I asked. 'She left Jimmy behind in Perth, didn't she?'

'She never mentioned a Jimmy. Is he cute?'

'Totally.'

'Well, like I told her, there's plenty of hot guys here.' Cream off. 'You know, you should consider an eyebrow shape and tint.'

Consider it I did, and at the end of it all, my face glistened like a ripe plum. I gave a ridiculous sum to the snotty cashier, and Sophie wished me good luck. With what, I didn't ask.

Now I headed to Peppermint Sherbet where the colourist coated my medium-brown hair with an ash-brown tint and applied a contrasting colour on strands that had been wrapped in foil. She set the timer and offered me magazines — but I could sit still no longer and spent the time pacing the room in my plastic gown. The problem with going to the hairdresser was all that staring in the mirror. I usually had my hair cut at a blue-rinse place, among pensioners with their curlers under the dryer — without fuss, and cheap.

When at last my colour had 'taken', the scissor artist cut my hair fully eight centimetres shorter than requested, significantly altering my appearance. I feigned joy and paid for it. Three figures.

At last, after three hours in the shopping bunker, with a clean face and straight silky hair, I emerged, blinking, into the daylight. But it was all so temporary. My hair would, on the next wash, return to its usual state — hair that was conscious, an autonomous and capricious life form.

It wasn't far from Knifepoint to my flat and I decided to walk. I crossed the footbridge and trespassed on the golf course, passed through the driving range, and entered a deserted Union Road. Squally winds tossed a flurry of plastic bags. I looked to the sky and, sure enough, it was thick with ominous storm clouds. Then came the first drops, and I covered my new hairdo with my jacket and hurried home. Once safely upstairs, I listened as the now driving rain beat down on the window. A fire hose could not have saturated my washing more thoroughly.

When it stopped, I went downstairs and put it all back in the machine to wash it again. I checked my watch; there was still two hours before I was due to meet Phuong. I put on my coat, grabbed an umbrella, and headed out.

As the automatic doors of the Ascot Vale public library slid apart, a familiar and reassuring hush greeted me. I took the empty seat at the information desk and waited. A woman wearing a *Rosamund* name-tag pushed her tortoiseshell bifocals down her nose. 'Can I help you?' She had on a lot of red lipstick.

'I need information on a company called CC Prospecting, in relation to a Nina Brodtmann.'

Rosamund, her manicured fingers hovering above the computer

keyboard, thought for a moment. 'Company information, business registrations?'

'Yes, everything you've got if it includes Nina Brodtmann.'

Flurry of finger tapping. 'Nothing in the ASIC register. I'll try the business journals.' Pause. 'No. Nothing for that name and CC Prospecting.'

'Try combining CC Prospecting and Blue Lagoon Corp.'

A short burst of typing. 'This might be something. The directors of CC Prospecting are on the board of Blue Lagoon Corp.'

There was no rivalry. Tania was not hiding Blue Lagoon Corp information from CC Prospecting, they *were* Blue Lagoon Corp.

Rosamund looked at me, her fingers waiting.

McKechnie said the Brodtmann's were litigious. 'Try legal cases, all jurisdictions.'

She typed and clicked and typed some more. 'There're two cases that mention both companies.' She cut and pasted the results onto a Word document and printed it out.

I took the documents to a quiet corner of the library and read. The first was about a contract being invalid for breach of corporations law — something about a quorum of directors. All very dull. My eyelids started to close involuntarily.

I flipped the page. The next case was a matter heard in the Supreme Court of Western Australia. Dated December 2009, the plaintiff was the liquidator of Bailey Range Metals Proprietary Limited. It appeared to be a routine bankruptcy. I studied the company name again: Bailey Range Metals. The other company on the mining report.

I tapped a finger on my lips, pondering. According to the report, the two companies anticipated mining for gold at Mount Percy Sutton in 2008. Then, in late 2009, one of those companies went bankrupt. I wondered what Blue Lagoon Corporation had to do with Bailey Range going into liquidation. My eyes darted across the page, looking for a mention of Blue Lagoon. I found it mentioned in passing as background information — and it was a tale of mining folly.

There had been a formal joint-venture agreement between Bailey Range and Blue Lagoon Corp. The two companies intended to combine their tenements, or mining claims, in a region west of Laverton, WA, looking for gold and sharing the exploration costs.

According to the terms of the joint venture, each company brought something to the arrangement that was of value to the other. Blue Lagoon had a large amount of land under its claim, about twice what Bailey Range had.

Bailey Range contributed tenements, approximately half the total land area of the venture. They also brought about thirty million dollars in capital, as well as permission to explore from the traditional owners. I wasn't sure if permission was hard to get, but against the vast area of land Blue Lagoon had access to, it must have been worth something.

So the two companies had made a deal to work together. So far, so good. Until exploratory drilling found nothing of value and both parties conceded reluctantly that there was insufficient gold to justify any further expensive extraction.

I sat back. Tania's mineral report told them that. If they had read it, it would have saved them a lot of time and money. I checked the dates. The joint venture was signed in December 2008. The report was written in August 2008.

Why did the directors of Bailey Range Metals and Blue Lagoon not know about the lack of gold? Maybe they did. Someone at Blue Lagoon certainly knew — since Tania had their report to that effect.

But a more puzzling question now arose. Since Crystal and Clayton Brodtmann were directors of both CC Prospecting and Blue Lagoon, they must have known there was no gold in the mountain — why, I wondered, would they deliberately set out to fail?

I checked my watch. There remained only fifteen minutes to get to the Station Hotel and see Phuong. I stuffed the documents in my bag and headed for the door. A taxi was turning into Union Road. I stepped from the pavement and waved as it approached. It pulled over and I asked the driver to take me to Footscray. The inscrutable movement of a turban told me he had heard of such a place.

27

PHOUNG WAS seated on a bar stool and had started without me. She looked ready for a photo-shoot, in a skin-tight mini-dress — long sleeved, floral print — and her hair loose. She raised her champagne flute in greeting. I spied oysters, three missing from a plate of six. I signalled *same for me* to the barman. He put a glass on the bar, filled it and gave it to Phuong. She slid it over to me. 'Here's to Ashwood's poor judgement.'

'Have they appointed you a new companion?'

'We're all friends in the force. One big happy family.'

I must have been thirsty. The champagne disappeared, and almost immediately a comforting wall rose up, separating me from the harsh reality of the day's events. It was a blessed relief.

Phuong glanced at me. 'That book of Adut's you had — we're still going over it. It's full of names and dates. All little people, but no leads on the Big Banana. No prints we can find, other than yours. It does confirm that Adut Chol was one of a group of young African boys selling ice for Cesarelli.'

I tried an oyster. 'A group of them?'

'Yes. They recruit them young and shower these impoverished kids with cash. And we're still trying to figure out the Funsail thing.'

'Don't ask *me*; I've been trying to work that out. Mrs Chol doesn't know either.'

This information displeased her. 'Bruce and I have been to see her. Trying to get in touch with Mabor — but it seems he's skipped town. Know anything about that?'

'No, sorry.'

She frowned. 'How long have you had that book? You didn't hand it over right away.'

'These oysters are good. Very fresh.'

Phuong scoffed and crossed her legs; I noted new high-heeled boots. 'What's with the break-in?'

'The location of the ice lab. Where Adut collected the merchandise. I have that information.'

A flicker of intent in her eyes. 'Mabor told you.'

I drank champagne and neither confirmed nor denied.

'Flemington?'

'Not Flemington.'

She picked up an oyster shell and passed it to me. 'Where?'

'Diggers Rest. A hobby farm.'

'You don't know exactly?'

'I've got directions, sort of. Landmarks. Not a street number.'

'Wait. Cesarelli's dead — is someone else working the place?'

'Probably. I heard there was other stuff going on at the house.'

'Like what?'

'Don't know.' I did the two-handed, two-fingered quotation sign in the air. 'Bad shit.'

Phuong tapped her lips with the flute. 'We go there — quick look. If it's a meth lab, we call in the uniforms, say it was an anonymous tip-off, and no names.'

I was sceptical. 'It has to be completely anonymous.'

She held up a hand and crossed her bare cleavage with the other. She never used to show cleavage. 'Trust me.'

'Detective material, you know that?' I said. 'I hope they appreciate you in Testosterone Central.'

Phuong tipped an oyster down her throat, finished her champagne. 'Some do.'

I left my oyster in its shell and my half-empty glass on the bar. A metaphor for my day. Outside, the rain had stopped. Phuong pressed a button on her keys and her car's lights flashed. I buckled up, thinking here I was, about to break into a meth lab, once operated by Gaetano Cesarelli; I'd come a long way. On the Tullamarine Interchange, as we flew past the 'red straws' and the cantilevered 'cheese stick' roadside sculpture, I remembered another matter of business. 'You know a Vince McKechnie?' I asked Phuong. 'He's a journalist?'

'Journalist?' She made a face of distaste at the word. 'Nope.'

'You sure? Finance reporter — likes to hold a blowtorch to the feet of tax-avoiding corporate fiends. He's old, one lung, half-dead?'

Phuong shook her head, and took the Calder turn-off. Peak hour was over — the road was almost uninhabited. 'What about him?'

'He came to see me, asking about Tania. Nina. Whichever.'

'I didn't think she was involved in the family business.'

'I didn't think so either but he said Tania had been in touch with him. They had arranged a meeting but she didn't show up.'

Phuong lifted her chin slightly as she drove — I had her full attention now. 'Why would she speak to a journalist?'

'I don't know,' I said, feigning bafflement. The report had become my number one theory. She was going to show McKechnie the mineral report for Mount Percy Sutton, but then for whatever reason, she had changed her mind.

Phuong glanced at me, across the dark interior of her silly little car. Her eyes called me a damn liar.

'I didn't tell him anything,' I said. 'About the case.'

'Okay,' she said slowly. 'And you're telling me this because —?'

'McKechnie phoned me this morning. A car was found in the desert: outback, Western Australia. A deceased male corpse inside.'

The news caused her brow to crinkle. 'McKechnie told you that? Why?'

'The area is leased by a mining company owned by Tania's father.'

'Why tell *you*, is what I'm asking.'

'He likes me.'

She guffawed.

'He came around to check out her flat, and a neighbour told him we were friends. He's under the impression I know all about her. But I haven't told him anything much.'

Phuong sniffed. 'I'll get the uniforms to talk to WA. I'm guessing burnt-out cars *litter* the outback.'

I pursed my lips and looked out the window. 'How's the investigation going?' I said to the blackness. 'What angles are they working?'

'They don't tell me anything,' Phuong said.

If I told her about the report, she'd want me to hand it in — she'd insist on it. I was pretty sure Tania did not want that to happen. 'I don't think Brodtmann has been completely forthcoming with your colleagues.'

We were approaching the Diggers Rest turn off. Phuong changed lanes and slowed to the speed limit. 'What makes you say that?'

I shrugged. 'I think he feels responsible for Tania's disappearance; he seems guilt-ridden, to me.'

She let that idea float around for a while, and then said. 'So, how are you?'

I hadn't mentioned Brophy — my almost-boyfriend, now dumped — thus avoiding the need now for a humiliating status update: Single. Again. 'Awesome.'

As she took the exit, I gave directions. We turned at the football oval and stopped in the shadows of a brick building. In the dim light, a faded sign read: *Home of the mighty Burras.*

'You're parking here?'

'It's not far.'

'I don't mind the *exercise*; I'm questioning your judgement. We will be completely exposed, walking from here.'

'I know what I'm doing.'

'One does not simply walk into Mordor,' I said, more to myself.

'Relax, will you? I thought this was your idea.' She unzipped her dress, slipped out of it, and took off her boots. Soon she was clothed in dark trackpants and black T-shirt.

'I can't imagine why you'd think that. I'm a very law-abiding person. I conform, I obey, I acquiesce to my betters — my political and social overlords.'

191

Phuong pulled the hood of her black jacket over her head, tied the laces on a pair of black Free Runs, and retrieved a sports bag from the boot. She unzipped it and let me see the police-issue Glock, two torches, bolt-cutters, and a couple of smaller tools that appeared to be of differing but specific purposes. 'Let's go.'

28

WE LEFT the township, heading out into a flat, open landscape. The road was dark, and the only light was from a thin moon that kept disappearing behind the clouds. Cold wind swept over us and hummed in the power lines; the only other sound was the crunch of our shoes on the gravel shoulder. After about forty minutes of brisk walking, a dirt road crossed our path. My nerves started doing burnouts. I checked my note from Mrs Chol. 'This fits.'

We went left on the rutted dirt track. There were fenced paddocks on both sides, and I heard a horse whinny in the dark. I could just make out a trotting track.

I was numb from cold when we came to the house. A rectangular kit-home, homestead-style, with a long, bull-nose veranda, sat on an angle about fifty metres from the road.

I nodded at Phuong and we stepped through a gap in the fence into the adjacent paddock. I prayed there wasn't a steer lurking in the blackness, quietly snorting and stamping and lining us up. The grass was damp underfoot. A tall cyclone fence measured the perimeter of the block, and we walked around it to the back boundary. Some of the posts had floodlights and CCTV cameras mounted on them — but our movements failed to trigger the lights. We inspected the fence until we found a padlocked gate, leading from the paddock to a yard at the rear of the building. Phuong pulled out a couple of pairs of latex gloves and the torches from her bag. Once we were gloved, I held a torch as she inserted a small tool into the lock and it released.

The back of the property was taken up on one side by a large shed. The other end was cleared and the ground was covered in small screenings, and not a blade of grass in sight. It probably served as a car park, but it was empty now. We walked between the shed and the fence. It was dark and quiet; no security lights came on. We reached the house and peered in a couple of windows, there were no lights on inside that I could see. We walked around, and halfway along there was a doorway with a wire door. It creaked loudly as Phuong opened it. The timber door behind it was locked. I pointed to the two deadlocks along its frame. Phuong tracked along the wall to an aluminium-framed sliding window. She unlatched the flywire screen with a screwdriver, and then started playing with the lock. It gave and she pushed the window mechanism, which moved about twenty centimetres and stopped. She threw her bag in, and with a smooth lift and sideways tumble manoeuvre she disappeared inside. Given the size of the gap, there was no point attempting to follow her, so I turned off my torch and waited.

A car travelled at speed on a distant road. I held my breath, but it kept going, heading towards Sunbury.

I could see the muted light of her torch moving through the rooms. 'Phuong,' I hissed into the window. 'Hurry up. Open the door.'

She was back. 'Hold this.' She handed me her torch through the window.

'The door's deadlocked from inside.'

'See anything?'

She eased her way out. 'Stinks. Filthy. Crap everywhere. No equipment though. I don't think this is it.'

'The shed?'

She nodded.

The handles of the double doors were threaded with a padlocked chain. Phuong tried the small tool in the lock again, but it was jammed and wouldn't budge. She pulled out the bolt cutters and snapped a link. The chain fell and we stepped inside, flashing our torches.

It was an office, of sorts: desk, office chair; a couple of low, metal filing cabinets; and all around us, stacks of plastic crates. There were doors on either side, a sliding door on the right and a regular door on the left. I pushed the sliding door open and Phuong shone the torch through. It was a larger space, set up like a factory.

194

A long, industrial-looking bench was in the centre of the room, and shelves lined the walls. A couple of free-standing industrial heaters attached to gas bottles stood in the far corner, near a table and three colonial-style dining chairs. A large freezer was chained and padlocked.

I left Phuong, who was shining her torch in the corners of the factory, and went back to the office for a proper look around. I opened the filing cabinet drawers but they were empty — ditto the desk drawers, except for an empty packet of cigarettes, a disposable lighter, and a bunch of keys. It had been completely cleaned out. Everything not nailed down had been stolen. I wondered if Mabor had plundered any decent spoils. I tried the door on the left. It was deadlocked, but there was a small dusty window above the door.

I dragged the office chair over to the door and tested it with my foot. It liked turning around. I put the torch between my teeth, steadied myself by holding the doorjamb, and with both feet on the seat, stood up on the chair. I shone the torch in the window and tried to see, but as I leaned forward the chair turned, pulling me with it. I let go of the door and slid to the floor.

I sat on the stupid chair and swivelled in the manner of a bored child. Like Marigold, in fact. What a life that kid led — a childhood effectively over by ten. But it wasn't exactly her fault. She had a weariness that implied she'd seen and heard some pretty nasty adult stuff in her time. My conventional Catholic upbringing in rural Victoria seemed idyllic in comparison. I folded my arms on the table and put my head down. It was likely that, in similar circumstances, I would have turned out like a Marigold — a know-all, cynical child, set on poisoning her father's relationships. I was woozy from swivelling when I thought of the keys.

Some genius had installed the deadlock at the top of the door. I had to stand on my tiptoes to reach it. There were three keys. The first was a long silver key that didn't make it past the opening. The next was small, probably a window key; I didn't try it. The last was brass, pretty standard-looking, and I slotted it. The lock released and the door swung open. The place stank of stale body odour and a rank rubbish-bin smell, same as when we found a rats' nest in a shed in Woolburn — sickening. I held my breath and, waving my torch, ventured inside. It was a storeroom, converted to a miserable little bedroom. No windows, save the one above the door. There was a mattress against one wall, a wooden chair lying on its side, a pile of blankets, a row of metallic shelving, and some big plastic containers on the floor and stacked in the back corner, where a small table had been placed at a ridiculous angle. Clearly these people had no appreciation for *feng shui*.

Phuong was back in the office and slid the factory door shut behind her. I came out to join her, glad to get away from the pong.

'This operation was massive,' Phuong said. 'You can see it's been dismantled. Only odd bits of equipment left. But the amount of storage — the output must have been ridiculous. Be good to get prints.'

'Just as long as you don't say how you found the place. And can you please not shine that in my face?'

'Wait. Look.'

Phuong was pointing at something on the table. 'There. Look at that.' She trained the light where her finger was tapping the tabletop. I looked at a long smear of dried goo across the surface of the table. 'Gross.'

Phuong met my eyes. 'He leaves a snot scrap wherever he goes. Like a calling card.'

'Clacker was here,' I squawked. We laughed hard, the tears streaming, trying to make no sound. I thought I might wet myself.

Phuong recovered first. 'Anything?' She nodded at the filing cabinet.

I shook my head. 'Nothing.'

'And what's that? A storeroom?'

I was about to say, when she held up a hand for silence. Outside, we heard the crunch of tyres rolling slowly over the stones and a large engine throbbing at low revs. Car doors slammed. Boots on the gravel. Voices. '… fuckin backwater.' A male voice, loud, not afraid of being overheard. 'Inbred cunts and hobbits, innit?'

'Not *inbred*.' The reply was higher pitched, with traces of indignation. 'Some of em don't know what day it is, but.' An untreated New Zealand accent.

'Sheep keep youse busy?'

'Give the sheep a rest, bro.'

'You're the one fuckin em.' The first voice was full-throttle alpha male, the one in charge: 'Can't see shit. Hey, fush'n'chups, put the headlights back on.'

My heart laboured like a two-stroke lawnmower. Phoung put her bag over her shoulder, turned the torch off and grabbed for my hand. To my horror, she was leading me into the stink chamber. Phuong closed the door behind us and the deadlock clicked. In the back of my mind, my one functioning brain cell noted that the door was the only way out. She kept moving, pulling me with her, easing her way along the side of the room. I followed, my back flat to the wall, terrified of bumping something. We came to the table and crouched behind it.

Feet stomped back and forth over the stones. Voices closer now. 'My uncles live there, bro. Fuckin lonely as, ay.'

'Mate, shut the fuck up for one second. Look at this.'

'What?'

'He's come back. The African cunt.'

They'd seen the chain and padlock, lying in a useless pile by the door. 'Blacks,' the Kiwi bloke was saying. 'They can surprise you, ay.'

The stench in the little room churned my stomach, and squatting under the table was taking its toll on my knees. I leaned backward, one hand on the wall, trying to keep steady. Electric waves shot through my back, the ache in my legs was becoming brutal.

The light in the office came on, shining through the grubby

window and casting shadows across the storeroom. I could see Phuong's face. She looked more annoyed than frightened. They were walking around in the office now, both of them. 'Come out, muddy,' the loud one yelled. 'Come on, mate. The money's here. Got your share if you want it.'

If they thought Mabor had come back, that he'd been and gone, we might — *might* — survive this. I heard them slide the door to the main shed, there was a faint click and then the buzz of fluorescent tubes. Their footsteps echoed in the empty factory. The loud one calling out: 'Muddy? Come on, muddy.'

The ache in my knee was getting worse. I needed to find something to support my weight. I pulled myself up and moved to the blankets about half a metre away. Up close, it was actually a small heap of Hessian sacks. I reached the mound and tested it with a hand. It was hard and lumpy. I lowered my bum and eased the muscles in my thighs. Outside, the wind picked up, showering the shed's tin roof with leaves and twigs.

They were back. 'Waste of fucking time. Cunt's gone, bro.'

I got off the sacks and picked up a plastic container and carefully put it upside-down beside the door. It held my weight, and I could just see out the window into the office.

Despite his girlish voice he was a big boy, this one — a Maori with broad shoulders, in an oversized, yellow hooded jacket and dark beanie.

'Yeah. But why'd he come back for?' Alpha was big, too; he had a shaved block head with a high forehead.

'Who fucking cares? Let's get this over with. Get home for a choof.'

'Mate, shut up while I think.'

'You keep telling me to shut up, bro — see where it gets ya.'

Alpha ignored him. He sat on the swivel chair and frowned. 'Someone's been in here.'

'Forget it. They're gone now. We should just get it and bury it and go home. Like when I stay with my uncles — go fishing, ay. Have a choof, sleep all afternoon, drink all night.'

'One more fuckin uncle story, I'm gonna deck ya.'

'Deck *me*, bro?' He asked, with a creepy giggle. 'Not if you're fuckin dead.'

'Yeah, right.' Alpha kicked the desk and got to his feet. 'Fuck it. Okay. Go get her.'

'In here?'

'Yeah.'

The Kiwi came over to the door I was standing behind. He rattled the doorknob. I lurched and lost my balance, wheeled my arms, and stepped back off the tub.

'It's locked, ay.'

They hadn't heard me. I breathed again. Phuong gave me a small apologetic smile. I don't know why she felt the need to say sorry. We might be about to die, sure, but it wasn't her fault. Poking around a known murderer's ice factory had been my stupid idea — up there with the dumbest. But the situation hadn't gone completely south. Besides the Glock, there was something else on our side. I held up the keys and wiggled them at her.

'I know, dickhead. Look for the key. Try the drawer.'

I heard both desk drawers open and close. 'Not here.'

'Shit.'

I tiptoed over to Phuong and sat on the pile of sacks beside her.

'There's a second set in the house. Go get it.'

'You go get it, ay.'

'Fuck you, you piece of —'

There was a deafening gunshot in the office, followed by a loud grunt and harsh rapid breathing. I heard a match strike, then footsteps, then the swivel chair squeaked.

'That's for the Kiwi bashin, ay.' A deep, sucking inhale; a pause, and a long exhale. 'All you Aussies are fuckin racist.'

'Dickhead.' Alpha's voice was hoarse now.

'*Dickhead*? Me? I'm not the one lying on the ground pissing out blood.' More giggling.

'No ... That's right. You're a big man ... A great big fuckin Kiwi dickhead.'

I wondered at the wisdom of Alpha using his final moments to be antagonistic — but each to their own. There was a hard *thump*, not unlike a booted foot meeting human flesh. 'And that's for Trevor Chappell. We don't forget shit like that, bro. Aussies are bad fuckin sports.'

A grunt. A cough. 'Still angry about losing ... are we?'

Another sickening, ringing blow. 'One all, bro. Series ended in a tie.'

'Time you moved on.' Alpha was breathing more slowly. 'Happened before you were born.'

'Time *you* moved on.'

I braced for another gunshot, but it didn't come. The sound was of struggling — the chair being knocked over, muffled grunts. Then quiet. He had a gun and he hated Australians. We had a gun and we were in a locked room. But what if he went for the keys? If he found us, it wouldn't help matters to explain my shame about bowling underarm, or to tell him how much I enjoyed Jane Campion movies.

He was moving around again. The chair scraped across the floor, heavy boots clomped around the office and went outside, and then footsteps tramped on the screenings.

Phuong had the gun in her hand. She cocked her head in the direction of the door. 'Open it,' she whispered.

He would be coming back, coming in here. My hands shook as I pulled out the keys. I rose and the top sack moved with me. Phuong looked down, then at me, her eyes wide. I looked back. An arm stuck out from under the bags. A long slender human arm — blue-grey, with the hand bent, fingers curled, so I could see glossy, red nails. And one bruised, enlarged knuckle. Tania.

Now I moved fast. I scrambled away as far as I could, to the opposite side of the room. I tried to suppress it, but an anguished howl escaped me.

'Stella, calm down. He's in the house. Let's go. Open the door,' Phuong said.

I stood on tiptoe, found the brass key, and put it in the lock. Then I froze. He was back. Keys jingled. He was humming the riff from 'A Slice of Heaven'.

I could see Phuong under the table. She shook her head at me, a signal I took to mean *change of plan*. She flashed the gun.

He was coming in and I needed a place to hide. I moved behind the door, squatting, ready to catch the door before it hit me.

The deadlock turned and the door swung open, nearly smacking me in the face. But my fingers were under it, holding it still by my fingernails.

The single fluorescent tube flickered, washing out the room with glare. He walked straight to Tania's body and, in one effortless scoop, picked her up, sacks and all. He lifted her to his shoulder, turned, and walked straight out. Through the crack in the door, I watched him go. A stubby troll with bison shoulders in a yellow hoodie.

I'd seen him loitering in my street.

After a moment his feet were stomping across the stones, and the car door opened. I tiptoed out from behind the door. Phuong was standing, gun in hand, and she nodded to me. I nodded back. We crept out into the office. There was a lot of blood on the floor, but no body. The external door was open and was swinging loose in the wind. I poked my head around it. The car was parked beside the shed, rear to the back fence, its headlights lighting the yard down to the road about a hundred metres away. The shed door was in shadow, on his blindside.

In the cool fresh air, Phuong behind me, we made directly for the side fence, not running, walking. The space between the shed and the fence was dark, and we stopped and waited.

The hooded troll was busy walking around, opening the car's

rear hatch, slamming it shut. He was muttering to himself. I heard the gate at the back of the yard — the one we'd first come through — swing open. Another minute passed and nothing happened. A cold breeze was at our backs. The wind carried the distant shoving and scraping sounds of a spade striking the ground.

I looked at Phuong. Time to go. Staying in the shadows of the perimeter, we picked our way around to the back of the house. We were standing on the compacted dirt that was the path between the fence and the house. Phuong ran now, holding the bag to her chest so the tools inside didn't make a sound. I did my best to keep up. We stopped at the corner of the house. The front yard was dead grass, bisected by a gravel driveway leading from the gates at the front to the car park at the back: a fifty-metre dash to the open gates. I wanted to run but Phuong held me back. With the headlights shining, we were exposed — better to stay hidden until he was gone. Phuong dropped her bag. 'Back in a tick,' she said, and ran back towards the shed.

I paced in the dark, waiting anxiously for her return. I'd become hardened to the suffering of others. People crushed by life, bad luck, or one too many setbacks — struggling families dealt one more bitter blow. I'd been the detached observer, making stark observations about life's unfairness. Tonight, everything had changed. Tania's death was on me, stuck to me — and it would likely stay there. Gaetano and his gang of morons had taken Tania and kept her locked up here. That part was the most difficult to accept. These drug dealers were idiots, yet they had been able to learn that Tania came from a wealthy family, find out where she lived, and then pull off a brazen kidnapping. Until the plan went wrong and one of them killed her — just left her body there — and days later sent two imbeciles to clean up the mess.

Phuong was back, panting. 'SUV. A Nissan. Got the rego.'

'He's the guy, the one who tried to break into my flat,' I said. 'I recognise him, the same hoodie.'

The car started. Hoodie gunned the engine, then roared through the gates, sending the gravel flying as he careened down the dirt track.

I watched the tail-lights disappear into the night. At last I could breathe. I felt giddy and light. Phuong started laughing. I chortled. Then we were both hooting and screeching, in the thrill and wonder of still being alive. And then we were running through the gates and onto the road. I was still laughing, but now I was shaking as well. We slowed our pace. Phuong walked in the centre of the road and I trotted along the verge. The clouds thinned and a thread of moon appeared. I looked back at the house. It was a compound, designed for security-conscious, paranoid criminals to cook crank, make pills, hide cash, deal, torture and murder in. It was a place where no one would hear the cries of a woman held against her will.

29

MY RADIO alarm woke me with the seven o'clock news bulletin and I hit the off button before there could be any mention of Tania's murder. I put my laptop in my bag, not wanting to let it out of my sight, and headed to Buffy's for my usual. The sun had the sky to itself, the air fresh but not cold. I avoided the pile of newspapers and stared at the walls while I waited for my coffee. My phone sounded in my bag as Lucas handed over a takeaway cup. It was work. I headed for the tram stop as I answered.

'They've increased our funding by twenty per cent,' said Boss. I could hear the joy in his voice.

'That's great,' I said, and meant it.

'So all the redundancies are off the table, no one's getting retrenched.'

'That's great,' I said, and did not mean it, not one bit.

At my desk I read a few emails, made a few calls. The JUNKIE project was in full swing and the Flemington cops were keen to be onboard. Raewyn Ross had arranged a meeting with me, and was waiting in our staff room on the dot of eleven. But when I sat down with two mugs of International Roast and a plate of Milk Arrowroot — left over from yesterday, the most unloved of all biscuits — she didn't want to discuss the project.

'They call me "the Khaleesi",' she said.

'Really?' I acted shocked. 'Maybe they mean it in a nice way; as in, she's as awesome as …'

'No.' She dunked her biscuit despondently; the end broke off and sank. 'They mean it in a mean way.'

'Can you speak to your senior sergeant about it?'

'Yeah,' she sighed. 'But then everyone'd know it bothers me.'

'How about I tell them how great you are on the JUNKIE project, how you're down with the kids and considered cool among the community workers. Stuff like that?'

She made a dubious face and started to scoop up the soggy biscuit with a teaspoon. I stared at my watch, stretched. 'Sorry, Rae,' I said, standing up. 'Gotta get back to work.'

Ross sighed, and leaving her cup for me to wash, headed for the door. 'By the way,' she said. 'Clacker's out on bail.'

When she'd gone I quickly sent a text to Phuong, and she fired one back. In fifteen minutes I was waiting in front of WORMS with my scarf around my face and my Department of Justice ID in my bag. The little, blue clown car pulled in and the door opened. 'He's home with his mum. In Deer Park,' Phuong said.

The car smelled like a bakery. I fastened my seatbelt. 'I need to see someone, get professional help.'

'You've been through a rough couple of days. Last night was —'

'I'm fine.' If I had to talk about last night, I'd cry. 'I mean, I need someone like a lawyer. Corporations law, finance, joint ventures — that kind of thing. Just a five-minute chat. Know someone?'

Phuong put on her indicator. 'Something you're holding onto? Another bloody book or something? I can't trust you now.'

'I'm not hiding anything,' I said, hugging my laptop. 'I'm just curious about corporations law.'

Phuong rolled her eyes.

'So,' I said. 'What's the latest?'

'The Diggers Rest place is rented in the name of Gaetano's cousin. Lives in Italy.'

'That's not news.'

She sighed. 'She died night before last, our blokes reckon. About thirty hours ago.'

That was while I was having dinner with Brophy. Before that, in the late afternoon, Mabor had been there, at the Diggers Rest house. 'How did she die?'

Phuong hesitated. 'Beaten.'

'Was she raped?'

'No.'

'Why beat her? I don't get it, those dickheads had guns.'

The corners of her mouth turned down. 'There's no logic to it. Don't even try. Can't comprehend these people.'

I could feel her looking at me.

'Stella, I have to tell you something.'

'Is it about Bruce Copeland?'

Phuong put her head to the side. 'You know?'

'That you're seeing Copeland?' I shrugged. 'Everyone knows.'

'Stella, there's something else.'

'Copeland's married.'

Her cheeks reddened. 'Actually, the marriage is over.'

I said nothing.

'He's been in his own place for months.'

'Right,' I said. I didn't feel vindicated, or even smug.

'I made you these.' She reached behind her to the back seat and brought out a wicker basket full of muffins. I took one. It was still warm, no doubt made with organic oat husks. I bit into it, tasted the sweetness of blueberries. It would do.

The roller-shutters on Clacker's mum's house were down. The weeds were high, and two chained-up staffies in the front yard were barking their heads off. Clacker answered the door with: 'Not youse a-fuckin-gain!'

He sat at the kitchen table and rode the chair, legs akimbo; the back of it came to rest against the wall, with Clacker's feet dangling, twitching. 'Must be in love with me. Wanna suck my cock?'

'No thanks,' said Phuong. 'Darren, we know you were at an address in Diggers Rest where the manufacture and distribution of methamphetamine took place.'

'Say what you like, gook.' He took on a frozen look, swinging

206

both feet to kick the table. 'Nothing to do with me.'

'Your friend Wayne Anthony Gage is dead.'

Clacker laughed. 'Who?'

'He was murdered by Tapahia Maurangi aka Titch. Heard of him?'

Clacker shook his head, but his Adam's apple bobbed.

Phuong took a folder from her bag and opened it. She shuffled through the papers. 'Cooperate now, it will help you in the long run.'

'About what?'

'About the drug operation of Gaetano Cesarelli. About the kidnap and murder of Nina Brodtmann. Her body was found last night at his meth lab. It's all over the news.'

Clacker sucked in his cheeks. 'Cesar? Wouldn't know. I've been in remand for the last two weeks. In case you hadn't noticed. Until today.'

'You and Wayne Gage were working for Cesar. Right?'

'Nuh.'

'You went there, though, didn't you? Diggers Rest. You were a part of Cesar's crew.'

'Who says?'

'Your DNA says.' She leaned towards him. 'You like to leave your snot on things.'

The DNA of the snot we found smeared across the table in the shed had not yet been analysed. But Clacker looked stricken, and his chair came crashing forward.

'Oh, snap,' I said. 'Busted.'

Phuong put her hand out to curb my behaviour.

'In the light of these developments, now would be a good time to tell the truth. Would you like to make a statement?'

'I told you. I don't know shit about some girl.' He made a fist and cradled it with the other hand, cracked the knuckles.

'Come on. Cesar must have been planning it for months. Was it him or Gage? Or was it you who knew the girl had rich parents? A girl who lived on her own, no security, easy to grab and shove in the back of your car. Someone made a secure room to hold her in. Wrote ransom notes.'

Ransom notes? I hadn't heard about that. Phuong was probably making that up too. Clacker fidgeted.

'If you were in on it, it's conspiracy.'

'Big whoop,' he sneered.

I cleared my throat. 'Maurangi — he's Funsail, isn't he?'

'Who? Hahaha. That's funny.' But he kicked his foot harder and faster.

I looked at Phuong. 'Maurangi doesn't know where Clacker lives, does he?'

She shrugged. 'Probably. But so what? Clacker has nothing to fear. He was never there, not involved. We can't offer protection if he keeps denying everything.'

'Jesus, youse don't ever give up.' His freckles stood out against his white face. He started mumbling.

'Sorry?' Phuong could be a stone-cold bitch when she wanted. 'Louder please, Darren.'

'I went to that shit hole. Okay? Only a couple of times.'

'Mr Cesarelli's meth factory?' Phuong clicked a pen and wrote it down.

'Yeah.'

'What were you doing there?'

'Collecting. Logistics, he called it. Thought he was a businessman or some shit.'

Phuong unclicked the pen and folded her hands on the table. Now she was acting friendly. 'How'd you come to work for Cesarelli?'

'Gage introduced us. He was working for Cesar and I ended up there too, driving around, putting the hard word on cunts, making good money — and I'm thinking *this is all right.*'

'He trusted you.'

'Yes. Gage and I were trustworthy.'

'He asked you to help when one of the kids in the flats was a problem.'

'Yeah,' he admitted. 'One day, he's got a different kind of job. This kid who's been selling, but now Cesar reckons he's a problem.'

Phuong kept her cool but I was gritting my teeth, wanting to smack him.

'What happened?' she asked.

Clacker's eyes darted around the room. 'If I say, youse can offer me protection or something?'

'Of course.' She nodded.

He wavered, then he shook his head, like that was his big mistake.

'Come on, Clacker,' I said. 'Explain it to us.'

He sniffed. 'I'm supposed ta meet Gage at that bar.'

Phuong was nodding. 'Adut Chol was there in the laneway. Then what happened.'

Darren shrugged like he didn't recognise the name. 'Fuckin Gage set me up.' He kicked the table. 'That's all I fuckin know. That lawyer made me cop this bullshit.'

Phuong closed her folder.

I pushed my chair back. 'Are you saying Cesarelli never mentioned Nina Brodtmann?'

'Never. I don't know anything about any girl getting kidnapped. Sounds like bullshit to me, the whole thing.'

'Why do you say that?'

'Because he was busy as. Every bit of shard west of Melbourne was his shit. Why risk all that for a dumb-arse kidnapping?' He turned to me, for some reason. 'Full-on security conscious, Cesar, and he gets cracked at his own fuckin fortress in sunny Keilor. How does that happen?'

Phuong dropped me back at work, and as I walked through the waiting room a discarded newspaper caught my eye:

ICE PRINCESS? Brodtmann daughter found dead in drug
den. An anonymous source said today that Ms Brodtmann
was addicted to the drug 'ice' and had been working as a
prostitute for Gaetano Cesarelli.

The anonymous source was the journalist's arse — and Brodtmann
would sue it. There was something else in the article about loose
morals and a wardrobe full of ten-thousand-dollar handbags. Utter
bullshit. She was no inheritance queen, for God's sake, she'd once
worked in a *mailroom*. That was menial, boring work. The kind of
work where having a friend made it bearable.

I thought about that for a moment. I had been thinking of a
James, but maybe this 'Jimmy' was a *she* — a Jimmi, or a Jamie, or
Ja'mie?

I went to my desk and stared at my computer. The time was
1.15pm, which was 11.15am in Western Australia. I had the office
to myself: Shaninder was out and Boss was on the phone with his
door shut. I searched for the Ladies' College in Perth and rang the
number. A receptionist called Pam answered, sounding overwhelmed
but polite. 'How may I help you?'

'I'm Stella Hardy, Clayton Brodtmann's PA. You may have heard
the terrible news Nina Brodtmann has passed away.'

'Oh yes, Miss Hardy, we are all devastated.'

'I'm contacting some of Nina's closest school friends to arrange
a memorial ceremony for immediate family and close friends. I
wondered if you could provide me with some contact details.'

'It's not standard practice.'

'Mr Brodtmann would appreciate your help. He is a very generous
donor, you know, to the school.'

'Yes. Quite. And what are the names?'

'The names. Of course. Well, I am mainly trying to reach Jimmy.'

'Jimmy?' A pause.

I had gambled and lost.

'...You don't mean Jemima Slattery? They were inseparable.'

'Yes. Jemima,' I said, calmly. 'Do you have her parents' number on file?'

'Just a minute.'

I listened to some piano music. I didn't like piano. If it had to be classical, I preferred strings, sad violins, maudlin cello.

'The parents are separated and I only have an address for her mother. But it hasn't been updated since 2006.'

'That's fine, I'll give Jemima's mother a call.'

'Eliza Slattery. Sixteen Purcell Street, Cottesloe.'

'Thank you, Pam. I am most grateful.'

I walked home via Union Road so I could buy a wine cask from the supermarket. Shopping was a necessary evil. I grabbed random items for eating and drinking and paid with a wave of plastic. As I entered my building, I met Brown Cardigan in the foyer, checking his mailbox.

'Most unfortunate,' said he of the gigantic understatement.

'Yes,' I said. He gave me a grave nod and ascended the stairs. I checked my own mail and found a single business-size envelope without a stamp. My name and address were written in a hand I did not recognise.

> Stella,
> I should have told you. I meant to. I was going to. I was stupid not to. I wish I could fix this. I'm sorry. Please let me explain.
> Peter

I put the letter back in the envelope and shoved it in my bag. Upstairs in my flat I rang Vince McKechnie.

'Jimmy is Jemima Slattery. Mother is Eliza Slattery, last known address is Purcell Street, Cottesloe.'

'I'll take it from here, Hardy. Good work. Be in touch.'

I went downstairs and took my washing out of the dryer, and headed back upstairs. Before I reached my door, my phone was singing.

McKechnie. 'Jimmy's in a palliative care hospice over here. Cancer.'

He said it like it was nothing. 'You're a first-class hard-arse, McKechnie, you know that? Anyway, well done. I'll see you tomorrow.'

'How so?'

A snap decision. 'I'm coming to Perth. First available.'

He gave me his address with a hint of astonishment that was highly satisfying.

I hung up, and opened my laptop and booked a seat on the next morning's red-eye special to Perth. Then I made a meal sourced from tins — four-bean mix, corn, tuna — and tossed it together with a dash from a bottle of ready-made French dressing. I ate standing up, and washed it down with a glass of Italian sparkling mineral water I'd just purchased in a moment of madness.

Clacker had a point about Tania. It seemed unlikely that Gaetano, an ice-selling kingpin, would dabble in kidnapping off his own bat. He had to be working with someone. Mr Funsail. But Maurangi was a thug, not a criminal mastermind. No way was he Funsail. How to find out? Who knew Gaetano intimately and was privy to his business affairs?

Price. Finchley Price. High-powered lawyer to the underworld. I googled his name and found his chambers on William Street. It was barrister central, handy to every type of court and half the law firms in the city. I rang the number and spoke to a secretary. 'I would like an appointment to see Finchley Price.'

'I'm afraid Mr Price is fully booked until October.'

'It concerns his client Mr Cesarelli.'

'And you are?'

The bottle of mineral water was near to hand. 'Galvanina

Monte, a friend of Gaetano, a very *close* friend, if you take my meaning — and tell Mr Price that Gaetano gave me something to give to him.'

'Just a minute.'

I waited, but not for long.

'Mr Price will see you in his chambers at three this afternoon.'

Galvanina, as I was now, called for the exotic — and that was exactly what I wasn't. I improvised with my best jeans, my sluttiest low-cut top, and a black blazer I'd bought years ago for a job interview but which I'd only worn to a funeral. I applied eyeliner and dark red lipstick. I tipped my head down and teased the underneath hair. Then I studied the results in the mirror: my face was now framed with big Italianate hair, foofed up yet still sleek after yesterday's cut. The overall effect was of a high-class, if mature, vamp. I was ready, but there was one more thing; if it all went to hell, I needed backup. I made a quick call to Raewyn Ross and fed her some crap about impressing the boys. She was more than willing.

I drew breath to keep the nausea from taking over. Thinking about my dad, for some inexplicable reason, I steadied myself against the wall. I'd done it — I killed his dog. Levelled the barrel and pulled the trigger. It was perverse of him to make me do it. I couldn't speak to him for three weeks. And then his Cessna stalled and fell out of the sky.

And I was thinking about Brophy; I knew the situation was settled. Despite his brainless letter, it was over. A bit sooner than even I had expected. I put on my scarf and smelled Brophy. The situation was not settled, not yet. It was decidedly unsettled. The terrible burning in my chest was proof of that.

30

LESS THAN an hour later, I was at the south-western end of the Melbourne CBD standing in front of the lockers at Southern Cross Station. I chose a locker and put the key in a yellow envelope I'd just bought at a newsagent along with a copy of the *Herald Sun*. From there, I walked north up Spencer Street. It was exactly 3 o'clock when I reached Price's chambers.

The brass name plate said *Mason Dickson Chambers*. Here they gathered — a billable hour of barristers, a picnic of lawyers, a murder of crows. And sure enough, a bewigged gentleman barged past me, followed by a woman in a dark suit pulling a wheeled suitcase. I entered, and after a bit of hunting, found Price's rooms. I let myself into the waiting room. It was empty; no associate to greet me. I sat on the edge of the chair and put the newspaper and the yellow envelope on my lap. From my handbag resting primly on my knees, I withdrew a tissue and proceeded to rub my nose and dab at my eyes.

Price appeared, silent as death, tall as Lurch — and bowed his head. 'Miss Monte, if you please,' he said, pointing to his office. The wood-panelling was dark, the rug Persian, the bookshelves vast, and the law reports many.

'Make yourself comfortable.'

I did; the armchair was yielding yet firm.

He sat behind his desk, put his elbows on the blotter, and touched his fingers together. It struck me as not unusual that he would use a blotter. There was a phone and a photo frame turned away from visitors, but no computer. Perhaps he used a tablet, or had a laptop stashed in a purpose-built drawer under the desk. His eyebrows were raised in mild interest. 'How may I be of assistance, Miss Monte?'

'Gaetano and I, we had a special relationship.'

The eyebrows came down. 'Special in what sense?'

'Private.'

'Quite,' he said. 'He certainly never mentioned you to me.'

'Well, why would he? You're his lawyer, not his priest.'

That sent the eyebrows up a good five centimetres.

'You see, Gaetano had needs. *Unusual* needs. That only I could satisfy. I think it was me being from an Italian background.'

'You don't look Italian,' Price said dryly.

'My mother was Irish. From County Clannad.'

He frowned. 'Is that a county?'

'As I was saying, sometimes he needed me to be his mother, sometimes a member of religious order specialising in harsh discipline, and sometimes,' I lowered my voice, 'a podiatrist.'

'I'm sorry, I don't quite —'

'His feet, Mr Price. I was required to —'

'I know what a podiatrist is.'

'— to touch them, do *things* on them, to put them —'

'Please, get to the point.'

'Well, it was strictly business at first, but after a few months we became close. Inseparable. It's only natural if you've done particular *activities* with a person. You know what I'm saying? We've been *exposed* to each other, vulnerable. And —'

'Miss Monte, I'm sure —'

'Call me Galvanina.'

'Yes, fine.' He cleared his throat. 'But my time is limited. And expensive. My associate said you had something for me, from Mr Cesarelli.'

'Gaetano had evidence.'

I held up the yellow envelope, waved it, and his eyes followed like a six-week-old kitten.

'What you want to see, it's not actually *in* here. There's no money, either, because I've looked.'

Appalled, the corners of his mouth came down. 'Indeed.'

'Hey, don't judge me. I've got bills to pay like everyone else. Seems to me that everyone's got their spot at the trough — politicians, union bosses. Why's it so bad if a working girl gets her turn?'

Price worked his jaw around, the long face stretched to one side and then the other. I could tell he was nearing the limit of his patience. 'Miss … I mean, Galvanina, what do you have in the envelope?'

I smiled. 'The thing is. He didn't exactly say who to give it to. He only said to give it to someone he trusted.'

Price let out an incredulous snort. 'Are you questioning my integrity?'

'Someone he *trusted* murdered him in cold blood, so …' I let that insinuation hang in the cool office air.

His inhale flared his great nostrils, but his eyes never strayed from the envelope. 'And how do you propose to assess my trustworthiness?'

Cometh the hour, cometh the pretend prostitute. I pulled the newspaper from my bag and threw it down on his desk, with the photo of Tania face up. 'Nina Brodtmann.'

'What about her?'

'If you can tell me all about Gaetano's involvement with this woman *then* I will know he confided in you. That you are a man he trusted.'

I thought I saw Price's version of a smile. It was pretty sexy actually. And then the phone on his desk rang. 'Yes,' he spoke into the receiver. 'Yes, that will be fine. Thank you.' He hung up and leaned back in his chair, hands behind his head.

A bead of sweat worked its way down my back. I sensed danger. 'Reason being, I need to know if she was a rival. I mean, it's bad enough to lose him, but to discover he was cheating on me with a skinny blonde bitch.'

Price rose and went to open an oak cabinet, where a whisky bottle and glasses waited on a silver tray. He held up the bottle.

'It's a bit early for me, thank you.'

He seemed surprised. He shrugged and poured a couple of fingers into a heavy glass.

'If that's lead crystal, you're gonna get a mushy brain.'

He let out a hoot and drained half the glass. 'Nina Brodtmann had no intrinsic interest for Mr Cesarelli.'

'Intrinsic? What the hell does that mean?'

'He didn't fancy her. Is that simple enough for you?'

'Hell no. Why did he lock her up if he didn't fancy her?'

Price sipped his drink, closed his eyes, allowing the whisky to linger in his mouth. 'Oh,' he said airily, 'he was helping out a friend.'

'Who?'

He smiled, amused. 'I think that is enough, don't you?'

'Enough? Um. Sure.' I shifted in the leather, the vibe of menace from him was disturbing. I had been slow to understand that Finchley Price was not the man I had imagined, the good and sober citizen. There was a hint of the sadistic in his cold stare. 'Good enough for me.' I stood and dropped the envelope on the desk. 'Here you go.'

He looked at it with disinterest. Why the change in attitude, I wondered.

'There's a key in there to a locker at Southern Cross Station,' I said. 'I haven't opened it so don't ask me what's in there.'

'Sit down, Galvanina.'

'No thanks, I'm late as it is. I'm meeting someone. If I don't show up, they'll worry.'

The door opened and in came a Maori man in shorts and thongs. He was not wearing his customary yellow hoodie but rather a black T-shirt, allowing us full view of his massive biceps and the sleeve tattoos that came down to his wrists. His long hair was tied with a sloppy elastic band.

I sat down as cold fear washed over me. Maurangi was a murderer. Price was in this up to his square jaw. Perhaps *he* was Funsail. Either way, I was going to die. Today, probably.

'Sorry I'm late, bro. Traffic, ay.' Maurangi said and flopped down in the other visitor's chair.

'This fellow is my … colleague. He will go with you to the locker.'

I assumed that Maurangi didn't know the police were looking for him — otherwise he would not risk being seen; this part of town was crawling with cops. One cop in particular I hoped was crawling outside, and knowing that was a small advantage to me. His advantage was that he was a cold-blooded killer who seemed not to care or think too much.

'Your colleague's a big boy, he can go by himself,' I said.

Maurangi nodded, being of the same opinion.

'He might get lost,' Price said coldly.

'I told you, I'm late for a client.'

'I doubt that very much, Galvanina.'

'This client is a stickler for punctuality.'

He bared his perfect teeth. 'That's a big word for a woman in your line of work.'

'Some women in my line of work have PhDs, you arrogant prick.'

'Titch, take Miss Monte to the station and get her to open the locker.' Price handed him the envelope. 'Depending on what you find, you'll know what to do.'

Maurangi shrugged. All he knew was busting heads. He came to me, side-on, and slid two hands under my armpits. It was unnecessary — I was up out of the chair and standing on my tiptoes.

31

'THOSE ALL BLACKS,' I said. 'They're pretty good at rugby.'

'Best fucking team in the world,' Maurangi said. At least, I think that's what he said. It sounded like *bustfeckintumuntheweerld*.

I was hoping like hell that Ross was waiting for me outside. I picked up my handbag and pretended to check its contents. 'You know what I like? Sauvignon Blanc. New Zealand makes the best, don't you reckon?'

Maurangi shrugged, though he seemed quietly pleased. 'Drink beer.'

'Enough!' Price said. 'Take this sickening conversation outside.'

Once in the hall, all I had to do was scream, half the Victorian Bar was within earshot, plus sundry tipstaffs, bailiffs, sheriffs, magistrates, and justices, not to mention sworn officers of the law. On the other hand, if I did make a fuss I'd have a lot of explaining to do. Instead, I scurried along beside Maurangi, listening to my heart pound. We went down some stairs at the back of the building and into a covered back lot, where a couple of dark, late-modelled European cars were parked. He led me to a SUV, the one I'd seen at the Diggers Rest house. The one the cops were looking for. If they pulled us over, there'd be a shootout. Maurangi struck me as the type to think it would be cool to die in a hail of bullets. If they didn't pull us over, and he found the locker at the station empty, I'd be in a ditch by evening. 'Why don't we walk?' I said. 'It's quicker. Besides you'll never get a park down there.'

I could tell from his frown that he was trying to think.

'It's only about four blocks from here. You've seen the traffic. It's crazy to drive.'

His frown deepened. 'Yeah.'

I set off out of the laneway to Little Lonsdale Street. He lumbered after me in his thongs, the yellow envelope in his hand.

'This way,' I said, and bolted in a stiff-legged power walk down the hill, west, towards Spencer Street. It was getting on to knock-off time and the nearby offices were expelling their workforce. Crowds in suits took over the narrow street, marching like defeated soldiers to Flagstaff Station. I strode against the flow, elbows up when necessary, ducking and weaving. All that walking along the Maribyrnong had paid off — I was not out of breath. On the contrary, adrenalin kicked in and I gazelled on my toes. I glanced around and saw Maurangi fifteen metres back. I kept going, staying close to the buildings. Ahead on the left was a narrow lane and from it a police car nosed out. I stopped. Constable Ross was out of the car and sprinting. I turned and started to run back up the hill. There was a chance both of us could take Maurangi down. Instead a hand grabbed my arm and pulled me around. 'No! Ross! Stop!'

'Shut up, you,' she said. She joined my hands behind me and cuffed them.

'You don't understand. It's him. Maurangi. He's just up there.'

Ross slammed me against the wall. 'You're under arrest, Monte.'

'No, stop,' I hissed. 'Listen. Maurangi is right behind me. If you let me go —'

'As if,' Ross said in a loud voice.

Maurangi, who had been thundering down the hill to catch up to me, stopped dead.

Ross cleared her throat. 'Galvanina Monte, I'm arresting you for solicitation.'

Maurangi backed up and slowly turned around. He walked back towards Prices's chambers, very nonchalant — and I groaned in disgust as Ross shoved me in the car. It would have been the arrest of her career. Not to mention justice for Tania and getting a dangerous psychopath off the streets. But she was playing her part too well and wouldn't listen. At least, I was grateful for one thing: I was alive. 'Thanks, Raewyn,' I said. 'I owe you one.'

'Nah,' Ross said with determined good humour. 'I'm always up for a prank. Think we fooled your lawyer friend?'

'Definitely. You're the best.'

'Drop you off somewhere?'

'Footscray.'

I found him in the Slacker. He was on his haunches, attaching wire with pliers to the back of a canvas. I coughed and he stood, looking wonderfully bereft.

'You look different. Don't tell me — the hair, nice haircut. And those clothes ... wow. Looking good.'

I let him gush. I felt I owed him that. 'I had an appointment,' I said.

'I don't know what you said, but that Mathilde from the Veldt Art Prize wants to offer me a bursary or something. I have to meet with them, work it through.'

I'd forgotten dropping his name to Van Zyl that night at the Dragon Bar. Who knew that it would have actually worked?

'I was hoping you'd get in touch, so I could thank you. I don't want to hassle you. I'm sorry about everything and I understand if you can't be with me, but at least let me say thank you.'

Okay. That was enough gushing. 'You've been a bit selective with some details about yourself,' I said.

He closed his eyes. 'I was going to tell you. In time.'

I believed him. Oh God. I was liquefying, and my words came out as a whisper. 'When you said it's too hard sometimes, you were right.' I started to laugh but it slipped, to my horror, into weeping. He moved to embrace me but I pushed him back. I wiped my eyes with the sleeve of my blazer. 'I look at you and I see someone who —'

He shook his head. 'Stella, I —'

My palm out, in front of his face, stopped him. '— Is basically a decent person. But you need help to get through.'

'I'm going to cut down, bit by bit, honestly.'

'Don't make any stupid promises. It doesn't matter. Take the damn methadone.'

With a rush he came forward, before I could step back. Our embrace was like two boxers at the end of round one. The scrape of bristles on my face was abrasive. We kissed. My hand found his waistband and slipped under it. He found his way under my jumper. We kissed, and the horrible things of the world went back into the shadows. I fell with him to the floor. His jeans were unzipped, peeled back. We were laughing. And I took him by the hand and led him to his room. 'Say goodbye to me properly. I'm going to Western Australia for a while.'

32

MEN WITH stop signs impeded my progress. A haphazard scattering of witches hats squeezed the morning peak into a single lane convoy that inched and tooted and raged. The taxi driver was not one to chat, preferring the radio so that only the business report, relayed in a low monotone, intruded upon my thoughts — gold up, iron down, crude oil down. I knew of at least three people in the country to whom that information mattered. Outside, Perth's industrial outer limits crawled by. The newsreader recapped the top stories: the murder of Nina Brodtmann, describing her as *enigmatic* and *reclusive*; and police had identified the body of an adult male found dead in an apparent suicide in a car in the Mount Percy Sutton region. His name would be released once his next of kin had been notified.

Eventually a skyscraper reared up, and another — city towers funded by the trade in expensive dirt. Then I was treated to the sight of a vast body of sapphire water and my pity for the locals, their isolation and the near irrelevance of their capital, gave way to sudden envy. While Melbourne's two main waterways were junk-strewn, oily sumps, Perth convened around an actual river. To my malnourished eyes, such splendour was almost painful to behold.

The taxi turned inland and stopped at a row of austerity-era houses, plain little dwellings immune to the disease of the dream bathroom and the national obsession with price. Vince's quarter-acre was overgrown with tea-tree and oleander. The house, built from cinder blocks, resembled a public convenience.

I knocked. Nothing stirred.

The garage door was up and I saw a battered Toyota HiLux, holiday stickers on the back window. I walked around the house, trying to see through the curtains; someone shambled past. The old bloke opened the door, panting.

'Jeez, Vince, you look like —'

'I know. Shut up. Come down here.'

He hunched his shoulders, and walked down the hall to the kitchen at the back of the house. I followed and leaned against a bench as he filled a kettle and put it on the gas burner. The kitchen table clearly doubled as his desk, with piles of newspapers and folders and books, even an in-tray.

'They feed you? Cheapo airlines now, no food.'

'I'm right.' I didn't fly cheapo. I looked at the many cupboards, that 1950s green, with odd press-button mechanisms. 'Did you speak to the hospital?'

He winced, irritated. 'Comfortable. That's all they tell you. Could mean anything.'

I thought he intended to say more, but he busied himself with mugs and a two-kilo packet of brand-less sugar, and opening and closing the cupboards. Maybe the kitchen was older than the house. Do they do that? Build a new house around an old kitchen? Vince scratched his neck, realising he lacked a teaspoon. I opened a drawer, found a few items of cutlery; some were clean. Apparently the act of feeding himself was too complex but investigating corporate malfeasance, biting on and not letting go, *that* he could do. I handed him a spoon. 'Getting support from the paper for your inquiries?'

'Not as much as I'd like.'

'Let me guess, they want to focus on celebrity stories for the online edition. Use dodgy Photoshop visuals and misleading headlines to suck people in. More clicks, more revenue. Typical.'

'Revenue pays my wages.'

'But Vince, this is how people get away with things for so long. There's no proper investigation. The WA police are not going to touch Brodtmann. For obvious reasons.'

He winced again. 'Of course there are proper investigations. The paper submits FOIs every day of the bloody week. Don't go all conspiracy on me. I thought you were the practical type.'

'I'm practical.'

Vince shrugged. 'Drink your tea and we'll head off. I've a secret lunch meeting with a fellow from the Department of Mines and Petroleum. It's not far, I'll drop you off at the hospital on me way. You can join us after.'

My mug, now that I looked, was a highly unsanitary thing, cracked, stained, never having had the benefit of detergent or a scourer. The boiling water, I reasoned, would kill most bacteria. I sipped obediently, hoping the meeting was at a pub.

The hospital was in a posh neighbourhood. I spotted a private school nearby, with several sprawling playing fields. He parked the Toyota outside a brown brick, single-storey building. I hopped out and slammed the door. Vince yelled out something about seeing me later at the restaurant as he motored away.

The hospital looked more like a motel, long and plain, with no emergency department or ambulance bays that I could see. It was surrounded by a low brick fence, and beyond that a garden of lawn. The occasional clipped bougainvillea and frangipani grew up the side of the brickwork. There were large windows at the front and I could see some patients sitting in the rooms, mainly elderly patients sitting up in bed or in armchairs, looking out the window. At the entrance, the automatic doors parted. I stepped forward, through a second pair of doors, and breathed in the warm, ailing air.

A woman in a pink cardigan smiled at me from behind a counter.

'Jemima Slattery, please.'

She looked startled, as though she'd misheard. 'Room seventeen. That way, all the way to the end. On the right.'

The door was ajar. I looked in and found the room empty. I put the magazines I brought on the table and sat on the bed. A fridge hummed somewhere. The room was overheated and smelled of fish cakes.

A shadow filled the doorway — a young woman, somehow elegant in grey trackpants and a T-shirt, came in pushing a mobile IV-drip stand.

'Jimmy. I'm Stella. I'm a friend of Nina's.'

She blinked. 'Tania, you mean.'

I smiled. 'Yes. Tania.'

She had an exotic beauty, with killer cheekbones and perfectly arched brows, her dark hair was long and swept up in a careless bun. Her hand came out to me and I went to shake but she nodded to the armchair. I held her by the arm as she sat.

'I wanted to ask you about Tania, if that's okay with you?'

She nodded.

'You heard she died?'

She closed her eyes, nodded again.

'When did you last speak to her? Before she left WA?'

'Yeah.' Her voice was breathy. 'Tania wanted to — she'd already changed her name — catch up for drinks one last time before her move to Melbourne.'

'Why did she move there? Was she trying to get away from someone?'

She shook her head, sad, resigned. 'She said she wanted a change. I think she wanted to get away from the mining business, switch career to beauty therapy.'

Her accent was refined, the white sugar of Australian English. I had heard the same elongated vowels squealed by trust-fund-enabled youths across the campuses of Melbourne University.

'Was Tania very involved?'

She gave me a look. 'She was seriously into it. The business. Doing all the testing, the science stuff. And when she needed to be there for some reason, she drove. That's a nine-hour one-way trip.'

'Really?'

'Yep. I went with her sometimes. There were some cute guys too. Not that she cared about that.' Jimmy gave me a sheepish grin.

I hesitated. 'Just you and Tania?'

'Sure. We drove nonstop from Perth, but it's fun too, you know? We used to sing, stupid songs — Dolly Parton, Simon and Garfunkel.' She looked down at her hands.

'Do you remember where you went, which mine?'

She looked tired. I thought I might have to leave, but she gathered herself and lifted her head. 'I don't know, sorry. I didn't keep up with all that.'

I was starting to think it had been a waste of time coming all the way here. It seemed that Tania hadn't confided in Jimmy.

'You're telling me that one minute she loved the business, lives and breathes ore samples, and the next she changes her name, moves interstate, and starts from scratch as a beauty therapist. What the hell happened, Jimmy? You must know!'

The girl shrank back into the chair, tears in her eyes. She started to tremble. 'I don't get it either.'

There was a plastic jug on the tray table. I handed her a cup and poured in some water. She took a couple of small sips. 'Sometimes I wondered if she put so much into the job because she was trying to impress *Daddy*.'

'Tania had to impress him?'

Jimmy nodded. 'He was pretty tough on her.'

'How?'

'Well he did threaten to cut her out of his will once.'

'For what?'

'She stuffed something up. I don't know what. But she was really upset, she thought she'd let him down. But the inheritance thing was no big deal to her. She totally didn't care about his money — she said the way Crystal spent money made her sick.'

The night at the Screaming Goat, Brodtmann acted like it was all Crystal's fault that Tania had run away, that it was Crystal who had made life difficult for her. It was a pretty big omission, failing to mention his threats to Tania's inheritance.

227

Jimmy scratched her cheek, staring out the window at the sky. Outside, a woman in a blue uniform dress was hanging a sheet on a long clothesline. The act had an anachronistic quality, like sitting and listening to a radio. I gave Jimmy a soft squeeze on the shoulder. The bones moved under my touch. 'I better get going.'

She whispered. 'Hey, Stella. Can I come with you?'

'But ...' I hesitated to state the obvious.

She pulled out the drip, held up both arms to show me. 'All they give me is tablets for the pain.' She swallowed; it was difficult to watch. 'I'm going crazy in here. Just for a few hours.'

In the garden, the woman had finished hanging out the washing. I thought for a moment. 'Let's go find a doctor.'

Jimmy stood up. 'The doctor will say no. Come on, Stella, help me get out of here.'

With a sigh like a deflating tyre, I agreed. I popped my head in the corridor, no pink cardigan woman, no one at all. I went down the corridor, away from the main entrance. More wards. At the end of the corridor was the cleaners' cupboard, then the laundry, and an exit door that led to the backyard and the clothesline.

Back in the room, Jimmy was waiting by the bed in a hoodie and runners, a bag over her shoulder. The drip line dangled from the stand.

'Come on.'

The exit door opened easily. In the back garden area an elderly patient was sitting on a wooden bench, uninterested in us. We rounded the building and came to a lane on the other side enclosed by a brick wall and lined with wheelie bins. A wrought-iron gate at the end was unlocked. After we walked a couple of blocks I pulled out my phone and called a cab to take us to a restaurant in Cottesloe.

'Jemima Slattery, I presume.'

'Jimmy.' She held out her hand and Vince shook it, but his eyes were on me. I smiled sweetly at him.

We pulled up an extra chair as a waiter took our order. Jimmy and I ordered martinis.

Vince waved a USB stick. 'My contact at the department just gave me a list of all the Brodtmann company tenements.'

'It's all on the public record,' Jimmy said. 'You can look up who's got what, any time you like.'

'He didn't tell me that.' Vince looked disgusted. 'I bought lunch for that prick.'

'Anything happening at Mount Percy Sutton?' I asked.

'Yes,' he said. 'CC Prospecting are mining the site — iron ore. Making a bloody fortune, because the price of iron is through the roof, record highs. Not paying tax.'

I took out the Bailey Range documents that Rosamund had printed out for me. 'According to this bankruptcy declaration, Bailey Range Metals, a private company, had claim to half of the Mount Percy Sutton area and capital in excess of thirty million. Bailey Range entered into a joint venture with Blue Lagoon, but it failed.' I eyeballed Vince. 'We know that Blue Lagoon Corp is basically a front for CC Prospecting. Seems like now they're sitting pretty with Percy Sutton all to themselves because Bailey Range went under in 2010 and their tenements went up for grabs.'

Vince cocked an eyebrow. 'Why'd the joint venture fail?'

'Stella, you want to go get a manicure later?' Jimmy asked, picking at a nail.

'Sure.' I turned to Vince. 'They were trying to find gold, but there wasn't any. Bailey Range realises they're in big trouble. But all the samples come back saying that there isn't any gold and oh by the way, there's *tonnes* of iron ore.' I glanced up at Vince.

He had a wry smile. 'Interesting.'

'By now the banks want their money; Bailey Range is broke. In order to recover their investment to this point they must switch to iron exploration, but Blue Lagoon are taking their time. They stall, say that the terms of the joint-venture agreement must be explicitly changed from gold to iron. They keep fussing over the wording. Any variation to the joint-venture agreement by one party and compensation must be paid to the other. They pay Blue Lagoon ten million dollars. The Bailey Range directors say that at least they can recoup their money once they start mining the iron ore.'

Vince nodded. 'Go on.'

'Bailey Range runs out of time. The bank calls in the liquidators.' I sat back and finished my martini.

'The Brodtmann's take over and now they have almost double the original size of their tenements. Double the profit on the ore, presumably,' Vince said.

'Yes,' I said, seeing what he was getting at. 'And now they have permission to mine from the traditional owners. It might have taken Brodtmann and Crystal years to get a new agreement, but the liquidators transferred the Bailey Range arrangement to the new operators.'

We sat in silence for a moment.

'So all the initial sample testing they did of the area was wrong?' Vince said.

'Yes, but wait, there's more.' I pulled Tania's DVD, back in its pirated *The Blue Lagoon* cover, out of my bag and slid it across the table.

'What's this?'

I knew the title by heart. 'It is the Report on the quality of Mount Percy Sutton alluvial samples for Blue Lagoon Corp and Bailey Range Metals. August 2010.

He stared at me. 'How did you get this?'

'Tania. It's proof that someone knew there was more iron ore than gold at Mount Percy Sutton before the joint venture.'

'Fuck me,' Vince said. 'That's devious.'

'You've been looking into their business activities, is it that surprising?'

'That's the first report, the proper one from the geologists,' Jimmy said, casually. 'Tania rewrote a whole new one. Had to forge it, put names of the geologists on it. She said it had to be way more positive about gold.'

We both looked at her. 'Why did she do that?'

'Crystal.'

33

TWO DOORS down from the pub was the Fancy Fingers Nail Salon. I selected a shade of crimson and I handed over my fingers, all ten. Jimmy seemed to be enjoying the experience. But I found it tedious and unsettling. I kept thinking about Tania and how I'd completely misjudged her.

When it was over I did not recognise my own hands. With our talons shining, Jimmy and I crossed the road, to where Vince was waiting for us.

We sat in the shadow of a late-nineteenth-century pavilion, watching the Indian Ocean; the slow repeat of waves as they smacked, retreated, curled, and smacked again into the sand. Though it was winter, and the breeze off the water was nippy, people were everywhere, walking, playing ball games, lounging on blankets spread out on the grass. Some game souls were jumping in the waves. Couples jogged together.

I stared at the horizon. 'Why call the mining company Blue Lagoon?'

'Crystal's choice,' Jimmy said. 'Her pet project, so she chose the name. She saw the movie as a kid — that's what Tania told me. The movie was banned in Croatia or Poland or wherever she's from. The communists didn't like Brooke Shields, I suppose. Anyway, she saw a smuggled-in video and after that the fantasy of total freedom in a tropical paradise became a kind of obsession for her.'

She went quiet and her head began to droop down to her chest.

'You okay? You look a little worn out.'

'I'm fine,' she said, snapping back upright and gazing at the waves.

'Time to go back to hospital, I think,' Vince said.

Back in Vince's shack, he handed me one of his lethal mugs of tea.

'Crystal asked Tania to procure a fraudulent mineral analysis.' Vince stabbed a finger at the DVD on the table. We'd been going over it together in the car since we dropped Jimmy off back at the hospital.

'Asked, or maybe coerced,' I said, wanting to give Tania the benefit of the doubt.

'Okay. Coerced. And Brodtmann made a fortune from the deal.'

'Correct,' I said.

'But Tania kept the original mining report. Why?'

'Insurance?'

'God, would her own parents —'

'I doubt it. But what about the Bailey Range directors and all those investors? They'd be interested to see that original report.'

Vince was attacking his laptop. 'Got the names of the directors of Bailey Range. You check them out — I've got to see a man about a horse.' Vince went outside and started to cough. A disgusting hacking, followed by gross spitting. He may have coughed up a lung. I heard a fart that lasted the better part of a minute. Then somewhere in his yard another door creaked open and closed. Now that was quaint, an outside toilet. I suspected he'd be there for some time.

I studied the list of Bailey Range directors. Three mega-rich, middle-aged white men. I imagined it would be easy to discover their movements in the last four years. They probably had publicists. You make the BRW rich list and get little puff pieces in the paper about your nice house in the country, your beautiful wife, your fucking cute dog.

After half an hour I was ready to give up. I'd tried all manner of business websites and not one of them was a director of anything anymore. And I was beginning to worry about Vince. Perhaps he'd died.

I was trawling through endless hits — they all had boring common names, and a basic Google search picked up half the western world: Colin Cartwright, John Billings, and Trevor Michaels. I finally tracked Colin down. A piece on NGOs said he was now a volunteer working in Africa. Okay, so maybe he wasn't such a bad guy. But he'd be impossible to contact. John turned up in an institution for the catatonic. He, too, was effectively unavailable for comment. Trevor was a greater challenge. My searches yielded no likely candidate. It seemed that he had dropped off the grid. I wondered if he had joined a hippy commune or something.

I switched to reading a news website while I waited for Vince to come back from the loo. That's when I found him — Trevor Michaels had been found dead in the car at Mount Percy Sutton.

When Vince returned, I gave him the bad news. No former Bailey Range director would be able to confirm our theory.

After my tea, I needed to venture outside, myself. The facility was a little tin shed down the back of the yard and it stank like a corpse flower. I pulled a rope by the door and the single bulb shed a dirty yellow light on a nightmarish scene: cobwebs, a wet concrete floor, a roll of paper on a stick protruding from a hole in the wall, dodgy magazines in a bucket. I propped myself on the toilet, shivering, ever on the lookout for spiders. I hoped it was too cold for them. When I finished I stood in the dark and cold McKechnie backyard. I could smell the sea in the air. I pictured Brophy in the empty gallery and felt sad.

Inside, McKechnie was pointing to his laptop. 'A full list of the investors,' he said.

'And?'

'Company names mostly.'

'Makes sense.'

'And a few of individuals. I checked a couple of names: Rodney and Ida Lloyd.' Vince looked up at me. 'They're interesting. I found a newspaper article that says they tried to force their way into the Blue Lagoon office after Bailey Range folded. Didn't get far. Tackled by security. I could have told them, the Blue Lagoon head office is like Fort Knox. They use thumb-print recognition.'

'Impressive. But if a couple of old people tried to storm into Blue Lagoon, wouldn't that be on the evening news?'

Vince winced at me. 'Seeing conspiracies again?'

'Just asking.'

'I gather Crystal kept it discreet; she came out and spoke to them, sorted it out before any camera crews arrived.'

'Of course.'

'Then later she slapped them with a restraining order.'

Vince snorted and went back to jabbing at the keyboard like it was an old typewriter. He looked at the screen, read silently, and bashed the keys some more. 'God bless them, they're in the *White Pages*. Nedlands.'

'Where's that?'

'Not far,' he said, picking up his keys and heading out to the car.

I felt uneasy in McKechnie's house when he wasn't home. I hung around in his front room, decorated in the same spartan theme as the rest of the house: green vinyl couch, bookshelf, circular glass-topped coffee table. Outside, a large, black four-wheel drive pulled up in front of the house. The driver, in a black suit and chauffeur's cap, opened a rear door. Crystal unfolded her legs from the back seat, sheathed in black leather, the front zip straining to contain her breasts, across which the designer's label appeared in gold letters.

The chauffeur slouched against the car and tipped back his cap. Broad, Brodtmann's right-hand man. Crystal wiggled some fingers at him, the sign for him to stay. I opened the door as she rang the bell. She raised her large, dark sunglasses and nestled them in her hairdo. Smudged eye-makeup deepened the melancholy. 'We are a mess ...' She dabbed her nose on a tissue. 'Clay, he can't eat, can't sleep, no interest to check stock price.'

'Would you like to come in?'

She looked with distaste at the room behind me. 'I'm here to ask you, Miss Hardly, personally, to leave all this alone.'

'It's Hardy.'

'Leave us to remember Nina in peace, and go back to Melbourne.'

'I'm just here visiting a friend.'

'No. Please. You listen to me. You don't need to be busy body. Clay has the police looking for those fucking animals,' she said. 'The New Zealand one, that fucking bastard.'

'I hope they catch him.'

'Oh, don't worry, he will pay,' she said, and showed her teeth, even and white. 'You go home, yes? Tonight?'

'Sorry,' I said, and started to close the door.

Crystal put a point-toed boot in the crack. She lowered her extended lashes and her voice. 'What were you thinking to take Jemima out of the hospital? The poor girl is dying.'

I was stunned. Who were these people? 'That's none of your business.'

'Last warning for you.' She gave me a threatening stare and sashayed to the car.

I rushed down the path after her. 'Hey!'

Crystal was at the car and the driver had the door open. I caught up and gripped Crystal's arm; it was like leather-covered rock. The driver landed a blow in my solar plexus that sent the air from my lungs in one huge puff. I dropped to my knees. He grabbed a handful of hair and yanked my head back. He growled in my ear. 'Go back to Melbourne, bitch.'

'It's … a … free … country.'

He pushed his cap back on his head and spat. 'You're one ugly dog, you know that?'

He let go of my hair before his steel-capped toe slammed into my kidneys. I fell sideways to the ground. From there I had a worm's eye view of the car as it edged away from the curb. I stayed there, trying to breathe through the searing pain in my back. It was several minutes before my breathing returned to normal, and I sat up just as Vince pulled into the driveway.

'They've moved.'

'Who?'

'The Lloyds. I asked the neighbours, there's no forwarding address.'

'Bugger.'

'What are you doing down there?'

'Resting.' I was on my feet now, walking to the house.

'What happened? What did I miss? Come on. Tell me and I'll make you some tea.'

'No tea, ever again,' I said, and gave him a genial pat on the shoulder. I moved on wobbly legs inside, with my shaking hands in my pockets. The buzzing in my head was possibly from shock.

He was not surprised to hear that Crystal had had me followed and had warned me off. He was surprised that her chauffeur had punched and kicked me in broad daylight on his street. I reassured him that I was fine, other than bruised and humiliated.

'That's who we are dealing with,' he said.

I took him to mean that I could call the cops if I wanted but not much would come of it. So I changed the subject. 'So, no luck with the Lloyds?'

'Oh, we had *some* luck.' He started going through his papers on the kitchen table. 'Not a total waste of time. The neighbour knows where the Lloyds were headed.'

'Where?'

Vince dug through his files for a while. 'Maybe it's in me briefcase.'

I checked my phone and found a missed call from Phuong. I also had one from Shane Farquar. Nothing from Brophy. I called Phuong first. 'Can you die from being winded?'

'Depends. No. I don't think so. What's happening over there?'

'My own stupidity.'

'Be careful.'

'Careful. Right. Will do. Got some news for you. Finchley Price — Maurangi works for him.'

'How do you know? Jesus, don't answer that.' Phuong paused.

'I've got news for you. A fire at Pickering's mother's house: place gutted, two bodies inside, a fifty-eight-year-old woman and a twenty-nine-year-old male. Suspicious, the deaths and the fire.'

'Mr Funsail?'

'We believe the crime is related to the case, yes.'

'But the case all revolves around Mr Funsail, doesn't it?'

I could hear her sigh. 'That Funsail thing, it's a doodle in a book, we don't know what it refers to — it's probably nothing.'

It was strange to hear Phuong say 'we'.

'Say hi to Bruce,' I said, genuinely happy for her.

'Found it.' Vince came back, flapping a folded map at me. He spread it across the table. The map covered 22,000 square kilometres, roughly half the size of Switzerland. It could have been a foreign country — large swathes of green, few roads, and lots of empty space.

I rubbed my aching back. 'So, where are the Lloyds?'

Vince pointed to a convergence of three roads. 'Laverton.'

34

AFTER A sleepless night on the floor in Vince's spare room, he offered to take me out for breakfast. My flight to Laverton was not due to leave until the afternoon. Both of us sat in grim silence in his Toyota. I was wearing a jacket I had brought with me that was too small and pulled across the shoulders. We crossed a bridge, heading south. Fremantle. I was getting the tour. The place had a past — lots of nineteenth-century statues, historical markers — and was now in various stages of reconstruction and renewal. Some tenants left over from the time before the gentrification were the tattoo parlours, the needle exchange, and the VD clinic; not that they advertised, but I was versed in the signs.

There was an outdoor café on a corner in the middle of town. Vince dropped me off, saying something about finding a park. Despite a fine drizzle, people were sitting at tables under large umbrellas. An adjacent doorway was open, with stairs leading up to a methadone clinic.

I made no conscious decision — I just went up the stairs.

It was a cruddy waiting room: one grubby window with bars, a couple of low counters built into a wall, each with a slot in the perspex big enough to talk through. Posters on the wall advised clients to ask for a smaller dose if it had been a while. I sat next to a fidgeting youth in a lumber jacket. His face covered in scratches, some dried blood. Next to him there was a girl in parachute pants, with a puppy in a shopping bag — no wait, it was a soft toy.

I took off my stupid jacket and noticed, seated near a pot plant, a large man in chinos and a clean check shirt. With his clean-shaven face and good haircut he looked like an industrialist headed to a Sunday barbeque. He radiated a 'fuck off' vibe.

A door opened and a woman in a zip-up nurse's uniform came out. 'Simon?'

The man in the chinos sprang up and bolted past her to the back room.

She looked at me, frowned. 'You registered here?'

'No.'

She handed me a clipboard and a pen. 'Fill this out. Got your Medicare card?'

'Yes.'

She went away and I sat there, looking around. Thinking of Brophy. Coming in here was a mistake, I wasn't going to learn anything about him by judging this place. Who knows why we love who we love? I put the clipboard down and made a coy little manoeuvre towards the door. I was thinking about Crystal forcing Tania to make a false report. Was she planning to expose the fraud? What would Crystal do if she got wind of the plan? The girls at the salon said Crystal had come in, abused her. There was stomping behind me and Simon, the chino man, came thundering down the stairs. 'Morning,' he said. 'Lovely day for it.'

'Shit-awful, actually.' I was trying to put the damn jacket back on, pulling at the sleeves.

He laughed, like that was funny. 'Sounds like you need a cup of coffee.' He had a British accent, somewhere between Prince Charles and Stephen Fry.

'Urgently,' I agreed.

Outside, he waved at a boy in a long apron standing in front of the café then pointed to a sidewalk table. I sent a quick text to Vince, and joined Simon. Hands flat on the laminex, knees wide, eyes closed, he breathed deeply, like a man lately released from prison. 'How long?'

'Hmm?' I was miles away. In Victoria, Melbourne, Footscray, in an art gallery, with an artist — and I was speaking to him of exoneration. Acceptance. Love. 'How long what?'

'Your habit?'

I had a habit. Of sorts. 'Too long.'

'Oh don't.'

'Don't what?'

'Feel sorry for yourself. You're alive, aren't you? It's a great time to be alive.' He spread his arms wide, beaming at the world.

'Aren't you worried about being seen? At the clinic, I mean.'

'Not at all,' he chuckled. 'Do it in plain sight and they'd still not believe it. Not the type.'

'Right.'

'Like you. Not too many users of the service have manicured nails. You are ... let me guess ... a manager? National manager of something?'

I hooted. 'Not even close. I'm in social ... policy.' A lie. I felt the need to be a rung or three up from the actual.

'A wonk? Good God. You bureaucrat beggars are running the country into the ground. Babies out of school, spending our dough on art classes for gay cats or some nonsense.'

'Hey!'

He laughed. 'Country's going to the dogs.'

'Some social policy makes sweet honey in a cup.'

He roared at that. 'Quite.'

'What do you do?'

'Oh me,' he sighed. 'Much worse, I'm afraid. Evil bastard.'

The waiter brought coffee in glasses. I stirred in some sugar. 'Oil baron?'

'Worse. Enabler of oil barons.'

'Enabling how?'

'Mergers, joint ventures. Brokering finance agreements. Sow the silver, no skin of mine on the table, reap the gold when it goes wrong. And it does, spectacularly.'

This development was almost too serendipitous. As though I'd tripped with my hands outstretched and caught a rare bird. I guessed luck was like that. Having spent days pouring over dense legal bumf, wishing and hoping for a translator, I find one at the methadone clinic. I was careful not to frighten him off. I looked at my froth, lifted some on a spoon. 'What might go wrong? Say, in a joint venture?'

'Very often it's insolvency. No one thinks it's going to happen. Everyone borrows, mortgaged up to the eyeballs, then the market turns bad, the project is incomplete. One partner has other assets and can dig itself out, but the other can't and calls the liquidator. The first partner is stuck with the project until the liquidator agrees to a deal. That might take years.'

'And the banks, they're exposed too?'

'The banks are eager whores. They offer their backsides to one hundred per cent of the project cost. But they spread out the risk among the investors. And they hold the deeds and the assets, take everything. Can't say I'm bothered. Capital of another kind, that's more of a concern.'

'Not banks?'

'Very wealthy individuals. Funny money.'

'Like?'

'Good heavens, what is this? Social policy research?'

'Just interested,' I said, trying to sound detached.

His glass was empty, and he pushed back his chair.

'Thanks for the coffee, Simon,' I said.

'Good luck with those gay cats.' He strode out into the street and flagged down a passing cab.

The liquidators on the Mount Percy Sutton venture sold everything to CC Prospecting. All the money from the sale went to the bank. Meanwhile the Lloyds lost everything. I would be seeing the Lloyds soon. But what of the other investors? Other companies had money in Bailey Range. Who were the other investors who'd taken a financial hit? I needed to know where every cent of investor money came from.

Multiple car horns blared, interrupting my thought processes. The tooting persisted. A brand new, red Maserati was blocking traffic; cars were trying to get around him. The driver leaned on his horn, treating everyone to the sound of Italian irritation.

Vince sat down and picked up a menu. 'Eggs,' he said to the waiter. 'Bacon, sausages, everything. And coffee. Strong.' He passed over the menu and eyeballed me. 'So who was that bloke you were yakking with?'

'No one,' I said. 'Tell me, Vince, how would your average ignorant thug launder money?'

'Thug, like who?'

'Like Gaetano Cesarelli or Wayne Gage. How does money laundering usually work?'

Vince shrugged. 'Lots of ways. Send small amounts through gaming, share trades, and trust funds. I heard about a gang that sent money out in international investments — came back clean in Aussie dollars.'

'Exactly. Shares. Maybe even in mining companies.'

'What are you on about?'

'Before they were killed, Cesarelli and Gage were making shitloads of money. But they had to clean it up before they could splurge on a gangster mansion or a *Maserati GranTurismo*.'

'A what?'

'That day in the café with Mabor, Cesarelli said he'd lost money on a bad deal.'

'You have to back up a bit.'

'I heard him. One day Gaetano Cesarelli said out loud, in *public*, that he had lost some money on a deal. *What deal?* I ask myself. Could he have tried to cleanse it through some complex financial transaction? No. Because he was a dummy.'

Vince winced. 'Twaddle. Mad about conspiracies, you. Too much internet.'

'But what if he had the help of a smart lawyer.'

'Eh?'

'Finchley Price.'

243

'Price?' Vince glanced across at me. 'All right, I'm listening now.'

'Suppose Price put Gaetano's money into the Mount Percy Sutton joint venture.'

'Via a third party?'

'Yes. A friend.'

35

THE ATMOSPHERE in the regional airline terminal had the strained quality of the visitor room at a prison. Some flight attendants with small suitcases were gathered in the foyer, groomed, fabulous, and bored. A man in a Dockers shirt, family in tow, passed the pre-boarding time nattering with a fellow worker. When the doors opened, he snatched up his bags and rushed out, failing to say goodbye to his children. His wife took them away, a boy and a girl, with the resignation of the forsaken.

On impulse I hugged Vince. He had come inside to wait with me even though I'd insisted it was not necessary. I suppose we had bonded, in a way — possibly during the fruitless hours we'd spent going over the companies who had invested in the Mount Percy Sutton venture, without making any connections, or progress, at all. On our own, it was difficult to work out which ones were legit and which were possible fronts for gangster money.

He gave me a hearty slap on the back and out I went with the other passengers, men mostly, across the tarmac into the swirling wind and the deafening drone of propellers. I stowed my bag under the seat in front — the overhead lockers were already full — and buckled up. A bear of a man, a stranger to soap, took the seat in front of me. I inhaled his stink as he strong-armed the hostie for a biscuit.

'When we start service.' No hint of revulsion in her smile.

An hour in the air and the patchwork farmland changed to oceans of sand and spinifex. From the window I could see the occasional incision of a road or open-cut mine; from the air they resembled ulcers, gaping holes of sickly green, and then a Nowheresville airstrip — and we were there. The plane touched down and taxied to a high fence, a covered waiting area, and a shed. None of my fellow passengers were in a hurry to leave the terminal. I started to compose a text to Vince but soon twigged to the lack of a signal. I cursed and a bloke in an airport uniform standing nearby had a good laugh. 'Telstra only, here,' he said. 'If you're lucky.'

'How do you get to town?'

'Got legs, don't ya? It's only two K.' He waited for hysterics. *Oh jocularity.* I played it straight and made a show of looking at my suitcase, back to him. 'Walk? Really?'

'Nah!' he giggled. 'I'll get you a lift.'

He went from group to group, having a good yak with each, and trotted back. 'Lockheed Martin. Always good for a lift.' He nodded to two men and a woman loading their bags into a four-wheel drive. The woman wore outback get-up: boots, jeans, and shirt. I smiled at her. 'Lockheed Martin? Don't they make nuclear bombs?'

She pursed her lips, looked at my bright red nails. 'Drop you where?'

I squeezed into the back seat and we drove past rusted car bodies on the side of the road to the edge of town, where the caravan park sprawled with squat, temporary-looking dwellings. I wheeled my bag over the gravel and into the tiny reception room that doubled as a shop and café and stank of yesterday's hamburgers. A grey little woman looked for my name in the book. She took a key from its nail and led the way through the park, full of empty tent sites, some vans, and row upon row of dongas.

'Rodney and Ida Lloyd, are they here?'

'Rod and Ida?'

'Yup.'

'Friend of theirs?'

'Uh huh.'

'Well, now. Sometimes they leave the van and go driving. Camp out.' She pointed out the Lloyd's van — locked up, no car beside it. 'Back around dusk. If they come back.'

My unit backed onto the fence; beyond the fence was the immeasurable desert.

She gave me the key. 'Need anything, come down the shop.'

The unit was one room with a kitchen, table and chairs, TV, two broken recliner-rockers, and a double bed. I opened a cupboard and found the bathroom — disintegrating fittings dripping brown water. I unpacked and opened my laptop. No wifi. I opened a few drawers in the kitchen: a couple of dessert spoons, one serrated knife, some mugs covered in grime. The fridge droned, cooling nothing.

Vince's background on the Lloyds was not wholly useful. 'They are your typical informed shareholders,' he'd said. 'In court every day for the Bailey Range case. When they went to the Blue Lagoon office, they knew who to ask for.'

'*Whom.* For *whom* to ask.'

'Catholic?'

'Is the Pope?'

'Explains a lot. No other mention of the Lloyds' stunt at the Blue Lagoon offices in the press. So I spoke to the journalist who wrote the article. The police were called and they were removed by force. The company didn't press charges, and the matter was forgotten. Certainly, no one took up their cause.'

'Tacit pressure from Brodtmann?'

Vince ignored me. 'If you show sympathy, they might open up a bit.'

'They lost everything. I have genuine sympathy for the Lloyds,' I said.

Vince frowned, thought for a moment. 'Talk to them. But be careful.'

I'd paid for the flight direct to Laverton. But the nearest hire car was in Leonora, over a hundred kilometres away. Consequently, I had no ride.

I left the unit and walked around the town. Every third house was boarded up. Some appeared abandoned but were actually occupied, a fact I registered when a mangy dog came out to see what I was up to. The main road was deserted. Truth was, I enjoyed that last-woman-on-earth feeling; the town resembled the aftermath of an apocalypse — zombie or otherwise. I passed a creepy-looking motel. Apart from the caravan park, it was the only accommodation in town — except for the pub, a handsome two-storey Victorian structure, with a lush apron of green lawn. But at night the noise in the pub would be insufferable. Next to the pub was a new-looking police station, the only building yet to acquire its sprinkle of moribund dust. A small office near a statue of a man on a bicycle served as a library, and I made plans to return and use the internet.

Further along was a museum with the fancy name of The Great Beyond. To kill some time I paid my twenty bucks and saw a ten-minute movie about the early explorers. A Black Keys song played in the gift shop. I hung around, looked at every item twice, and then bought a NATMAP of the area and a hand-dyed silk scarf.

'Made by a local Aboriginal artist,' the woman behind the counter said, with the detached affability of a nurse about to inject.

The supermarket, more of a last-chance supply depot, was closed due to fire damage. 'Try the BP,' a man in the post office suggested. This did not sound promising, but the service station was part warehouse and its shelves were filled with tinned goods. I bought some tuna and a gigantic can of peaches and a loaf of bread.

In the public library, I found an unoccupied public computer and checked my emails. There was one from Vince: *Mount Percy Sutton coordinates attached. I've checked — it's about a hundred and fifty K from Laverton. Between the Anne Beadell Hwy and the Great Central Rd.*

Before I left, Vince and I had speculated that if the meeting with Lloyds proved to be a dead end then perhaps it might be worth my time checking out the location of the Brodtmann mine. Since I was already in the area, having a look up-close might yield some worthwhile information. If one of the Bailey Range directors had chosen that area to commit suicide, there must be something significant to it. I spread my NATMAP across a table and marked the site. The closest geological landmark was a depression called Dead Mans Soak, a vacancy between two dirt roads.

I folded up the map and went back to the computer. I took the DVD from my bag and slotted it. I clicked on the file and opened the report. I made one more futile attempt to drag it onto the desktop. The little box came up asking for the password. I typed: *Tania.*

Nothing.

Goldtriple.

Nothing. It was probably some obscure thing only she knew.

I typed: *microdermabrasion.*

The box closed. The document was free. I performed a *control-P* and hit *OK*, and the printer on the librarian's desk sprang into action.

I made use of the stapler and went out to call Brophy from one of three public phones on the main drag. The last one worked.

'S'up, yo,' Marigold said. 'We cool?'

'No.'

'But I told you straight. And you wanted to know, am I right?'

'We are not cool. You need to make a grovelling apology to your dad and an even bigger one to me.'

'Wha?'

'You heard. Get your dad.'

The time it took to drag Brophy from the studio used up most of my coins. He sounded sleepy. 'When you coming back?'

'Soon. I don't know. I miss you.'

I headed back to the caravan park and passed a group of people walking up the middle of the road. A woman, whose face bore the scars of many bashings, stopped. 'Hey,' she said, and we shook hands. 'They call me Walkabout Annie.' A broken smile.

'I'm Stella. Good to meet you.'

'You got any money, Stella?'

'No. Sorry.'

'No worries. You have a nice day.'

'You too.'

'I like your nails.'

The group walked up to the pub and joined the people sitting on the lawn in groups of two or three, waiting for something to happen, or just passing the time.

The Lockheed Martin woman was in the shop when I got back to the caravan park. The cashier whispered to me. 'She's with that over-the-horizon radar mob; they manage it.'

'Keeping us safe. Excellent.'

I caught up to her in the car park. 'Hey, I don't suppose I could get a lift out to Dead Mans Soak? Not far — north-east, only a hundred and fifty K.'

'Afraid not,' she said. 'Try the pub.'

It was getting on to evening when I returned to the unit. The Lloyds' van was in darkness. A falcate moon drifted between clouds. I ate the tuna and some peaches and watched an SBS documentary interrupted by bursts of static interference. Male voices drifted across from the pub, drunken, booming. It was not the kind of revelry I felt inclined to join.

Later, I tested the shower; it was no more than a trickle of warm water. I closed the window and put on a clean T-shirt — an extra-large I scored at a conference — and my last pair of fresh undies, and slipped under the covers. As I lay not sleeping on the bed, other voices reached in from the desert. A woman's anguished howl, a man's menacing bellow. The shouting echoed back and forth for a long time. Something bad was happening out there.

36

AROUND MIDDAY I was reading in my unit when I heard a four-wheel drive on the gravel outside. I pulled back the blind on my window and saw a dusty Patrol parked in front of the Lloyds' van. I put on my corporate-looking striped jacket and the scarf from The Great Beyond. I put the printout of the report in the folder Vince had prepared and grabbed a pen. I gave them ten minutes to settle then walked around to their van.

'Hello?' I called from the path. A woman in sandals, shorts, and a T-shirt flung open the wire door. 'Yes?'

'Stella Hardy.' My hand out ready to shake, smiling.

'Yes?'

'I wondered if I could speak to you about Blue Lagoon Corp.'

'I don't believe it.' She came down the narrow steps. 'Ida Lloyd.' She gripped my hand in both of hers. 'Those crooks are finally getting looked into.' She turned. 'You there, Rod?'

'Been out prospecting?' I asked Ida.

'Ten days. No TV, no phone. After a while you get sick of tinned food and trying to bathe in a mug of water.'

I made an ostentatious shudder. 'How'd you go?'

'Not much. Don't get me wrong — it's magic, the big sky, the desert. We love it.'

'Where were you?'

'Bailey Range,' Ida said. 'How's that for irony.'

A man came from the back of the van, wiping his hands on a rag. 'Cleared the pipes. Won't last. Connections are buggered.' Once upon a time, Rod had been a spunk: tall, square chin. He raised his head, flicked the mop of peppery hair away. 'Who's this?'

'The Blue Lagoon business,' Ida said. 'Her name's Stella Hardy.'

'Is that so?' The grip of Rod's handshake was a touch too strong.

251

He nodded. 'You better come inside.'

The seating was cramped but an improvement on the recliners. I slid around the table and put the folder on top.

'They got you, too?' Ida asked.

I fiddled with my pen. 'Not me personally, a friend.' Vince had advised me to go in soft, hedge and hint. To draw out their information. Cover my arse. 'I said I'd have a look at it for them. See if there was any recourse.'

'Lot of people got fleeced,' Rod said. He had a blank stare but there was a tremor at his temple. 'Good people. Not a legal leg to stand on.'

'The other investors, you mean. Did you get to know them, personally?'

'All those creditors meetings we sat through, but we never really spoke. I saw the same people each time. There was a couple of retired folks like us, but the rest seemed to be investment groups, represented by lawyers and sometimes they didn't even show up.'

'And when Blue Lagoon stalled on changing the terms, Bailey Range was out of time?'

'Correct,' Rod said. 'When the bank called in the debt, Bailey Range had no option but to go into receivership.'

'We lost everything,' Ida said to the table. 'All our savings.'

'And you know that a company called CC Prospecting, a parent company of Blue Lagoon Corp, has the Bailey Range tenements now?'

Rod held my gaze. 'We know.'

'Tell me why you tried to crash the Blue Lagoon offices.'

Rod's hands rested on the table in front of him. 'We made official complaints to ASIC. We went to the police. Got us nowhere.' The voice was calm but the knuckles were white.

'Got us an intervention order — and a hell of an anecdote at dinner parties,' Ida said.

'If we ever get invited to one.'

'You accused Blue Lagoon of making false statements regarding the gold deposits, and demanded their test samples.'

Rod nodded. 'We had time to go over it all. When we looked back on the fiasco from the beginning, we realised the entire venture hinged on their geology report. In hindsight, we thought this bloody gold business was fishy. Too positive. These geologists use equivocal language, but this report was all certainty and over-confidence.'

'You think Blue Lagoon Corp was aware that the gold deposits were minimal before 2010?'

The Lloyds swapped a glance. Rod nodded and Ida said, 'Yes. But we couldn't prove it.'

I cleared my throat. 'Some evidence has come to light.'

Rod's eyes travelled to the file on the table in front of me.

'It's not conclusive, but it may provide grounds for further scrutiny.'

Ida's eyes were bright in the gloom. 'What evidence, Stella?'

I put the printout of the original report on the table. 'This is an analysis of samples from the area, written a year before the joint venture.'

Rod put his head to the side. 'The original report?'

'Yes. Stating that the likelihood of gold deposits in the claim area was slight. Essentially unlikely.'

Ida's mouth fell open.

'We believe the directors of Blue Lagoon withheld that report and had another report written. The one they submitted to Bailey Range.'

'You believe? Why don't we ask the bastard who wrote it?' Ida said. 'Get the police to interview him, get sworn testimony?'

'You can't speak to her, because she's dead.'

Ida put a hand to her mouth, with an audible inhale.

'I need a beer,' Rod said. 'You thirsty, Stella?'

They locked the van and we walked to the pub. In the main lounge, Rod went to the bar and came back with a jug of beer and three glasses held in his fingers.

Ida pointed at my bag, where I'd put the printout. 'What do you intend to do?'

'As yet, I haven't revealed its existence to anyone. The fact that the report is not public yet gives us some leverage with Blue Lagoon Corp,' I said.

'No point,' said Rod. 'Whatever you've got there, it won't hold up in court. The lawyers Brodtmann has — unbelievable. We can't win that way.'

Ida drew a tissue from her sleeve and sniffed. 'That girl who wrote the dodgy report? What happened to her?'

'She was found murdered in a drug den near Melbourne.' I hesitated. 'Brodtmann's daughter.'

'His daughter? Good heavens. We didn't ... I mean, we've been out prospecting for the last two weeks, no contact with civilisation. No wonder we haven't heard about it,' Ida said.

'Then you probably haven't heard that one of the directors of Bailey Range committed suicide in a car near the mine site.'

'Which one?' Rod asked, his steely eyes unblinking.

'Trevor Michaels. The police have pieced together his last known movements. About two weeks ago he checked into the motel here in Laverton, left some of his stuff there, and headed out to the desert. His car was found at the site.'

A few blokes in bright orange boiler suits gathered round the bar, others stood smoking in the small courtyard. Jugs of beer were handed around. The noise level steadily increased.

'I was thinking I might go out there, have a look around,' I said.

'Why?' asked Ida.

'Does the name Funsail mean anything to you?'

Ida shook her head. 'Never heard that name.'

'Look out, here's Chris.' Rod topped up our glasses.

'Who?'

'Chris Randall, the local sergeant.' Rod nodded at the bar, where a fellow with a pink face and white, feathery hair was sharing a joke with the barmaid. He picked up his beer and scanned the room, clocked Rod and Ida and ambled over. 'Rodney, old son. Ida, lovely as usual. Any luck?'

'Some. You know Miss Hardy?'

'Have not had the pleasure.'

'Stella.' I put out my hand. He grabbed it in his paw, turned it sideways, and planted his gob onto it. 'You work for?'

'On holiday.'

He pulled up a chair. 'And what are you folks chatting about so earnestly over here? Lasseter's vein of gold?'

'A bloke died in the desert,' Rod said.

'Which bloke? Not the tool out on Yamarna Road? Up to the axles in sand. He rings his mate with the winch — he comes to get him. *He* gets bogged. Had to rescue the pair of them.'

'Not those men,' I said. 'Trevor Michaels, from the motel.'

'Terrible,' Randall said. 'Search and Rescue came up from Perth. They're handling it after the Germans found the car.' He drank half the glass. 'Place called Dead Mans Soak.'

'What's the best way to get there?' Rod asked.

'Two choices. A well-prepared adventurous type might take the Great Central Road and turn right near Cosmo Newbery territory.'

'Cosmo Newbery?' I asked.

'A great whack of Aboriginal land north of here. You need permits to go through it. Keep going and in three days — non-stop, mind you — you end up in Alice Springs.'

'Great Central Road sounds the way to go,' I said to Rod.

Randall agreed. 'The other way's quicker but only a suicidal lunatic would risk it. The White Cliffs road to Yamarna goes all the way to Coober Pedy. Half of it is loose sand. Zero water, food, fuel on the way — and that's if the road's open. There's corrugation two-feet deep, with the added fun of rocks and breakaways. So, you know, I wouldn't advise it.' Randall spoke without condescension. I sensed only the concern of someone who didn't want to get a call for the use of his winch.

'Okay. Great Central it is,' said Rod.

'Go off-road and there's abandoned bores and mines all over the shop. Tell me you're not going to do something stupid.'

'Don't worry, Randall.' It was Ida. 'We know what we're doing.'

'Rightio,' said Randall. 'I'll follow you out there. Good excuse to have a look around. Been meaning to do that ever since the poor bastard dropped off the radar.' Randall's name was called out and he placed both hands on the table and heaved himself to standing. 'That'll be my lunch. See you all later — say, meet back here in about an hour?' He hitched up his shorts and elbowed a path to the counter.

Rod stared at his beer. 'She has peacocks,' he said quietly.

'Who?'

'Crystal,' Ida said. 'We got a call one day. After she'd had us removed from the Blue Lagoon offices, she invited us to afternoon tea at her house.'

Stunned, I burped and said, 'Are you fucking kidding me?'

'You go up the drive, a good hundred metres of city real estate before you see the house, and there's someone feeding peacocks on the lawn.'

'What did they say?'

'Not *they*, only Crystal. He was overseas.'

'He doesn't know the half of what that woman is capable of,' Ida said. 'The blonde airhead thing is an act. Behind those sad eyes lurks the business acumen of Kerry Packer.'

'She offered us money to back off, stop the protests.' Rod finished his beer. 'We took it, too.'

Behind the bar was an open window, through which an Aboriginal man with a bushy beard was buying a carton of beer. I recognised him as one of Walkabout Annie's companions. And for some reason I wondered why the museum was called The Great Beyond. The idea made me vaguely nauseous. I thought of Trevor Michaels — going into the great beyond and not coming back.

I turned to Ida. 'I might get changed, if we're going out to the desert; pack a few essentials.'

The air outside was cool and pleasant, and baking aromas drifted from the pub kitchen, something buttery with lots of sugar and fruit. Rhubarb? I was tempted to head back inside, get that sweetness into me. Surely it could drive out this awful sense of everything being wrong. I felt a loneliness that bordered on the existential and found myself drifting over to the public phones across the street, but I changed my mind and started to walk back to my unit at the caravan park. It was quiet out and only a few people were sitting under the trees in front of the pub. The lady in the caravan-park office was sweeping the path out the front. All the way back to my unit, I had a strong sensation of being watched.

37

I PACKED the bread and pinched the knife from the drawer, and filled my water bottle from the tap. The printout was still in my backpack and it seemed prudent to keep it with me — as well as my laptop, even though it was heavy. I didn't trust the dodgy locks on the unit. For company, I turned on the TV and caught the news.

Flamboyant South African mining magnate Merritt Van Zyl discusses the new Shine Point refinery deal, said to be worth billions of dollars, and which will create thousands of new jobs and boost the flagging economy. He sat down with Shelley Swindon in Darwin:

Swindon: Mr Van Zyl, this deal was a long time coming, what sealed it?

Van Zyl: Veldt Minerals required certain guarantees from its partner.

Swindon: You mean the Australian government?

Van Zyl: Yes.

Swindon: And what has the Australian government brought to the table?

Van Zyl: That's confidential, but the deal is done. And it's a win-win.

Swindon: Can you explain how you were able to secure the deal when you're facing fraud charges in South Africa related to the manipulation of share prices to prevent the hostile takeover of one of your companies.

Van Zyl: I deny all charges. It's a beat up by my competitors. I will be found innocent and then I will take legal action to clear my name.

Swindon: One of your top executives was beaten nearly

258

to death at his home in Port Elizabeth, rumours abound that you were involved.

Van Zyl: I assure you I had nothing to do with the assault on that man, a man who is a personal friend. I have done everything in my power to see that he and his family are taken care of. Now, if you will excuse me, I have a busy schedule and I'm due in a meeting.

There was something odd about the way the journalist pronounced Van Zyl's name, like Vun Zail — *Mr Vun Zail.*

I turned off the set and stood still as the room began to move. I was plastered in a film of sweat.

Mr Funsail.

Outside, the wind picked up, moving through the power lines and making them howl, stirring the dirt on the road. I could feel it stealing through the gaps in the unit, rattling the roof. Worse noises were coming from inside the room: groaning, and the agonised repetition of *oh fuck, oh fuck.*

Van Zyl knew Finchley; they were members of the 'Bow-Tie Club' with Brodtmann. It was possible that Finchley introduced him to Cesarelli because Cesarelli was looking to launder his money. Along comes Van Zyl with a proposal about the Bailey Range joint venture. Anonymous investors, hiding behind various company names — so that even Brodtmann didn't know Van Zyl had money in Bailey Range. But Van Zyl and Cesarelli both lost millions on the deal. Only to see Brodtmann prosper, mining iron ore.

But how did Merritt Van Zyl become the *Mr Funsail* in Adut Chol's book? That a man like Merritt Van Zyl even knew Adut Chol was absurd.

I held my arms across my chest, trembling. Van Zyl wanted revenge on Brodtmann. He had lost millions, not to mention costing Cesarelli a small fortune. Had Van Zyl suggested to Cesarelli that he might kidnap Tania? Van Zyl knew Tania was really Nina, heir to the Brodtmann's billions. In one horrible crime, he could have his retribution on Brodtmann and Cesarelli could have the ransom.

And Cesarelli had given that task to Adut Chol. And the boy had dutifully written down Tania's address and the name of the client. Mr Funsail.

But then Adut changed his mind — kidnapping was way more serious a crime — and had refused to go ahead with it. So Cesarelli had him killed.

The room was tight around me; I felt trapped. I needed fresh air in my lungs and I made a dash for the door and flung it open, breathing, gasping. Ida was standing on the step.

'You're early,' I said, trying to compose myself.

'Rod wants to get a good start.'

'But what about Randall? He won't know where we are.'

'He knows, Rod's told him.'

'I just have to make a call first.' I had to tell Phuong about Van Zyl.

Rod tooted the horn on their four-wheel drive. 'No time,' Ida said. 'Do it when we get back.'

Rod gave me a curt nod. 'All set?'

I patted my bag. 'I suppose.' We drove around the edge of town until we were on the main highway, a single lane of bitumen that soon turned to dirt. After that, the going was slow and rough and vaguely sickening. In the empty, continuous desert — and with the sun directly above — I had no point of reference other than the low hills to the east. It really was a nice day. Clear skies, nice breeze wafting. We were a dull party though, with no games of I-Spy, or idle chitchat.

'Here,' said Ida, the first words anyone had said for an hour. She had a map spread out on her knees and was checking it against their GPS. Rod slowed and turned onto a track without a signpost. The road was rutted and progress was difficult, and we passed another hour of tedious lurching and reeling. Ida pointed to a rocky point around a depression in the sand, near a sad stand of saltbush and a bunch of spinifex. 'This is it,' she said. 'Dead Mans Soak.'

Rod stopped and we all got out. There was nothing special about it that I could see. It was a scrubby plain, swept by a continuous gritty breeze — and circling high above, a lonely wedge-tailed eagle. Other than the low whistle of the wind, silence was all around. Ida opened the rear door to get some water. I pulled out the backpack, heaved it over my shoulder and ventured out to the ridge, glad to be out of the car. I walked a short distance, about a hundred metres, to the rock formation. From across the hills to the east, I heard a melancholy cry, like the bellowing of a sick animal, possibly a donkey's bray.

Rod was moving the car, searching, I assumed, among the rocky peaks for some shade to park under.

I climbed the rocks to see the nothingness beyond them. The sweep of the desert gave me a woozy rush and I was grateful for the wafting air that lifted my hair and cooled my neck. The problem was one of scale: here you had one small human, and her little problems; and over here, inconceivable breadth, bearing witness for a gazillion years. But now was not the time to dwell on such things. The sooner we checked the place out, the sooner I could get back and report Van Zyl to Phuong — or if not her then Randall or one of the local police.

Michaels had not come here for the peace and quiet, or to kill himself, but to meet Crystal. The poor fellow probably had no idea he was a threat to Van Zyl, as was anyone who understood the financial workings of the deal. I was convinced, now, that Michaels was just one more casualty in Van Zyl's insane war against Crystal. If I could find evidence linking Van Zyl to Michael's death, it would add more weight to my case when I spoke to the police.

I looked about me. Below, stamped upon the soft red dust, were tyre tracks. Big fat tyres, like those on a Range Rover or a Hummer. There'd been no rain for weeks and the tracks were perfectly preserved. I turned around to announce my discovery to the Lloyds but I couldn't see their car, only a rising line of dust that continued into the distance.

The beer at the pub had made me slow-witted — the comprehension dawned in slow-motion: they had left me behind.

I sat on a precipice of orange boulder. I picked up a stone and flicked it down onto the tyre tracks. This place wasn't Bourke Street, but surely, sooner or later, a car would come.

No. Not sooner. Maybe not even later. Maybe never.

Trying to walk back to town was dumb. Waiting was suicide. Oh silly, silly me.

The eagle circled. It looked menacing.

I tried to think. I could do this — I just had to use my brain. Survival required a few simple things. I had some water and some bread. Out here, that would probably last me a day or two. Maybe three. Then I'd die.

To make matters worse, I was busting. The art of outdoor urination had always eluded me. Whenever I attempted it, some disaster befell me. I'd squat and lose my balance and tumble backwards, arse-first, into the bushes. Once, a bug crawled into my undies. Usually, I'd just get wee all over my shoes, socks, and jeans. With a sigh, I climbed down and looked for a suitable place. Not many trees to go behind. But then who was going to see me? In the curve of rock, I took off my shoes and socks, and to be extra sure, my jeans as well. I crouched down and felt sweet relief.

At that exact moment, I heard an engine in the distance. I tried to hurry but some things can't be rushed. At last, I pulled up my undies and ran out to see what was coming. It was about five hundred metres away, a four-wheel drive, large, probably a Land Cruiser, approaching from Laverton and travelling east of me. There was not enough time to run back and put my jeans on; if I wanted this car to stop I had to start jumping up and down now. I was about to start flapping my arms but realised this was unnecessary. The car had turned, and moved with determined speed towards me. An unsettling thought came to me then; there was nothing out this way, no facilities, no town, nothing to see. Either this vehicle was off-course, or it was coming for me.

Panic rose in my chest. I pushed away thoughts of outback horror stories. I tried to still my shaking hands, the tingle in my nerves.

Calm down, I told myself. You're being melodramatic. Or perhaps not. A man had died in suspicious circumstances not far from where I stood. Some caution might be called for. I went to the backpack, took out the breadknife and folded it under the elastic of my undies.

The car stopped about twenty metres from where I was standing. Crystal Watt stepped out, wearing a khaki skirt and pink satin shirt.

'Hi, Crystal,' I yelled, relieved. 'Wow! Perfect timing.' Under normal circumstances I'd avoid her. She was corrupt and conniving and she'd had me beaten up. But if she gave me a lift out of here all would be forgiven.

'See? She has no pants. She is an idiot,' Crystal said to someone in the car.

'Oh,' I laughed, feeling a little bashful. 'I had to take a p—'

'I offer my advice. But you don't take it.' She was walking towards me.

'Huh?'

'In good faith, I come to you. I ask you, leave us alone. All you had to do.'

'I don't understand. You're here to give me a lift back, right?'

The driver's-side door opened and the racist and contemptible Tom Ashwood, former Victorian police constable, now — what? — some kind of dodgy body guard, stepped out. To my amazement he had a pistol in his hand and was pointing it at me.

'You could have done the decent thing,' Crystal was saying. 'I imagine now you're sorry?'

I was. I should have run back and put my pants on. And my shoes — why didn't I just leave them on? The knife in my undies was digging into my hip. Ashwood had a gun pointed at me. Tania had died a horrible death. 'I'm very sorry.'

Crystal laughed. 'Yes. Now. But it's too late. So give me the report.'

'No.'

Crystal rushed at me and grabbed a chunk of my hair before I could react. 'I beg your pardon?'

263

'Let go,' I yelled, trying to push her away.

She yanked my hair upwards. 'Just tell me where the report is.'

Hair follicles stretched the skin on my nape. But I could handle it; I'd spent four hours in the hairdresser — my hair had been yanked, peroxided, and blow-dried. *That* was torture. This was nothing. 'I don't have it. It's back in the unit.'

'Liar!' she said. 'We've been all through your stuff. You have it with you. Now, give it to me.' Crystal let go of my hair.

Ashwood made a show of aiming the gun at my head. A bullet to the head is more persuasive than hair pulling. I nodded to the backpack. 'There.'

Crystal ripped it open and found the laptop. She walked around to the front of the car in her fancy high-heeled boots and placed it on the ground in front of the front tyre. Then Ashwood and I watched as she got in the car and drove over it. It crunched into pieces.

'You didn't have to do that — wreck the whole computer. Couldn't you just break the DVD?'

Tendons in Crystal's neck protruded as she left the car and strode around, strutting like one of her peacocks. She started going through the backpack, pulling things out, and discovered the printed version, the one I showed the Lloyds. And then it hit me. The Lloyds. Those poor, shattered fools were thralls of this woman. Crystal took a lighter from Ashwood's front pocket and flicked it. Flame lapped the pages and caught. She waved the burning mess about until it was completely alight, allowing the smouldering ashes to fall to the ground and die out on the dirt. 'Your little game is over.'

'It wasn't a game,' I said, one hand creeping towards my undies. If she grabbed my hair again, I'd be ready.

She looked at Ashwood, shaking her head. 'She's completely deranged.'

'Once again, Crystal, you have underestimated me.'

'Darling, I don't estimate you at all!'

'But I know all about what you did to Tania. I know how you

hounded her to make a false sample report for your precious Blue Lagoon.'

'What you must understand,' Crystal said, 'is that Nina was clever. She was good at all that geology business. She knew all the right things to put in to make it convincing.' She was walking around, coming towards me then moving back.

I put my hand down my undies and held the knife, thinking I'd wait till she was close enough to take a swipe at. They traded looks.

'Really, darling,' Crystal said. 'Are you hormonal or something?'

Ashwood put an arm around her shoulder and they stood there, having a good laugh.

I withdrew my hand and pointed a finger at them. 'Nina didn't want to do your dirty work.'

'It is true. She resisted this idea.'

'So you *forced* her to do it.'

Crystal sighed. 'Forced. That's a strong word. I like *persuaded*.'

Ashwood laughed. 'Forceful persuasion.'

'How?'

'Oh, family matters,' Crystal said airily.

'You threatened to tell Brodtmann about some error of Nina's. You'd done it before, told Brodtmann she'd stuffed up?'

Crystal shrugged. 'We put on some pressure and she caved in.' Her face darkened. Making this admission annoyed her. She inhaled, put her hands on her hips. 'You little heart bleeder, you don't understand. This is business — it's how we do it. You have to be tough. There's no room for the sweetie darlings who go around all kind and *after you* and *please* and *thank you*.'

Ashwood was nodding. 'You're as tough as they come.'

'You have to be.' She flashed her teeth at him, then she turned back to me. 'But after she made her new report, Nina became devious. She left for Melbourne and threatened to go public with the first report if I didn't leave her alone.'

'So why didn't you?'

She shook her head and her glossy hair swished around like in a shampoo commercial. 'She had the report. She had the power.'

'So you went to her salon and threatened her.'

'Threaten? No. I asked her for little favour, just to break the silly thing.'

'When she went missing, you had your muscle trash my flat.'

Ashwood grinned; he liked being called muscle. 'We anticipated that the girl would keep the DVD off-site. The likelihood was she gave it to you,' he said. He still had the gun aimed in my general direction.

'*Likelihood*? You broke every DVD in my place.'

Somewhere in the distance, a mining company chopper thrashed the air. I was starting to wonder if it was one of the last things I would ever hear. We were in an isolated part of the desert, they were going to shoot me, and my body would be picked over by the slow-wheeling birds flying above me.

It was time for plain speaking. 'I know who kidnapped Nina.'

Crystal put her head to the side. 'We all do. Idiot gangland drug dealer and his Maori thug. For ransom money.'

'And how did those idiot criminals know that Tania was Nina Brodtmann? Who told them *that*, huh?'

Crystal was quiet, her exquisite eyes studied the dust for a second then she planted them on me again. She was now looking irritated. 'You tell me.'

'Ask yourself, who stands to gain?'

'Just fucking tell us,' Ashwood growled.

'Merritt Van Zyl.' I pronounced it 'Funsail'.

'What? Happy Hammond? Why would he?'

'All because of you, Crystal. Your crazy scheme to acquire the Bailey Range tenements made you some powerful enemies.'

'He wasn't involved in Bailey Range. Those guys are all gone now. They've moved on. Even Trevor Michaels — he moved himself on, just last week.' Crystal was sniggering.

'Van Zyl and that criminal Cesarelli were investors. They were laundering money through mining projects.'

I watched as Crystal's skin tone went from rose bronze to whitish pink. 'I didn't realise —'

Ashwood's head moved from his boss to me like a sideshow clown. 'What's she saying?'

'I'm saying Van Zyl wanted revenge. And he got it. He killed Nina, and he outbid you on Shine Point. He wants to undermine CC Prospecting every chance he gets. And he won't stop until he destroys you, Crystal.'

'What's she on about?' Ashwood asked Crystal.

'Nothing, darling. She's lost her marbles. Put the gun away. I think.'

I started to relax the tiniest bit. 'Do you plan to kill me?'

'No.'

'So why did you arrange for the Lloyds to bring me out here?'

'To give you a fright. I have frightened you? I think so. I want you to forget about this business.'

I was so relieved, I started to laugh.

'You forget about the DVD, and Happy Hammond, everything. I'll take care of him.'

I had no doubt she would. She operated in a different stratosphere — ordinary laws did not apply.

'We go back now. You will behave, yes?'

I was happy to agree to that, and to anything else she wanted me to say, but the blare of the helicopter made hearing impossible. It was loud and getting louder. It came closer, flying low.

Ashwood observed the chopper with consternation. Then his eyes widened and he ran to Crystal, trying to shield her. A shot, like a whip crack, cut the air and Crystal dropped to the ground.

'Crystal!' Ashwood yelled. 'Oh fuck.' He knelt down and put an ear on her chest. 'No, baby. Don't die. Baby.' She was motionless, one eye open, the other leaking blood. He started frantic mouth-to-mouth but blood flowed from her head. It trickled down Crystal's neck, over her diamonds, and soaked into the sand. Ashwood left her, tears dripping from his nose. He levelled the gun at the chopper.

It descended to a flat patch of earth about a hundred metres away and sent up a cloud of dust. The engine shut off. A man ran out from under its still-rotating blades. Ashwood fired off a couple of wild shots — who knows where they went.

My bare legs were shaking, holding myself up was a struggle. With trembling hands, I pulled the knife from my undies and held it beside my leg. I watched the man approach us, he was carrying a long-barrelled gun. He stopped and put a telescopic sight to his eye and fired. Ashwood twisted at the shoulder and fell back on the sand.

That was a good idea. I threw out my arms and hit the dirt. Perhaps they'd think I was dead too. Out of the corner of my eye, I saw the man drawing closer — that bow tie, that candy-stripe jacket, befitting to only one man: Merritt Van Zyl.

38

VAN ZYL WALKED like a man approaching the 18th hole for a two-foot putt after an entire round of birdies. A relaxed hand held the rifle.

'Stella Hardy? We meet again,' Van Zyl said. 'Or should I say Galvanina Monte?'

I said nothing.

'You are a hard woman to find, do you know that?'

I didn't move.

'Get up, Stella. I know you are not dead.'

I didn't budge.

Van Zyl looked back to the chopper expectantly. I followed his gaze. It was Maurangi who stepped out of the helicopter and trotted over on his stubby legs. I stayed still in the dust, but the knife was no longer in my hand.

'Get her up,' Van Zyl said.

Maurangi lifted me to my feet like I was hollow.

'Not very bright this one,' Van Zyl said to Maurangi, and handed him the rifle.

There was sudden movement in the dust as Ashwood scrambled to his feet and took off into the spinifex. Almost lazily, Maurangi lined him up with the rifle.

'No!' I screamed. I waved my arms to distract him. 'Don't do it!'

He fired but Ashwood dodged and kept going, a haze of dust kicking up behind him through the scrub. I prayed he'd make it out to the main road. The odds were against it. He was wounded and distraught. He probably didn't know which way to go.

'You'll have to work on your aim,' Van Zyl said, dryly.

I looked down at my feet and saw a glimpse of knife. 'Why were you looking for me?'

'You have something I want,' Van Zyl said.

'What? The DVD? It's gone.' I pointed to the squashed laptop near Crystal's car. 'I made a copy and she burned that, too. There's nothing of the original report left.'

'Thank you, *darling*,' he said to Crystal's lifeless body. 'Maurangi, get this one in the chopper — have her dropped further out.'

Maurangi slung the weapon over his shoulder and scooped up Crystal's body.

'So, Crystal has beaten me to it. Gone ahead and destroyed the only proof that she defrauded me on the Mount Percy Sutton deal.'

'Well, that's that then.' I put my hands on my hips, job done. Smoko time. Crystal was dead. Cesarelli was dead. 'You've eliminated anyone who knew anything. So, ah, we good?' But as I said it, I realised the answer.

'*A clean slate*, is how Finchley put it to me.'

Finchley Price, of course. He was up to his wig in it. Probably had money in the deal with the rest of them.

Van Zyl paced around, waiting for Maurangi to come back, waiting for him to sling that rifle around and shoot me. He wanted Maurangi to do it so he didn't have to get his hands dirty.

'I bet it was easy for you to convince Cesarelli to rinse his drug money through Bailey Range.'

His eyes were on me. 'Easy?'

'Yes. It was a gold mine, literally, a fucking gold mine. It wouldn't be a hard sell.'

He shrugged. 'That proposition did hold some appeal for the man.'

'What else? Promises of big returns: *no worries, mate; it's safe, can't go wrong*? After all you had your own capital on the line, and you wouldn't throw that around foolishly, would you?'

Van Zyl was laughing. 'Very good, Hardy.'

'But it went down the toilet and you both lost millions.'

Van Zyl closed his eyes, the memory too much perhaps. 'A lot of money.'

'How'd you find out it was Crystal who brought the whole venture crashing down?'

'She told me herself,' he said. 'She boasted about it. She was drunk and started complaining to me that Nina had betrayed her.'

The wind picked up and an uncontrollable shiver took over my legs.

'Can you imagine,' he said, 'telling a madman like Cesarelli his money was gone?'

'No. How did it go?'

'I confess I had to soften the blow.'

'How?'

'I made certain offers. I suggested that he kidnap the girl and hold her to ransom. Two birds. I get revenge on Crystal and Cesarelli gets the ransom.'

'After you took her to Cesarelli's farm, Nina told you I had the DVD?'

'Eventually,' Van Zyl said simply. Maurangi had joined him now, and was picking his nose. 'He persuaded her to tell us.'

Maurangi shrugged. 'Reminds me, where's me money? Haven't seen a cent yet.'

'And what would you spend it on?' Van Zyl asked. 'A new pair of — what do you call them — jandals?'

Maurangi sucked something out of his teeth, spat it on the dirt.

'But you got Brodtmann back with the Shine Point deal,' I said to Van Zyl. 'Wasn't that enough for you? You won. He lost. Why kill Nina? She was one of them, she wanted to get away from them.'

'One must not simply win,' Van Zyl sighed. 'It is not nearly enough. Competitors are one thing, but Crystal put me dangerously close to bankruptcy. And Cesarelli, he wanted blood.'

Maurangi held the rifle, slung by a strap over his shoulder, loosely pointing at the ground.

'Now,' Van Zyl said. 'How about a nice ride in my helicopter?'

'I don't want to. You're going to clean-slate me.'

Van Zyl nodded to Maurangi, who then took the rifle from his shoulder — and, as he raised it, it went off. I felt a searing heat in my foot. The pain was blinding. I dropped, rolling around on the ground, holding my foot and whimpering.

'That's enough,' Van Zyl said, holding his hand out for the rifle.

'It just went off. Something wrong with it.'

'Learn to shoot, you idiot.'

Maurangi's head lolled back like an exasperated adolescent. 'Yes, *boss.*' He held the gun out for Van Zyl.

I rolled to the side and there in the dirt, right beside me, was the knife. I could reach it. Maybe stick it in Maurangi's fat calf.

Van Zyl regarded Maurangi contemptuously. 'You know, I don't like your tone.'

Maurangi put his head on the side. 'My tone? You fucking racist *pakeha,* you just called me an idiot.'

'I'm not saying that because you're black. It's just that you *are* rather slow.'

I watched a sly smile curl the corners of Maurangi's mouth.

'We had a mess on our hands,' Van Zyl said to me. 'I had to kill Cesarelli *myself.* Can you imagine? With a knife. Then the girl.'

Behind them, I saw the blades of the helicopter gather speed, the engine whined.

'Let it go, man. So what?'

Van Zyl leaned right up into Maurangi's face. 'My dear, dumb Tapahia,' he said. 'Gage told me you were not to be trusted.'

Maurangi stopped laughing. 'Gage? That psycho? When did he talk to you?'

'I once heard him say the All Blacks are cheats,' I offered.

'No way,' Maurangi almost whispered it.

Behind them, the chopper lifted off. These two took no notice. 'That's what I heard,' I said. 'And he reckons the *haka* is a dirty trick.'

Van Zyl squinted at me. 'Oh, please. That's pathetic, Hardy. Even for you.'

'What'd he say then, bro?' Maurangi squared his stance.

'Nothing,' Van Zyl said. 'We never discussed rugby.'

'Like hell.'

Van Zyl swung the rifle around to his shoulder. The gun went off but Maurangi was ready. He twisted away and tried to grab Van Zyl's arms — but Van Zyl shoved him away and shot him in the stomach. Blood gushed through Maurangi's fingers like water from a burst pipe as he sank to his knees and dropped face-first on the ground.

I scrambled up and hopped frantically towards Crystal's car, waiting for the sting of another bullet. But Van Zyl dropped the rifle and ran after me. In five strides, he had hold of me around the waist. I kicked and punched and landed a few blows, but Van Zyl was hanging on and we hit the ground and rolled.

I heard the driver's door open. We both stopped to look. It was Ashwood, he was trying to start the car — engine revving, tyres spinning dust. Van Zyl lept up and sprinted to the car before Ashwood could get traction. He grabbed Ashwood, trying to drag him out. They struggled. A foot came out and kicked Van Zyl hard in the chest, and he fell back.

I hobbled away from them and picked up the rifle. I pointed it at Van Zyl and he ducked. Ashwood tried again to accelerate. Now the tyres gripped and the car lurched forward. I closed my eyes and squeezed the trigger. There was a blast. The recoil put me on my arse. The rear window exploded. The vehicle kept going, bouncing over the corrugations and potholes. The car crested a hill and was gone. At the same time, the sound of the helicopter faded into the distance. Van Zyl continued to stare after the car.

The silence of the desert returned.

A far-off cockatoo shrieked.

Van Zyl was standing still, staring into the desert. I got to my feet and put the butt hard up against my shoulder again, the barrel pointed at his chest. Now he was walking slowly towards me, my knife in his hand.

'Die,' he said quietly. 'Just fucking die.'

I squeezed the trigger. The air cracked and the bullet whizzed but Van Zyl kept coming. I tried again. The dead *click* surprised us both.

He came at me and I forced myself forwards, shoulder down. I pushed into his chest. We fell back. The knife was moving, darting, as he slashed and stabbed the air around me. I tried to grab the knife. His other hand found a fistful of my hair. My poor head wouldn't have a hair left on it. I swept up a handful of dust and rubbed it into his face. He released my hair and made wild, blind stabs in my direction with the blade. I dodged out of his reach and ploughed at the dirt with my fingers, smearing his face in another fistful. And another. He had lost his grip on the knife and pushed at my face with both hands. I felt around for a sharp-edge. The point pierced my hand, but I seized the handle. I rose up on my knees and brought it down, heard the grunt. I was all movement, no thinking — only the heat in my head and arm as the knife found Van Zyl's face again and again.

In the air around me, there was suddenly too much noise. Screaming in my ears. A car pulling up, sirens.

I stared down at Van Zyl.

'Stella Hardy?' someone called. 'Drop the knife!'

Full of dread and triumph, I held the knife out to the side. 'This is the ancient and beautiful sword the Green Destiny. Its edge has killed too many men. It is time to leave it behind.' And I dropped it.

39

BEN'S MAZDA was mine while he was serving a short sentence for receiving stolen goods. In it, I motored north on the Hume Highway. I was a licensed driver and my destination was Shepparton and the country estate of Mrs Chol. Along the way, two magpies flew for several seconds in front of the car, low over the road, a kind of avian escort. The birds flew together, wings touching, only metres from the car, then veered right to survey a dry paddock. A certain type of person might regard that sight as a sign. I was humming as I drove and reflecting on how far I'd come since that day at Dead Mans Soak.

Of that day, much that happened was still a blur. I was cleaned up, dressed, and fed. Randall slipped me a beer, bless him. The Lloyds were questioned about what exactly they had told Crystal. And later, the bodies of Maurangi and Merritt Van Zyl were taken back to the morgue in Perth. The autopsy report said his face was a mess but the knife didn't penetrate his brain — it was a myocardial infarction that killed him. Crystal Watt's body had not yet been found.

At one point the Laverton librarian, who had heard some gossip about a rumble in the desert, came to the police station. Turns out I had left Tania's DVD in the computer I'd used at the library. The police told her they would hand it to me, but she wanted to give it to me personally, which she did.

A lovely afternoon — we went outside to a terrace where I listened to Mrs Chol explain that Mabor was back at school and was dux of his class. And she showed me around her newly acquired property, a seven-bedroom house with a swimming pool. The three little girls were in local schools and doing very well, and were also taking tennis lessons and had joined the pony club. Mrs Chol then let slip that she had sent a large donation to a charity for the education of girls in Sudan.

Where she got the funds for these things was not explained. And I did not ask. She was invited by Mucous Pukus to be a JUNKIE champion, for the so far less-than-successful Justice and Community Services program known as Justice Uniting Neighbourhood Knowledge with Inter-agency Expertise, but she declined.

In the afternoon, I bade her farewell and travelled back to Melbourne to prepare for an evening celebration at the Station Hotel.

The Hume Highway started to get busy when I got closer to town. It was later than expected when I finally got home and drove my little car into its parking space.

Upstairs I opened the door. The painting I had been working on was still on the kitchen table. Every part of the flat now served as a studio. It would have to do until I found something more suitable. The painting was a bad copy of a Boyd landscape. It needed a lot of work.

I showered and dressed, and thought about the desert.

Randall had found Ashwood still in Crystal's car. He'd got bogged trying to escape and was stuck in loose sand. And Finchley Price had been arrested.

As for the death of Merritt Van Zyl, Randall had backed me up. And no charges were brought.

So I was free.

And I was now looking forward to meeting up with Phuong and Bruce Copeland at the Station Hotel.

'Word on the street is Cesarelli had close to a million in cash stashed at his farm, but so far there's still no sign of it,' Copeland said to me over an oyster.

'Well, that *is* careless, Detective.'

He frowned at me. 'How is Mrs Chol?'

'Oh, she's grand.' I sipped my champagne and smiled to myself.

Bruce finished his drink. 'I better call it a night. Court in the morning.'

When he'd gone I gave Phuong a gentle nudge. 'Why didn't you leave with him?'

She ordered another round. 'I don't have court in the morning.' Her trademark smile was like a Zen koan, cryptic and beautiful. 'And what are your plans for tonight?'

I tried to match her air of mystery. 'A night of debauchery with a depraved artist in his garret.'

She raised her flute. 'Good for you.'

After a few more oysters and more champagne, I snuck out of the pub and walked alone through the Footscray streets towards Brophy's studio. I chose the backstreets, past the rows of narrow-fronted workers cottages — TVs on in front rooms. Some had housed the same immigrant families for more than fifty years, some were gentrified restorations and others were junkie squats. I found the clamour of the inner city soothing. Distant trucks roared down Whitehall Street — and brought Russell Hardy to mind. What I had of my father now, whether from the Hardy stamp on my cells or as the result of my early years in Russell's company, manifested in me, sporadically, as strength. Sometimes that was the strength to succeed. Sometimes, it was only the will to survive. It was like Brophy said: courage. That was my inheritance. It was there in the desert. The alternative was to be not walking, not breathing.

From the studio windows, the light glowed yellow. I waited outside, taking my time, enjoying the anticipation.

Two weeks before, Brophy and I had been swinging in a hammock built for two, on a tropical island, as a gentle South-Pacific breeze warmed our Melbourne-white skin. We were passing the day in idle chat, quizzing each other on such things as popular culture and our views on western civilisation.

'Best invention of the twentieth century?'

'The shower cap.'

He laughed, but didn't argue with me. And because of that, and because he was looking at the ocean, I decided to tell him about the money. He listened without interruption as I explained that I'd received a call in the middle of the night from a client. He wanted me to come over, straight away, he had said, because he and his friend had been threatened; he said they were going to the police and they wanted a witness, because they'd had trouble with cops in the past. When I got there, they were in their twelfth-floor apartment of the Flemington Housing Commission flats, already dead. Blue faces, cold to the touch. I called the ambulance, because there's always a chance to bring them around, I guess. I saw the fit on the filthy mattress beside them. And I knew he had a habit, and his friend was a junkie, too. Skin and bones, they both were. The place was a rat-infested hole and stunk of old garbage. I was waiting for the ambulance and I saw a plastic shopping bag near the bodies, and it'd tipped on its side, open. Spilling out were wads of cash — twenties in bundles.

'It was late, like about three in the morning. I was tired,' I thought for a moment. 'No. I'm just making excuses.'

'How much?'

'Thirty-four thousand.'

'Fuck me.'

'Six years of waiting to be found out.'

'Stella, Cesarelli's dead. It's over. You're free.'

I looked up now and saw Brophy through the window, walking around in the studio. I lingered for a moment longer. It had been the first proper hot day of summer, and the descending cool of night was a welcome relief.

Acknowledgements

This book would not have been possible without Henry Rosenbloom, who believed in the manuscript enough to put his John Hancock on a contract next to mine. I am grateful to him and to my editor Lesley Halm, and to everyone at Scribe, for always making me feel so welcome and for their unstinting professionalism.

To the judges and organisers of the Victorian Premier's Literary Award for an Unpublished Manuscript 2014, for which *Good Money* was shortlisted, thank you for what turned out to be a life-changing opportunity. And I'm grateful to my agent, Clare Forster, for her patient efforts on my behalf.

Many thanks to the teachers and students at the RMIT professional writing program, especially Toni Jordan, who is a national treasure — I am grateful for her encouragement. My thanks also to Antoni Jach and the students of his Master Class, especially Leigh Redhead, the kick-arse crime writer, whose generosity with her time and expertise was amazing.

Maurice McNamara read early drafts of the manuscript and gave me valuable advice and encouragement, and I owe him heartfelt thanks and another bottle of red wine.

To Trish Bolton, Dana Miltins, Kate Richards, Clare Strahan, and Lucy Treloar, dear and supportive friends and fellow travellers: thank you. I'm fortunate to know such talented and dedicated writers.

Natalie Thomas and Ming Lu Chen gave their time and friendship, and Anna Dusk and Michelle Towers never waivered in their faith in me, and I am grateful for their existence in this world.

And finally to Clinton and Morrigan, without whom I'd have drifted out to sea long ago, love and a lifetime's indebtedness.